DEADFALL

Books by Bill Pronzini

"Nameless Detective" mysteries

Bones
Double (with Marcia Muller)
Nightshades
Quicksilver
Bindlestiff
Dragonfire
Scattershot
Hoodwink
Labyrinth
Twospot (with Colin Wilcox)
Blowback
Undercurrent
The Vanished
The Snatch

Other novels

Quincannon
The Eye (with John Lutz)
Starvation Camp
The Gallows Land
Masques
The Cambodia File (with Jack Anderson)
Prose Bowl (with Barry N. Malzberg)
Night Screams (with Barry N. Malzberg)
Acts of Mercy (with Barry N. Malzberg)
Games
The Running of the Beasts (with Barry N. Malzberg)
Snowbound
Panic!
The Stalker

Collections

Graveyard Plots
Casefile

DEADFALL

Bill Pronzini

St. Martin's Press/New York

Library of Congress Cataloging-in-Publication Data

Pronzini, Bill.
  Deadfall.

  I. Title.
PS3566.R67D43 1986   813'.54   86–3669
ISBN 0-312-18525-1

First Edition

10 9 8 7 6 5 4 3 2 1

For Marty Greenberg

DEADFALL

ONE

S takeouts are a pain in the ass.

On rolling night stakeouts this is true literally as well as figuratively. During the day you can people-watch, read a little, get out of the car and walk around for short periods. After dark you're pretty much confined, particularly when the weather is bad and even more particularly when you're staked out in a residential neighborhood. Citizens might not notice a strange car, or somebody hunkered down in the shadows inside, but once you start prowling around on foot they notice you damned quick—and the next thing you know, you're exchanging amenities with a couple of prowl-car cops. About all you *can* do on a rolling night stakeout is sit and think and try not to fall asleep while you wait for something to happen.

That was what I was doing for the second night in a row, on Cerritos Street in San Francisco's Ingleside District, at eleven o'clock of a cold, overcast, but no longer rainy November Thursday: bored to tears, developing calluses on my backside, and reflecting on the metaphysical nature of stakeouts. I had been in the neighborhood since 8:15, at three different locations within two blocks, from all of which I could watch a particular gray-stucco house that belonged to a woman named Eileen Kyner. She hadn't shown up yet; neither had the guy I was waiting for, one Alfred Henry Umblinger, Jr. For all I knew they had run off to the North Woods or the North Pole, never to be seen or heard from again. Another long, dull, empty night. And for what? Was I suffering like this in order to apprehend a dangerous felon? I was not. Nothing half so glamorous or noble as that.

1

I was sitting here waiting to swipe a car.

Admittedly, Alfred Henry Umblinger, Jr., was what they used to call a blot on society's escutcheon. Not that he was a crook, not precisely. Alfred Henry was, in fact, a deadbeat of the first magnitude. He had a charming habit of buying things on credit and then forgetting to pay for them. He also moved around a lot, so that when people like me got hired by finance companies and/or various merchants to either collect what was owed them or repossess the goods, Alfred Henry was nowhere to be found. Why merchants kept selling things to him was beyond me, but they did; and of course he kept disappearing. He was very good at disappearing, Alfred Henry was. It had taken me almost a week to get a line on him, the line being Eileen Kyner. La Kyner, a recent divorcée, was reputed to be his current lady friend; she was also reputed to be harboring his silver 1985 Mercedes XL in her garage. Said Mercedes having been purchased by Alfred Henry from a dealer in Burlingame, and said dealer now wanting it back because Alfred Henry had neglected to pay him a dime on it in four months. The Mercedes had not been in Eileen Kyner's garage yesterday morning, when I'd first come out here, and it hadn't been there last night or today at any time. Neither had Eileen Kyner or Alfred Henry or anybody else, so far as I knew. I was beginning to view the past two days as a wild-goose squat. Still and all, I was getting paid to sit here, and so here I would sit for at least one more day and night, if necessary, gathering additional proof (as if I needed any) that stakeouts are a pain in the ass and that the life of the private eye is generally overrated as far as excitement is concerned.

I shifted position on the seat for the two-hundredth time, to ease the pressure on my tailbone, and stared out at the street. After two nights here I knew it as well as I ever wanted to know any street in the city. It was a very ordinary street, lined with medium-sized houses of several different architectural styles, the dominant one being Spanish. The houses on the north side, where I was parked in the heavy shadow of a Monterey pine, were built on higher ground ten feet or so above street level; the ones on the south side were at street level, set back behind short lawns or gardens. Among the latter group was Eileen Kyner's gray-stucco. Nothing much happened on Cerritos after dark, it seemed, which meant that there was hardly anything to occupy my attention while I waited. Once, an hour ago, a guy had come out of a house down the block, hauling a fat schnauzer on a leash, and I had been so grateful for something to look at that I had watched with rapt attention while the schnauzer lifted his leg against a tree and then left his calling card on a neighbor's nice green lawn. The dog's owner made no attempt to scoop up the calling card, so I had got another couple of minutes out of cursing inconsiderate dog owners who made no attempt to curb their mutts.

More time passed—at least an hour, I thought. I glanced at my watch to confirm that, and saw that seven minutes had elapsed since the last time I'd looked at it. I shifted position for the two-hundred-and-first time. It was stuffy in the car, probably because I was wrapped up in my heavy tweed overcoat—I was just getting over a touch of bronchitis—and so I opened the window a little to let in some of the cold night air. From somewhere nearby I could hear the faint sound of a television turned to a late-evening rerun of a sitcom: the rise and fall of canned laughter. That was how quiet it was in this neighborhood.

I glanced over at the GTE mobile telephone unit mounted under the dash. It was brand new, that unit. I had always felt that mobile telephones were an unnecessary affectation, and I had put up something of a squawk before yielding to Eberhardt's insistence that we each outfit our cars with one. Now, after two nights on Cerritos, with the most interesting thing I'd witnessed being a schnauzer having a bowel movement, I had begun to change my mind. I had used the mobile phone twice already tonight, once to check in with Eberhardt and once to let Kerry know that she was probably going to have to sleep alone again—a fact that depressed me, if not her. Too late to call either of them again, much as I would have liked to. Besides which, the mobile phone was for business and emergency use, not for idle chitchat to alleviate the boredom of a rolling stakeout. I had gotten through thirty-odd years of stakeouts without a telephone as a steady companion; I could likewise get through the next couple of hours of this one.

Come on, Alfred Henry, I thought. Come *on,* you deadbeat son of a bitch.

I sighed. I shifted position again. I poured a little more coffee from the thermos I'd brought along and tried to drink it too fast and spilled half of it down my chin onto the front of my coat. I said some rude words. I sighed again. I poured more coffee and managed this time to find my mouth with the cup. I yawned. I stared out at the street. I switched on my Sony portable radio and listened to five minutes of news, local and national, none of which was worth listening to. I switched off the radio and looked at my watch again.

11:28.

Headlights appeared in the rearview mirror. I pulled my head down lower on the seat and sat still, watching and listening to the sound of the car as it approached and then glided past. It might have been a Mercedes XL; it had the shape of one. But if so it wasn't Alfred Henry's Mercedes XL. It drifted on past Eileen Kyner's house and turned right on Moncada and disappeared.

11:29.

I had hung around until after two last night. Not tonight, Alfred Henry. If he and his Mercedes didn't show by 1:00 A.M. I was going home to sleep. Alone, damn it.

I thought about Kerry again. She was nice to think about—the love of your life always is. Almost always, anyway. I wondered what she was doing right now. Probably getting ready for bed in her Diamond Heights apartment. That coppery hair of hers brushed out smooth and shiny, her face scrubbed free of makeup. Wearing that flimsy peach-colored thing, maybe, the one that ended halfway down her thighs and was sheer all around except for little wisps of lace here and there, here and there. . . .

Terrific, I thought. As if this stakeout isn't difficult enough. Now you're having erotic thoughts and giving yourself an erection.

I forced myself to quit thinking about anything and stared out

4

at the street some more. Most of the nearby houses were dark now; the only ones that showed light were the two directly opposite where I was parked—a smallish Spanish-style job with a red tile roof and a round, squat central tower that bisected it into wings, and its east-side neighbor, a bulky wood-and-brick structure that had an old-fashioned front porch. A chest-high hedge separated the two. The TV sounds—the droning voices of news commentators, now, replacing the canned laughter—were coming from one of them, but I couldn't tell which.

Another set of headlights appeared, headed toward me this time from the other end of Cerritos. But *they* didn't mark the appearance of Alfred Henry, either; they came past the Kyner house, past me without slowing, and eventually swung into a driveway back near Ocean Avenue.

I told myself I was not going to check the time again. I told myself it was pointless and counterproductive and besides, a watched pot never boils. So then, having convinced myself not to look at my watch, I proceeded to look at my watch.

11:37.

Across the street, in one of the two lighted houses, somebody fired a gun.

I sat up straight, tensing, on the seat. TV, I thought—but it hadn't been the TV. I had heard enough guns going off in my life, too many guns going off, not to recognize the real thing even at a distance.

After a couple of seconds there was another bang, followed this time by a series of muffled noises that I couldn't identify. I was out of the car by then, acting on impulse and instinct, running across the empty street. It was the Spanish-style house that the shots had come from; the television noise was pouring out of the bulky one next door. The lights in the Spanish house were at the back; the front part was obscured by darkness. I cut over onto an asphalt drive that paralleled the hedge, ran past a Chrysler parked there, through heavy darkness toward the rear.

I was twenty yards from the corner when I heard a door whack open around back, then the thud of running footfalls. But whoever

5

it was didn't come my way. I pounded around the corner, into a shrub-cluttered yard bloated with shadow. At the far end I could make out a human form pushing through a gate in a tall grape-stake fence—somebody wearing a floppy rain hat and a trench coat, the tails of the coat flapping like half-folded wings.

I yelled, "Hey, you there!" but whoever it was didn't break stride or turn his head. Two seconds later he was gone, melted into the deeper blackness thrown by a yucca tree that leaned out above the fence. I ran across the yard, dodged past some kind of fountain . . . and something caught hold of my foot, pitched me sideways and down onto a damp patch of lawn. The thing still had hold of my foot when I rolled over onto hands and knees; I kicked loose of it—damned garden hose—and lumbered up and made it to the fence in time to hear a car engine surge to life, tires squeal on pavement a moment later. There was a narrow alley back there, of the type that runs through the middle of some residential blocks in this part of the city to give access to rear garages or parking spaces; the car, running without lights—another shapeless blob—was sawing along it forty yards away, pointed in the opposite direction. Then it was gone, too, and the night got quiet again except for vague disturbed sounds in the nearby houses.

My right knee began to throb: I had whacked it pretty good when I'd tripped over the hose. I limped back across the yard, bent over so I could rub it and so I could see to avoid any other obstacles. The rear door of the house was wide open; a wedge of light spilled out across a shadowed interior porch, coming from a brightly lit kitchen. I went that way, fighting myself a little because I didn't want to have to go inside, I did not want to see what was in there.

I was ten paces from the open door when a window went up in the bulky house adjacent and a bald guy in a bathrobe leaned out and called nervously, "What's going on over there? Who are you?"

"Detective," I said, because I didn't want to get into a discussion with him. "Everything's under control, sir." He took it the way I'd intended—that I was a police detective, not a private one.

He ducked back inside and the window sash slammed shut. But he was still there behind the pane as I went ahead, peering out through it marble-eyed like a kid watching a bug do something ugly and fascinating inside a big glass jar.

When I got to the open door I stopped and poked my head inside and listened. Faint sounds, not quite identifiable—a kind of dragging, a kind of crunching. The hackles were up on my neck now; the sweat that came rolling down out of my armpits had a cold oily feel. I thought about calling out, but that would have been stalling, wasting time. Get it over with, I thought. And I went inside.

Laundry porch, with nothing in it to hold my attention. I kept going into the kitchen. Empty. Wall telephone, table with a coffee mug on it, chair with a dark blue gabardine suit coat draped over the back—I saw those things, and then I heard the dragging, crunching sounds again. They were coming from beyond an archway on the far side, past a breakfast bar that divided the kitchen into two halves. I went around the bar to the archway. The room on the other side was a lamp-lit formal dining room, and when I saw what was inside it my stomach heaved and I said something half reverent, half profane under my breath and then tried to swallow the bile that pumped up into my throat.

The room looked like a war zone.

Blood, that was the first thing that struck the senses—a trail of it, smeary and glistening in the ochre-colored light, like an obscene parody of a slug's passage. Mahogany dining table broken in half, chairs overturned and two of them smashed, matching china cabinet lying face down across the other wreckage. Broken glass on the hardwood floor, broken china plates and cups and saucers, blue-and-white patterned stuff with some of the shards speckled with crimson. And the man crawling away toward another archway at the opposite end, a big man, fortyish, mane of gray-black hair, wearing dark blue gabardine trousers and a light blue shirt with a wet red front; one hand clawing at the wood, the other crooked under him in a vain effort to stem the flow of bright arterial blood. Dragging sounds, crunching sounds: trying to crawl away from death. Moaning, too, as he crawled, little rattles of sound that were not quite words.

For a couple of seconds I leaned hard against the inside of the arch, struggling to get the wall up between what I was seeing and my emotions. It wasn't much of a wall, it never had been, but when I got it in place it allowed me to function. I took a couple of deep breaths, keeping my throat clamped shut against the bile, and picked my way across the room—avoiding the trail of blood, the shards of glass and china. When I reached the wounded man he was almost to the far archway. I got down on one knee beside him, gripped his shoulder gently and put my mouth close to his ear.

"Easy, I'm here to help you. Don't move, just lie still while I call an ambulance. You're going to be okay."

A lie, that last; he wasn't going to be okay. Up close like this I could see that his face was gray, pustuled with sweat, already waxlike—stamped with the unmistakable imprint of death. But the lie didn't matter: shock and pain had deafened him. He kept trying to crawl, not getting anywhere now, just wriggling in place as the strength and the life ebbed out of him. Gut-shot once, maybe twice—I couldn't tell for sure with all the blood. No exit wounds. And no sign of the gun. Standing in here when he got it, I thought; force of the slug knocked him back into the china cabinet and he pulled it over with him when he fell.

I started to lift up away from him, to go call the ambulance even though he couldn't have more than a couple of minutes left, but the rattling in his throat stopped me. It formed a word now, a liquidly audible word.

"Deadfall," he said.

He said it again, not quite as clearly, and kept trying to crawl out from under my hand, away from the grinning skull-face that beckoned him. And then he said, mumbling, delirious words that I had to strain to hear: "So sorry . . . fall, how could you . . ." And then he died.

I *felt* him die. I felt him shudder, stiffen; I felt the life force desert him all at once, as if it somehow came winging out *through* my hand. The sensation put racking chills on my back, drove me to my feet, and sent me stumbling back into the kitchen. I leaned against the sink, staring at my left hand, willing the shakes to go away so I could use the telephone.

Deadfall. So sorry . . . fall, how could you . . .

There was a stain of blood on my left palm, like a vestige of the life force that had passed through it.

TWO

The dead man's name was Leonard Purcell. He lived in this house and apparently had for some time; he had been forty-four years old and unmarried; he had practiced law out of an office in Stonestown. I got all of that from a billfold—driver's license with his picture on it, one of several embossed business cards—that had been visible in an inside pocket of the gabardine suit coat draped over the kitchen chair. I used my handkerchief to take it out; I thought it was all right to do that because I needed to know who he was before I called the police, and I also needed to know the exact address without having to go out front and try to find the house number. I did not touch anything else in the kitchen except for the telephone, and I used my handkerchief on that too.

The Ingleside Police Station was not far away, so I put the call in there. The desk sergeant told me to stand by, he'd have officers there in five minutes. He meant uniformed officers; it would take a team of homicide inspectors at least a half hour to make it out from the Hall of Justice downtown. I said I wasn't going anywhere, and he said fine, and I put the receiver down and held my hand up in front of my face. The shaking had stopped. Outwardly, anyway. Inside I was still churning like an old dryer full of laundry.

9

I looked around the kitchen again. I did not want to do my waiting in here; the place had a heavy closed-in feel, for one thing, and for another I could smell the blood, all that blood in the dining room. Never mind that blood has no odor: I could smell it just the same. I considered going outside. I was still considering it when I heard the car come thrumming into the driveway.

The police already? Maybe, although black-and-whites usually pulled up on the street, even at a homicide scene. I went through the laundry porch, through the back door. A car door—just one —slammed on the side drive. I hurried over that way, around the corner. The car that had pulled in behind the Chrysler was definitely not a police cruiser. Some kind of sports car, an older model —an MG, maybe. There was no sign of the driver; he must have gone the other way, to the front of the house.

I retraced my steps, back inside. Just as I entered the kitchen, a door I took to be the front door opened and then closed again. A male voice called, "Leonard? I'm home."

There was a passageway off the near side of the kitchen that appeared to lead up front. It took me into a big tile-floored foyer decorated with multicolored Mexican pottery jars full of pampas grass. The man standing there had his back to me, hanging up a topcoat in a narrow closet that wasn't much more than a vertical slit in the wall. He said without turning, "What's going on? Some of the neighbors are looking out their windows."

I didn't answer him.

He swung around, saying, "Leonard, I asked you—" and broke off when he saw that I wasn't Leonard. He stiffened a little, not much, showing more surprise than anything else: he wasn't the panicky type. "Who are you?"

I told him my name. It didn't mean anything to him; I would have been surprised myself if it had. He was in his thirties, slight, sandy-haired, with a wispy mustache and gentle blue eyes and lashes that had been shaped and lengthened with mascara. A small circle of gold dangled from his right ear. He was wearing Levi's, a blue pullover sweater, a pair of beaded moccasins. The way he moved, the way he held himself, the lilt of his voice—all of those suggested a woman trapped in a man's body. Now I knew why Leonard Purcell was not married.

"Are you a friend of Leonard's?" he asked.

"No. I'm afraid not."

"One of his clients?"

"No. Mind telling me *your* name?"

"Tom Washburn, if it's any of your business. What are you doing in my house?"

"You live here too, then?"

He made an impatient gesture. "Certainly I live here. Now what's going on? Where's Leonard?"

I took a breath, let it out slowly. Telling somebody about the death of a friend, a loved one, is never easy. Doesn't matter if you know the person or not—it's never easy. I said, "There's been some trouble here. I'm a detective and I happened in on it. I wish I hadn't."

"Trouble? What do you mean, 'trouble'?"

"Your housemate is dead, Mr. Washburn. He was shot a few minutes ago."

Washburn stood there for a couple of seconds without moving; it took that long for the words to penetrate, to mean anything to him. Then they rocked him, as if some invisible force had struck him a sharp blow. He put a hand up to his mouth and said between the splayed fingers, "Dead? Leonard?"

"I'm sorry."

"Somebody *shot* him?"

"I've already called the police. They'll be here any minute—"

"Who? Who would do a thing like that?"

"I don't know. I heard the shots and I saw the person run out of the house, but I didn't get a good look at him."

Washburn still had his hand over his mouth; he was swaying slightly now, with his eyes squeezed shut. I was afraid he might faint, but that didn't happen. After a time he said in a low, tremulous voice, "Where is he? I want to see him."

"I don't think that's a good idea."

"I want to see him. I have a right to see him."

11

"Mr. Washburn, for your own sake—"

His eyes popped open and he said with sudden savagery, "Goddamn you, I want to see him! You tell me where he is! Tell me or I'll scratch your fucking eyes out!"

He meant it. Shock and grief and confusion make people irrational. I said, "In the dining room," and he spun away and ran through a big beam-ceilinged living room, the rear part of which was raised by three steps. I went after him; I did not want him touching anything, by accident or for any other reason. But he didn't go into the dining room. He stopped when he got to the archway and saw what lay beyond. Stopped, and then screamed —a shrill keening cry full of anguish and horror that put goosebumps on my arms and across my shoulders. He turned blindly, stumbling, his face all twisted up. I caught his arm to keep him from falling. And he made a little whimpering noise and came in against me, threw his arms around my neck and buried his face against my chest and began to weep hysterically.

I didn't know what to do. For a couple of seconds I just stood awkwardly, letting him hold onto me; there was a lump of something dry and bitter in my throat. Then I put an arm around him, turned him a little so that I could walk with him. He came along without resistance. I could feel the tremors racking him, paroxysm after paroxysm, so that his sobbing breaths came out like hiccups. I got him to a blocky Spanish couch set at an angle away from the arch so that you couldn't see into the dining room from there, and sat him down on that. There was a quilted afghan draped over the back; I shook the thing open and wrapped it around his shoulders, folded it over the front of him. It didn't stop his shaking but it seemed to take the chill away, help him get his breathing under control.

I stood off at a distance, not looking at him because I didn't want to face any more of his grief. Not looking at much of anything, just waiting.

There wasn't much longer to wait. In less than a minute pulsing red light stained the curtains over the front window and I heard the cars—two of them—come to fast stops out front. The officers made some noise, more than they had to, getting out and coming to the house. Cops don't show enough respect for death sometimes —the young ones, especially.

I went into the foyer to let them in.

The next couple of hours were bad, although not half as bad for me as they must have been for Tom Washburn. There was a vague sense of surrealism to the events, of déjà vu: I had gone through them all before, so many times that they blended together and became the same ordeal relived. Only the surroundings and the faces were different. The routine was the same. And so was the despair.

I didn't know any of the uniformed cops, but one of them knew me by reputation, so there was no hassle. I answered their preliminary questions. I took them in and showed them what was left of Leonard Purcell. I answered more questions. Washburn had stopped crying at some point and had made an effort to get himself under control; but he stayed seated on the couch with the afghan wrapped tightly around him. I listened to him answer questions in a small, empty voice, but his responses were just words to me, without any real significance. I felt removed from everything, even more so than at other scenes like this because I didn't know any of the principals, I wasn't an integral part of it personally or professionally. Just a bystander, that was all—in the wrong place at the wrong time. The only things Washburn said that I could remember later were that he worked in a bank and that he'd gone to a movie tonight, gone alone because it was R-rated and Leonard didn't approve of graphic violence in films.

The homicide team arrived; so did the assistant coroner and an ambulance and the lab crew. One of the inspectors was Ben Klein. Ben and I went back a long way, back to the days when I'd been on the cops myself; he and I had once shared a black-and-white out of the Taraval station. I repeated to him what had happened here, and answered his questions, and he told me to wait in the kitchen in case he needed to ask me anything else.

But I didn't wait in the kitchen: I could still smell the blood from in there. I went out into the back yard, but that wasn't the place for me either. Half a dozen neighbors were grouped in the alleyway, gawking the way they do, and the guy in the bathrobe was again hanging out of his window next door. One of the people in the alley called out to me, "What happened in there? Was somebody killed?"

Yeah, I thought, somebody was killed. I went back inside without answering and found a chair on the laundry porch, near the washer-and-dryer combination, and did my waiting in private.

Nobody bothered me for half an hour or so. Then one of the lab technicians came out and seemed surprised to find me sitting there in the shadows. He located the light switch and flipped it on with a knuckle, so he wouldn't smudge any prints that might be on it.

I said, "You want me out of the way?"

"Be easier to work."

"Sure."

I walked outside again. The guy was gone from the window next door; I'd have bet money he had come outside himself, finally, to see if he could get a better look at things. The other neighbors were still in the alley, but a couple of uniformed officers were questioning them and nobody was paying any attention to me. I went over and stood in the darkness under some kind of puffy shrub; watched rain clouds roll in overhead and smelled the good clean odors of ozone and damp grass and evergreens.

Another of the lab men and the other inspector, a young guy named Tucker, came out together and began poking around the yard with flashlights. I stayed out of their way. Then they went out through the gate and along the alley toward where the car belonging to Leonard Purcell's assailant had been parked. From under the shrub I watched the play of their light beams, but I couldn't tell if they found anything.

Pretty soon it began to rain—a misty drizzle at first, then a hard slanting downpour. Everybody beat it out of the alley. I didn't want to go back inside, but I didn't want to stand out here and get soaked either. At my age, you worry about things like pneumonia. The laundry porch was empty again, the light shut off, so I sat down on the same chair I'd occupied earlier and waited some more, listening to the heavy beat of the rain on the tile roof.

After what seemed like a long time, Klein called my name from the kitchen. I got up and went in, and he cocked an eyebrow and said, "What were you doing? Sitting back there in the dark?"

"Yeah."

"How come?"

"No reason. It was just a place to sit, out of the way."

"You sure you're all right? You look a little pale."

"I'm okay. Been a long night."

"Sure. Well, you might as well go on home. I'll call you if there's anything else. Otherwise, come down to the Hall tomorrow sometime, sign your statement."

I nodded. "How's Washburn holding up?"

"Not too well, poor guy."

"He won't be spending the night here, will he?"

"No. He gave us the name of a friend to call."

"Listen, you figure him for a suspect?"

"Too soon to tell. Why?"

"I was right there when he saw Purcell's body," I said. "He screamed, Ben—the kind of scream you can't fake. You know what I mean?"

"I guess I do."

"He didn't kill Purcell. For what it's worth."

"Worth something to me. I'll keep it in mind."

I pulled the collar of my coat up around my neck. It had been warm in the kitchen before; now it was cold. I could still smell the blood in the dining room.

"Whoever did do it," I said, "I hope you nail him for it. Fast and hard."

He knew what I meant; you couldn't have been in that dining room and not know. He put a hand on my shoulder and said, "So do I."

The nightmares started as soon as I went to sleep.

I knew they would; they always do after an ugly scene like tonight's. So I didn't go to bed right away, after I got home to my flat in Pacific Heights. It was too late to call Kerry or Eberhardt, as much as I wanted to talk to somebody. I opened a beer and turned on the TV and watched an old Edmond O'Brien movie without making sense out of half of it. Then I tried to read for a while—one of the seven thousand pulp magazines on shelves ringing my living room—but the words kept running together like ink under a stream of water. Three A.M., and my eyes just wouldn't stay open any longer. I was so exhausted it was an effort to drag myself into the bedroom and shuck out of my clothes. Still I fought sleep, lying there listening to the hollow beat of the rain —but not for long. And when I lost the struggle the nightmares came and put a bad end to a bad night.

Blood in them, jetting up bright red out of a fountain in a yard grown high with dead trees and shrubs. A bird on the wing, and I touched it somehow and felt the life leave its body and pass through my fingers, and it fell in a long spiral—a deadfall. Then I was on the floor, crawling, crippled with pain and leaving a trail of blood behind me—but it was the floor of Eberhardt's house, not Purcell's, the afternoon Eb and I had been shot by a hired Chinese gunman. And then I was on one knee, looking down at myself, putting a hand on my own shoulder and saying, "Easy, I'm here to help you, you're going to be okay," and I shuddered at the lie and felt myself shudder, felt the life go rushing out of my own body this time. And then somebody yelled, a thin wailing cry full of anguish—

—and I woke myself up, because it was me doing the yelling.

THREE

N othing much happened over the next week. I avoid reading the newspapers most of the time, but I had a look at the *Chronicle* twice during that week; I also called Ben Klein at the Hall and talked with him. But there just weren't any developments in the Leonard Purcell case. Or at least none that the police were admitting to. According to Klein, Tom Washburn had been unable to attach any particular significance to Purcell's dying words, except as an obscure reference to Leonard's brother, Kenneth Purcell, who had died in a fall this past May. None of the neighbors had seen or heard anything useful. No solid motive had surfaced. There were no suspects. Possible leads were still being checked, Klein said, but he didn't sound confident that they would point him anywhere.

I had no real stake in the case, yet I could not keep it out of my head. You don't watch a man die—*feel* a man die—and then just forget about it as if it never happened. Especially not with reruns of those nightmares every couple of nights. So I read the newspaper stories, and talked to Klein and a few other people, and found out some things about Leonard Purcell and his brother. Eberhardt thought this was morbid and a waste of time, and maybe it was. But Eberhardt has thicker skin than I do; after more than thirty years on the San Francisco cops, it's just a job to him. Sometimes I wish it was just a job to me, too. Sometimes.

The fact that Leonard was the second member of the Purcell family to die within six months might not have interested me if his brother's death hadn't been the result of a fall and hadn't also been on the odd side. Kenneth Purcell, a wealthy real estate broker and art collector, had lost his life during a Thursday-night party at his Moss Beach home. There had been a lot of drinking at this party, evidently—Kenneth had thrown it to show off a valuable antique snuff box he'd acquired—and he had done the lion's share of it. Sometime between nine-thirty and ten he had disappeared; he hadn't been missed until ten, by his wife Alicia. When a search of the house and immediate grounds failed to turn him up, the wife and a couple of the guests had gone out to check the cliffs at the rear of the property. His body had been caught on the rocks a hundred feet below.

There had been no witnesses to his fall. And no evidence of foul play, although Kenneth hadn't been well liked and there were rumors that some of his real estate brokerings were of the quasi-legal variety. The official theory was that he had wandered out

17

onto the cliffs to clear his head—it had been a cold, windy, but clear night—and lost his footing somehow. The valuable snuff box, which Kenneth had had on his person earlier, had not been found on the body; his coat pocket had been torn in the fall and presumably the box had been lost in the ocean. County coroner's verdict: accidental death.

Klein didn't think there was any connection between the deaths of the two brothers. Tom Washburn, on the other hand, *did* think so—apparently for more reasons than just those half-delirious words I had heard Leonard speak before he died. Klein hadn't wanted to go into Washburn's reasons but did say he'd had them checked out thoroughly. He'd also checked out Leonard thoroughly. And was satisfied that Leonard had had no violent old enemies, hadn't professionally or personally offended or antagonized any individual or group of individuals in recent weeks, was not in serious debt to anyone, had no ties to any criminal element. His law practice had been small but thriving, with a mixed client list of gays and straights; and he was financially well off. The official police theory in his case was that he had been shot by an intruder on the hunt for money or valuables.

That was the way things stood—more or less in limbo—when I got to the office at nine o'clock on a Thursday morning, one week after the shooting. Eberhardt wasn't in yet; he likes to keep executive hours, a habit that irritates me sometimes because the agency is mine, not his, and he wouldn't be a part of it if I hadn't felt sorry for him after his early retirement from the SFPD a couple of years ago and taken him in as a full partner. Still, coming in late most mornings was a minor annoyance. He was a good man to work with where and when it counted—a good friend. All things considered, the partnership had turned out much better than I'd expected it would.

I got coffee brewing on the hot plate and wished there were some way to turn the heat up; it was cold and drizzly outside and chilly in here. But no, the landlord—Sam Crawford, a cigar-smoking fat cat who owned buildings in every slum and depressed neighborhood in the city and referred to his tenants as "my people"—had decreed that the cost of heating *this* building was much too high. And to insure that the real estate outfit on the first floor, the Slim-Taper Shirt Company on the second floor, and us on the third floor didn't try to countermand his dictates, he kept the furnace turned on just twelve hours each day, as required by San Francisco law, and had it regulated so that just enough heat reached the radiators to maintain a sixty-degree maximum, no matter what the weather was like outside. Consequently, on mornings like this you had to either wear heavy sweaters or keep your overcoat on while you worked. The only reason Eberhardt and I were still here was that office space was at a premium in the city these days; we couldn't have found a place as large as this, anywhere in the general downtown area where we needed to be, for less than the eight hundred a month we were paying Crawford. The son of a bitch knew that as well as we did. If you'd asked him he would have said he was taking care of "my people" by regulating the heat instead of raising the rent. He was a cutey, he was. About as cute as a vulture on a fence post.

Without taking off my coat I sat down and poked through the papers on my desk. Not much there; things were a little lean at the moment. I had wrapped up some work for the plaintiff in a civil case yesterday, a simple skip-trace two days before that; and last Saturday I'd had the matter of Alfred Henry Umblinger, Jr., and his unpaid-for Mercedes XL wrapped up for me.

The reason Alfred Henry and his lady friend, Eileen Kyner, hadn't shown up at her house was that they'd been on a gambling and boozing spree in Nevada. At approximately four A.M. on Saturday, they had staggered out of a casino in downtown Reno, gotten into the Mercedes parked in a nearby lot, and Alfred Henry had gunned it out into the street. Unfortunately for him, the street happened to be occupied at the time by a Reno police car on patrol. The cops up there take a dim view of drunks running into them at four A.M., particularly deadbeat drunks from California, so Alfred Henry was still in the slammer. Eileen Kyner had bailed herself out and come home; she had not bailed Alfred Henry out because, she had told the police, he (a) had lost a thousand dollars of her money playing blackjack; (b) had made a drunken pass at one of the lady blackjack dealers when he thought she'd gone off to the potty; (c) was lousy in bed anyway; and (d) deserved to rot in jail, schmuck that he was, for doing something so monumentally stupid as mating his Mercedes with a police car. The Burlingame auto dealer who actually owned the Mercedes was not amused, considering that Alfred Henry's monumental stupidity had caused several hundred dollars' damage to the front end of said Mercedes. Once the damage was repaired he'd either have somebody drive it back from Reno or sell it up there at a loss, just to be rid of it. As for me I got paid for my time even though I hadn't managed to repossess the Mercedes; it wasn't *my* fault Alfred Henry was a drunken schmuck as well as a deadbeat.

All I had working now was a background investigation on a guy in San Rafael who had applied to Great Western Insurance for a very large double indemnity policy on his life. Insurance companies get edgy when private individuals apply for such policies. Skeptics and cynics all, they worry that maybe there is some ulterior motive behind the application. Fraud, for instance. Such as an intention to commit suicide under the guise of a fatal accident. My job was to gather as much background material on the individual as possible and turn it over to the insurance people; I could also provide a recommendation, if I was so inclined, but they were the ones who made a final decision as to whether or not to issue a policy. If they did issue it and they got burned, they couldn't put the onus on me. Not legally, anyhow. There were a couple of companies in the Bay Area who *had* got burned and who *had* refused to hire me anymore because of it. But I didn't have to worry about that happening with Great Western: their chief claims adjustor, Barney Rivera, had been a poker buddy for years. He threw a good deal of business my way, and I handed it back with plenty of care.

I was looking through the application and the other papers Barney had given me yesterday when I heard the door open. I glanced up, expecting to see Eberhardt, but instead I was looking at somebody I had never expected to see again: Tom Washburn.

He said formally, "Good morning. I'd like to talk to you, if you have the time."

"Of course, Mr. Washburn."

He shut the door, looked briefly around the office before he came ahead to my desk. The place didn't seem to make much of an impression on him, but that was all right: it had never impressed me either. It had once been an art studio and the owner of the studio had got permission to put in a skylight; the skylight was the place's only attractive feature. Otherwise it was just a big room full of furniture, a couple of pieces of which—Eberhardt's mustard-yellow fiberboard file cabinets—were pretty hideous to look at. Also hideous to look at was a hanging light fixture that just missed being obscene, intentionally on the part of its manufacturer or otherwise.

Washburn sat stiff-backed on one of the clients' chairs, leaning forward with his elbows on his knees and his hands clasped. He was wearing black shoes, black slacks, a black shirt, and a black leather coat—a typical getup for some gays in the city. But it didn't look right on him, and the thought struck me that it was a mourning outfit. There was no question that the death of his lover had affected him profoundly: his face was pale, haggard, with discolored pouches under his eyes; and the eyes themselves had a tragic, haunted look. I felt a sharp twinge of pity for him. I understood what he was going through, because I had known too many others who had suffered the same kind of pain. It was what I would have been going through myself if I had lost Kerry the way he had lost Leonard.

I said, "Can I get you a cup of coffee?"

He didn't answer for a time. Then he seemed to shiver slightly and said, "Yes, all right. It's cold in here."

"The landlord's a jerk. He won't allow the heat turned up past sixty."

I got up and poured two cups of coffee. When I asked him if he took anything in his he said no, just black. I gave him his cup, took mine around the desk, and reoccupied my chair. He sat holding the cup between both hands, as if they were cold; they were pale hands, delicate-looking, the skin almost translucent, so that you could see the fine blue tracery of veins running through them.

At length he said, "I came here because I want to hire you. I don't know what else to do, who else to turn to. You were kind the night Leonard . . . the night it happened, and I thought . . ." He let the words run out and looked down into his cup, as if he might find more words in there.

"Hire me to do what, Mr. Washburn?"

"Find the man who killed Leonard."

"There's nothing I can do that the police aren't doing," I said gently. "Give them enough time and they—"

His head jerked up. "Enough time? My God, they've had a week, haven't they? They haven't found him yet. They *won't* find him, damn them, because they won't listen to me. They simply won't *listen.*"

"Listen to you about what?"

"About the phone call and the missing money," he said. "About Leonard's brother, Kenneth. I can't make them believe me!"

"Take it easy," I said, "slow down a little. You think there's a connection between Kenneth's death and Leonard's?"

"I don't think there is, I *know* there is."

"How do you know it? Leonard's last words aren't really much to—"

"No, not that. The call last week, three days before Leonard was shot. The man on the phone."

"What man?"

"I don't know. A stranger—a voice I didn't recognize."

"He called you, this stranger?"

"No, he was calling Leonard. He thought I was Leonard." Washburn quit talking, gave me a muddled sort of frown, shook himself like a cat, and then said, "Am I making any sense?"

"You're starting to. Just go slow. This man on the phone mistook you for Leonard?"

"Yes. I'd just come home from work; Leonard wasn't in yet. I

22

said hello and this man's voice said, 'Mr. Purcell?' Then he went right on talking before I could tell him I wasn't."

"What did he say?"

"I can quote his exact words. He said, 'Your brother didn't fall off the cliff that night, Mr. Purcell. He was pushed. And I know who pushed him.' "

"That's all?"

"Not quite. I was shocked; I said, 'Who is this? What do you want?' He said, 'Money, Mr. Purcell, that's what I want.' I heard Leonard's car just then, and I was so upset I blurted out that I *wasn't* Mr. Purcell, that Mr. Purcell had just come home and would take the call. He hung up without another word."

"Did you tell Leonard all this when he came in?"

"Of course."

"How did he take it?"

"He said the man must have been a crank. He said Kenneth's death had been an accident, there was no question of that." Washburn's mouth quirked bitterly. "The same things the police said. But Leonard was as upset as I was. I knew him so well—I could always tell when he was upset. He and his brother were very close; he just hadn't been himself since Kenneth's death. If there was even a remote chance Kenneth's fall wasn't an accident, Leonard would have pursued it."

"Did the man call again?"

"Not as far as I know. But I'm convinced he contacted Leonard later on, at his office."

"Even though Leonard didn't mention it to you?"

Washburn nodded emphatically.

"What makes you so sure?" I asked.

"The missing money. Two thousand dollars from the house safe."

"Two thousand *cash?*"

"Yes."

"That's a lot of money to keep around the house."

"I suppose so," he said. "But the safe is hidden in the master bathroom; Leonard had it specially built. No one could find it if he didn't know it was there."

I had heard that one before; professional burglars fell all over themselves laughing when *they* heard it. But all I said was, "Why did the two of you need that much cash on hand?"

"Grocery money. Mad money. Spur-of-the-moment trips to Nevada. Emergencies. All sorts of reasons. We each put in a percentage of our income every month."

I said, "Nevada?"

"Leonard liked to gamble. Poker, blackjack, roulette. Nothing compulsive; he only went three or four times a year. I usually went with him. And he won more than he lost, so I didn't mind. Gambling was his only bad habit."

"When did you find the two thousand missing?"

"The day after the . . . after Leonard's death. The police asked me to make an inventory to find out if anything was missing."

"*Was* anything missing, other than the cash?"

"No. The safe hadn't been touched; there was still five hundred dollars left in it. No one but Leonard and I had the combination. No one but Leonard could have taken the money."

"And you think he took it to pay this mysterious caller. For the name of the person who allegedly murdered his brother."

"Yes," Washburn said. "He had absolutely no other reason to take that much cash out of the safe."

"What about for gambling purposes?"

"That's what the police think. Leonard sometimes gambled here in the city—just poker—but he *never* used house money unless he asked me first, and then only if it was for a Nevada trip. Besides, the most he ever risked at one sitting was two hundred dollars. He had an ironclad rule about that."

"Did he tell you when he took house money for other reasons?"

"Usually."

"Why not this time? Why would he buy information that way without confiding in you?"

"You'd have to have known Leonard," Washburn said, and there was something different in his voice now: a kind of sadness seasoned with hurt and a touch of bitterness. "He was a very private man. We loved each other, and yet when it came to his family and his business, he . . . well, sometimes he shut me out. Particularly where his brother was concerned."

"Why is that?"

"Kenneth didn't like me, didn't like anyone who wasn't straight. He told Leonard once that he didn't want anything to do with his faggot boyfriend, and Leonard didn't stand up to him. It was as if, underneath, he . . . he was ashamed of me." Washburn looked away, over at Eberhardt's empty desk. He seemed very small, sitting there—and very alone. "Anyhow," he said after a time, "that was why I wasn't invited to the party the night Kenneth died."

"Was Leonard invited?"

"Oh yes. And he went, even though he knew it hurt me."

I was beginning to get a picture of what kind of man Leonard Purcell had been. And I didn't particularly like what I saw. I watched Washburn finish what was left in his cup, put the cup down carefully on the edge of my desk. Watched him hunch a little inside his jacket. Damn Sam Crawford and his mandates about the heat.

I said, "More coffee, Mr. Washburn?"

"No, thank you. It's a bit too strong for me."

"I can add some water . . ."

"No, really, I'm fine."

I got up and poured another half-cup for myself. When I sat down again I said, "About Kenneth. How did he feel about Leonard being gay?"

"I don't really know. I suppose he ignored it, as if it were a temporary aberration on Leonard's part. Leonard was married once, you know."

"No, I didn't know."

"For five years. Ruth divorced him when she found out he had male lovers." A faint smile. "I was one of them."

"Do you know his ex-wife?"

"No, not really."

"Was the divorce bitter or amicable?"

"Not as bitter as it might have been, I guess—Leonard didn't talk about that much, either. She did let him have the house." Pain moved through his expression again, like something dark and restive just beneath the surface of his features. "He really loved that house. So did I, until . . . well, now it's as dead for me as he is."

"How long had you been living there with him?"

"Two years, ever since Ruth moved out. It was a permanent relationship."

"I'm sure it was."

"We were going to be married one day," he said.

I knew that gays sometimes had unofficial wedding ceremonies, without benefit of marriage licenses, presided over by ministers from the Unitarian church or some other liberal congregation. But I did not want to discuss that sort of thing with Washburn. It was a private matter, and painful for him now—and I was still old-fashioned enough to feel uncomfortable with some of the more open and iconoclastic attitudes of the homosexual community.

I said, "Let's get back to the man on the telephone. Do you have any idea who he might be?"

"No, none."

"Was he young, old?"

"Young—twenties or thirties, I'd say."

"Black, white, Oriental?"

"I'm not sure. Latin, perhaps."

"Did he have an accent?"

"A faint one. I couldn't quite place it."

"Anything else distinctive about his voice?"

"No. No, I don't think so."

"Did he sound educated?"

"Well, he used proper English. But he didn't seem very well-spoken."

"Any other impression of him?"

"I'm afraid that's all."

"If what he said to you is true he must either have been at

Kenneth's house that night and witnessed what happened, or he's close to someone who was there and witnessed it."

Washburn worried his lower lip for a time. Then he said, "He didn't strike me as the type Kenneth would invite to one of his fancy parties. His friends were mostly rich people."

"An acquaintance of one of the guests, then?"

"Kenneth's daughter," Washburn said musingly. "She's the wild type."

"Wild in what way?"

"Oh, you know, drugs. The whole scene."

"Where does she live, do you know?"

"With some fellow on Mission Creek. She has a houseboat there. At least she did a few months ago."

"What's the fellow's name?"

"I don't remember Leonard mentioning it."

"What's *her* name? Purcell?"

"Yes. Melanie Purcell. Kenneth's daughter by his first marriage."

"Would you know if she was at the party that night?"

"I'm not sure. I think she might have been."

"What can you tell me about the other guests?"

"Very little, I'm afraid. Alicia is the person to ask."

"Kenneth's widow?"

"Yes. She's his second wife."

"What happened to the first one?"

"They were divorced."

"Where would I find Alicia?"

"Well, I think she's still living at the house."

"In Moss Beach, you mean."

"Yes."

"Did Leonard handle his brother's legal affairs?"

"No. He didn't feel it was proper."

"Who did?"

"An attorney here in the city. I don't remember his name."

"I can get it from the police. Did Kenneth leave a will?"

"Oh, yes."

27

"Who inherited the bulk of his estate?"

"Alicia, Melanie, and Leonard."

"How much was the estate worth?"

"I don't know exactly. Quite a lot."

"What was Leonard's share?"

"I don't know that either," Washburn said. "Talking about it was so painful for him; I tried not to pry."

"Do you know if the will has cleared probate yet? If the inheritance has been paid?"

"I'm sure it hasn't. I'd know if it had been."

"Let's assume Kenneth *was* pushed off that cliff," I said. "Who do you think did the pushing?"

He spread his hands. "I just have no idea. Someone he was involved with on one of his real estate deals, possibly."

"Quasi-legitimate, some of those deals, according to the papers."

"Yes. So I understand."

"In what way?"

"I really couldn't say."

"Did Leonard know?"

"I suppose he did."

"But he wouldn't discuss it?"

"No. He didn't approve, I can tell you that."

"Did Leonard happen to say anything about his brother's missing snuff box?"

"No, nothing."

"Kenneth collected snuff boxes, didn't he?"

"Snuff bottles, too," Washburn said. "And humidors, cigarette boxes—anything rare and valuable connected with tobacco."

I made a note on the pad in front of me; I had been making notes right along. While I was doing that Eberhardt burst in. He doesn't just walk into a room, like most people; he barrels in as if he's one of the vanguards in a raiding party. Washburn, looking startled, swung around on his chair. I got up, saying, "Just my partner," and introduced them.

Eberhardt wanted to know if he was intruding; I said no, Washburn's and my business was about finished. He nodded, muttered something about it being like an icebox in here, poured himself some coffee, and went to his desk and picked up his phone.

I said to Washburn, "So your theory is both Kenneth and Leonard were killed by the same person—Leonard so he wouldn't expose the truth about his brother's death."

Washburn nodded. He seemed a little ill at ease now that someone else was in the room.

"But why *didn't* Leonard expose the truth? Why contact the murderer instead of the police? Why let him or her know that the crime against Kenneth had been found out?"

"Leonard might have been trying to make him admit something incriminating, just so he could be sure. He had to've known the person; he must not have believed his own life was in danger."

Plausible answers—up to a point. But it still didn't quite add up for me. I said as much to Washburn. I also pointed out to him that Leonard's murderer didn't have to be the same person who had pushed Kenneth to his death—*if* Kenneth had been pushed. It could just as easily have been the man on the telephone.

"But what motive would he have? Leonard must have paid him the two thousand dollars; the police didn't find it in his office and it certainly isn't in the house."

"Maybe he didn't give Leonard the name once he had the payoff," I said. "Maybe he didn't *have* a name; it could have been a straight extortion ploy, no truth to it at all. And maybe he demanded another payoff and went to the house to collect it. Leonard refused, the man threatened him with a gun, something happened to make him use it . . ."

"Yes, I see what you mean. But I don't really care *who* it was, or why; I just want him caught and put in the gas chamber." He folded his pale, delicate hands together again. "You know, it's funny," he said. "I never believed in capital punishment until now. Now I want to go to San Quentin when the time comes and watch that motherfucker *die.*"

I didn't say anything. There was nothing to say to that.

"You will work for me?" he said. "Do what you can to find him?"

I kept silent a while longer. The thing was, I felt sorry for him.

He was so small and alone, sitting there, so empty; and I kept seeing him the way he'd been last Thursday night, after he had looked into the dining room and seen what was left of his lover. I couldn't turn him down. How could I turn him down?

"If the police have no objections," I said finally, "yes, I'll investigate what you've told me. But you have to understand that if they don't think Kenneth was murdered, or that there's any connection between his death and Leonard's, chances are they're right and I won't find out anything."

"I understand. But they're not right, I know they're not."

"Also I don't come cheap," I said. "I get two hundred and fifty dollars a day plus expenses."

"That doesn't matter. Money doesn't matter. I have enough."

"All right then." I got one of the agency contracts out of the desk and filled it in and had him sign it. Then I asked, "Where can I reach you? You're not staying at the house?"

"No. I couldn't spend a night there, not any more. It was all I could do to make myself go back last Friday to take inventory for the police. I'm staying with a friend." He gave me a name and an address on upper Market, on the fringe of the Castro district, and said that he would be there days as well as nights, at least until next Monday: he had taken a leave of absence from his job at Bank of America. He also gave me a check for a thousand dollars and insisted I let him know when I wanted more.

When all of that was done I went with him to the door, and shook his hand, and watched him walk away to the stairs. And I thought: It's not just for him. It's for Leonard, no matter what kind of man he was—and for me, too. Because I saw Leonard crawling in his own blood in that dining room; because I was there with my hand on him when he died.

FOUR

M y second visitor of the morning showed up fifteen minutes after Tom Washburn left. And if I had been surprised to see Washburn, I was literally struck dumb by the appearance of this one.

I might have been gone when he came in—I had plenty of things to do, now, outside the office—but Eberhardt insisted on telling me a couple of jokes he'd heard at some party in Noe Valley the night before. Eb is a social animal, a party-goer, whereas I prefer Kerry's company whenever possible, or a pulp magazine's if I can't have hers. He was forever trying to drag me to this or that shindig, large and small, stag and co-ed. The first time I'd weakened and given in, I had been bored and uncomfortable. The second and last time, I had gotten sick on somebody's lousy fish canapés that turned out to be loaded with salmonella. Eberhardt's circle of friends does not include any gourmet cooks.

Anyhow, he'd heard these two jokes and thought they were hilarious. The first one had to do with a beautiful blonde, a well-endowed Texan, a copy of the *Kama Sutra,* and a billy goat; it was long and involved and had a punchline that was not worth waiting for and that I promptly forgot, along with the rest of the joke. The second story was much shorter and somewhat funnier, not that it was exactly a tickler of ribs or a splitter of sides.

"So this guy goes into a drugstore one night. He's just been married, it's his wedding night, and he's kind of nervous. He tells this to the druggist and then he says his new wife doesn't want to get pregnant on their honeymoon so she sent him in to buy some protection. He doesn't know much about stuff like that, he says

31

—he's still a virgin, see—so could the druggist show him what to buy."

"Uh-huh," I said.

"So the druggist shows him a rack of condoms, right? The guy looks 'em over, picks a brand, and asks how much. The druggist says, 'Two dollars plus tax.' The guy turns pale. 'Tacks?' he says. 'Jeez, I thought those things were supposed to stay on by themselves.' "

Eberhardt was laughing uproariously, and I was chuckling a little, when the door opened and the second visitor walked in. I had never seen him before and as it turned out, neither had Eberhardt; but one look at him and both of us quit laughing. He was that kind of guy. Mid-forties, six-two or so, lank brown hair, handsome in a saturnine sort of way; stiff-backed and solemn-eyed and pinch-mouthed. Wearing a three-piece charcoal-gray suit, a slender blue-checked tie, and black shoes polished to a high gloss. He reminded me of an undertaker. You just knew, looking at him, that there wasn't a funny bone in his body. If he'd come in in time to hear either of Eberhardt's jokes he wouldn't have cracked a smile. He might not even know *how* to crack a smile.

He stood just inside the door, looking around in a disapproving way, like an investigator for the Board of Health. He studied Eberhardt; he studied me. Then he nodded once, strictly to himself, and came my way and stopped in front of my desk.

I said, "May I help you?"

He said, "Fornication is a sin, sayeth the Lord."

I said, "Huh?"

"You're a fornicator—you lust after men's wives. You stand on the brink of eternal damnation."

I couldn't have said anything then if my life depended on it. I just gawped at him.

" 'Woe unto them that draw iniquity with cords of vanity,' " he said, " 'and sin as it were with a cart rope.' The Book of the Prophet Isaiah, five: eighteen."

"Listen," I said, and then stopped because the word came out like a frog croaking. I tried again. "Listen, uh . . ."

" 'Be not deceived; God is not mocked: for whatsoever a man soweth, that shall he also reap.' Galatians, six: seven."

I opened my mouth, and closed it again. Eberhardt's was hanging open like a Venus's-flytrap.

The guy reached inside his suit coat. I thought for a second that he was going after a weapon of some kind and got ready to launch myself at him; but all he came out with was a business card. He put the card down in front of me. Then he folded his arms and waited stoically.

I looked at the card. And then stared at it. In blue letters on a virginal white background it said:

THE REVEREND RAYMOND P. DUNSTON
Church of the Holy Mission

THE MORAL CRUSADE
1243 Langford Street   San Jose, CA. 95190

I put my eyes back on him and said, "Jesus Christ!"

"No," he said, "merely one of His servants. You know who *I* am."

I knew who he was, all right. Ray Dunston, Kerry's whackoid ex-husband. What I had trouble believing was that he was standing here in my office, looking and talking the way he was. Five years ago, when Kerry had divorced him, he had been a woman-chasing, small-time criminal lawyer in Los Angeles. Two years ago he had taken a dive off the deep end: given up his practice and any number of normal activities, including sex, and joined one of those off-the-wall Southern California cults, where he had shaved his head and worn robes and spent his days chanting things like "Om mani padme hum." Now here he was, wearing a three-piece suit again and with his hair grown back, calling himself the Reverend Raymond P. Dunston of the Church of the Holy Mission, involved in something called the Moral Crusade, quoting scripture and accusing me of being a fornicator. If that wasn't enough to boggle a reasonably sane man's mind I did not want to find out what was.

I said, "What are you doing here? What do you want?"

"I've come to claim what is mine."

"I don't have anything that belongs to you."

"Of course you do. My wife."

"Your . . . you mean Kerry?"

"Kerry Anne Dunston."

"For God's sake, she divorced you five years ago!"

"For *God's* sake," he said piously, "she did not. Divorce is a pernicious invention of man. God does not recognize divorce."

"He doesn't, huh? Did He tell you that Himself?"

"Yes, He did."

"He . . . what?"

"He told me so. We speak often, God and I."

Oh boy. He had clear brown eyes that met mine steadily, all full of righteousness and calm reason, but behind them he was as mad as a hatter. I shifted uneasily in my chair and pushed back from the desk. I had figured him for a loony when Kerry first told me about the cult, and I had figured there might be trouble with him when she confessed that he'd been bothering her, trying to talk her into remarrying him and joining in a life of wholesome chanting in the commune. She had managed to keep him at a distance, and after a while he seemed to have given up and gone away for good: she hadn't heard anything more from or about him in months. Or she *said* she hadn't, anyway. What he'd been doing in the interim, obviously, was climbing another rung on the ladder of lunacy, and now he'd come in person to claim his soul mate. No commune this time, though. No sir. This time he expected her to live with him in San Jose, if not in the Church of the Holy Mission; to join him on the Moral Crusade, whatever *that* was; and to sit in on his fireside chats with God.

I stood up. He didn't look violent, but with loonies you never know. God might have told him that if reason didn't work, it was all right to murder fornicators.

"Have you talked to Kerry about this?" I asked him. Out of the corner of my eye I saw that Eberhardt was also on his feet. His mouth was still hanging open; he looked like a man trying to wake up from a confusing dream.

Dunston said, "No. She refuses to listen to the Voice of Truth. You've cast some sort of spell over her."

"Spell?" I said. "What do you think I am, a witch?"

"Warlock," he said.

"What?"

"She was never like this before you seduced her," he said. "She always listened to me, obeyed me. But you enticed her, bewitched her, made her lie down in your bed."

"I didn't even know her when she divorced you!"

" 'How shall I pardon thee for this? Thy children have forsaken me, and sworn by them that are no gods: when I had fed them to the full, they then committed adultery, and assembled themselves by troops in the harlots' houses. They were as fed horses in the morning: every one neighed after his neighbor's wife.' Jeremiah, five: seven and eight."

"Look, Dunston—"

"The Reverend Dunston. I am ordained."

"Sure you are. Ordained."

"But I do pardon thee, just as God will if you seek Him out. I forgive your sins and I forgive hers. I hold no animosity. I mean only to have her back."

"She won't go back to you."

"She will. Yes, she will. God has decreed it."

"He told you that too, did He?"

"Yes. That too." Dunston turned abruptly and went to the door, opened it. At which point he looked at me again and said, " 'Many waters cannot quench love, neither can the floods drown it.' The Song of Solomon, eight: seven. Those whom God has joined together, no man can put asunder." And he was gone.

I stood there. Eberhardt stood there. Neither of us moved or said anything for at least fifteen seconds. Then Eb blew out his breath gustily and said with awe in his voice, "Now I've seen it all."

"That makes two of us."

"I thought he was in some kind of commune. The Hare Krishnas or something."

"Yeah. Or something."

Eberhardt came over to my desk and picked up Dunston's card. "Church of the Holy Mission. The Moral Crusade." He flicked a fingernail against the card and said, "From the Hare Krishnas to Jerry Falwell—that's some leap."

"You're telling me?"

"You ever hear of either one, the church or the crusade?"

"No. You?"

"No. I can check 'em out, if you want."

"I want. Thanks, Eb."

He went back to his desk. I picked up the phone and dialed the number of Bates and Carpenter, the ad agency where Kerry worked as a chief copywriter. The switchboard put me through to her secretary, who said that Kerry was in conference, could she call me back in about an hour? I said, "No, she can't call me back in about an hour. I don't care what she's doing, I want to talk to her *now*. Tell her it's an emergency." There was something in my voice that made the secretary decide not to argue; she went away meekly. I waited. A full minute went by. Then there was a clattering noise, followed by another clattering noise, as if the phone had been dropped, and Kerry came on sounding out of breath.

"What is it?" she said. "What's the matter? Are you all right?"

"That depends on your definition of all right. Your ex-husband just showed up here at the office."

"What!"

"We had a nice chat," I said. "He called me a fornicator and a witch, or maybe it was a warlock, and accused me of seducing you and then casting a spell on you to keep you from going back to him."

Silence for three or four seconds. Then she said, "Oh my God."

"But that's not the best part. No more commune for old Ray; no more shaved heads and robes and chants. He's back to wearing three-piece suits, he lives in San Jose, and he's an ordained minister—he says—in something called the Church of the Holy Mission."

"Oh my *God!*"

"God, right," I said. "I almost forgot. He talks to God now. Personally."

"Talks to . . ." She made a funny little strangled noise.

"Yes indeed," I said. "And God told him divorce is a pernicious invention of man, so as far as he's concerned the two of you are still married." I waited a while, and when she stayed silent I said, "He wants me to give you up. He said if I don't I'm going to hell."

"You mean he *threatened* you?"

"Not exactly. No."

"Thank God for that. He was never violent when I knew him." Pause. "He's living in San Jose, you said?"

"Apparently. You didn't know that, huh?"

"No. How would I know?"

"He hasn't been in touch with you?"

"Not in months. You don't think—?"

"I don't think anything. I'm just asking."

Another pause. "This new church—what kind is it?"

"Good question. It has something to do with the Moral Crusade. Him too."

"I never heard of the Moral Crusade. Like the Moral Majority?"

"Probably. Eberhardt's checking on it."

She said nervously, "What are you going to do?"

"About what?"

"About Ray."

"I don't know yet. You got any suggestions?"

"No. Just don't *do* anything until we talk this out."

"What are you afraid I might do? Drown him in holy water?"

"Don't grouch at me. It's not my fault, is it?"

"Well, you married him."

"He wasn't a lunatic when I married him, for God's sake. He was *normal.*"

"Yeah," I said. "Normal."

"Well, he was." There was some mumbling in the background. Pretty soon she said, "Listen, I have to go now. I was in an important meeting with a client. . . . I've got to get back. We'll talk about this tonight, okay?"

She sounded flustered and edgy, and all at once I was sorry that I'd shaken her up like this. It *wasn't* her fault she had an ex-husband who claimed a personal relationship with God, or that he'd decided to walk into my office this morning. Why take it out on her?

I said, "Okay. Babe, I'm sorry, I didn't mean to upset you. It's just that he got me all worked up . . ."

"No, I'm glad you called. For all we know he might be on his way over *here.*"

I hadn't thought of that. I said, "You'd better alert the receptionist."

"Don't worry, I will. See you tonight."

I put the receiver down, and sighed, and looked at Eberhardt. He was still on the phone. I sighed again and looked at my watch. 10:40. Most of the morning shot already. Tom Washburn was paying me good money, and all I was doing was hanging around here, stewing about Ray Dunston and feeling sorry for myself.

Eberhardt cradled his handset and said, "That was a guy I know on the San Jose cops. Ed Berg. He never heard of the Church of the Holy Mission or the Moral Crusade."

"Terrific."

"But it won't take him long to find out. I told him if nobody's here when he calls back, leave a message on the answering machine and one of us'll call him back."

"Right. You got anything pressing today, Eb?"

"Nothing that won't wait. Why?"

"Take over that insurance investigation for Barney Rivera, will you? I want to get moving on the Purcell thing."

He shrugged. "I figured," he said. "It's personal with you, right? Because you were there when it happened. You're glad Washburn showed up this morning and hired you."

"Maybe. A little."

"Just don't let it get too personal, paisan. You make waves somewhere, there'll be trouble. There always is."

"It's not that personal," I said.

"Uh-huh. I've heard that one before."

I got my hat and moved to the door.

Eberhardt said musingly, "What do you suppose God thinks about guys like Dunston? You know, religious nuts that claim they got a pipeline Upstairs. You think He finds 'em comical?"

"No," I said. "And neither do I."

He frowned. "What if they *do* have a pipeline, some of 'em? Guys like Falwell. What if they're delivering the right message?"

I didn't answer that; I didn't even want to think about it. I went out quietly and shut the door.

There are some things you just have to take on faith.

FIVE

The first place I went was to the Hall of Justice. Ben Klein was in and willing to talk over an early lunch; I spent twenty-five minutes with him and a tuna salad sandwich in the ground-floor cafeteria. He had no objection to my investigating Tom Washburn's theory, but he made it plain that he thought it was a waste of my time and Washburn's money.

"A tie-in between Purcell's murder and his brother's death was one of the first things we checked out," he said. "I told you that before. There's just no evidence that Kenneth Purcell's death was anything but an accident."

"From what I understand, more than one person had a strong motive for knocking him off."

"Sure. His wife and his daughter, among others; nobody seemed to like him much. But the world is full of assholes, and how many of them get wasted by people who don't like them?"

"Not many, maybe," I admitted. "But some do."

"Not Kenneth Purcell. Everybody at the party was with everybody else: all nicely alibied for the time of his death."

"Somebody else, then. Somebody who wasn't invited to the party."

"Theoretically possible. But again, no evidence to even suggest it."

"That real estate business of Purcell's—what put it on the shady side?"

"He was brokering for foreign interests," Klein said. "The kind with dubious ethics and political orientations. You know, buying property under his own name without telling anybody he was using foreign capital; helping unscrupulous investors from countries like Lebanon, South Africa, the Philippines get into positions of financial power in this country that they wouldn't be able to if property owners and legitimate brokers knew who they were. He peddled influence, too—arranged for high-powered legal representation for his clients."

"Could his brother have been mixed up in that?"

"No. Not powerful enough. We're talking big money here. VIPs."

"Sounds like the kind of business where you could make a lot of enemies," I said.

"Absolutely. But it's also the kind of business where the lid is screwed down tight. The feds might be able to unscrew it, given enough time and provocation; the authorities in San Mateo County couldn't, and neither can we."

"What about the missing snuff box? Any chance of an angle in that?"

Klein shook his head. "Purcell apparently had it on him when he went off the cliff. The body got beat up pretty bad on the rocks before it was recovered; San Mateo figures the box got ripped loose and lost."

"Washburn told me the dingus was valuable. How valuable?"

"Fifty thousand dollars in the collectors' market."

"That much? Lot of money for a snuff box."

"You're telling me. One of a kind item, though, made out of gold and dating back to Napoleon's time. So Eldon Summerhayes says."

"Who's he?"

"Owns the Summerhayes Gallery, up on Post Street. He deals in rare snuff containers, among other items. He and his wife were at the party."

"Other dealers and collectors there too?"

"Two other collectors. Purcell got them all together so he could gloat, evidently; he'd just bought the box."

"From?"

"Nobody seems to know. He kept his source a secret."

"Illegal deal, maybe?"

"Maybe. But there doesn't seem to be any way it could tie in to his death, or to his brother's. And those other collectors he invited are blue-chip citizens."

"Okay," I said. "So you figure the guy Washburn talked to on the phone was just a crank."

"Probably. Or somebody with a bright idea on how to make a fast buck."

"Either way, Ben, why would he wait six months? Why not make the call within a few days of Kenneth's death?"

"Your guess is as good as mine," Klein said. "But don't forget the same thing applies if the caller really did have knowledge that it was a homicide. Why wait six months?"

Good question either way. And one of several weak points in Washburn's theory. I said, "Nothing in Leonard's effects to indicate he ever talked to the guy?"

"Nothing."

"Or what might have happened to the missing two thousand?"

"No."

I asked him about Kenneth Purcell's wife and daughter. He smiled wryly. "A couple of sweethearts, those two," he said.

"How so?"

"You'll see when you meet them. I wouldn't want to spoil your fun by tipping you off ahead of time."

"Yeah, I'll bet. Can I get a list of the people at the party? Names and addresses?"

"I don't see why not. Come upstairs with me after we finish."

So I went back upstairs with him, and he gave me a computer printout of the list. He also gave me the address and telephone number of the Moss Beach house where Alicia Purcell now lived alone, the name of the attorney who had handled Kenneth's legal affairs, and the name of the guy that Melanie Purcell was living with on Mission Creek.

I thought about asking him to let me look over the complete file on the Leonard Purcell homicide, but I didn't do it. Cops don't mind helping out private detectives now and then, if you maintain a good professional rapport with them, but they get testy if you hang around and ask too many favors. They have to slog along assembling facts on their own; they figure you ought to be doing the same thing. In the detective business, there is no such thing as a free ride. Or, for that matter, a free lunch: I had paid for Klein's, and gladly.

Kenneth Purcell's attorney, Lawrence Rossiter, had a suite of offices on the twentieth floor of a newish high-rise in Embarcadero Center. Both the offices and the address were impressive, and so was Rossiter himself: sixtyish, graying, with a beautifully groomed walrus mustache and the kind of courtly manner you seldom find these days in any lawyer under the age of fifty. He kept me waiting less than fifteen minutes before he had his secretary usher me into his rosewood-paneled inner sanctum, which was another point in his favor.

He was helpful, too, although he made it clear from the start that he was willing to discuss the terms of Kenneth's will only because it was in probate and therefore a matter of public record. It was due to clear probate, he said, in less than two weeks.

"How much is the estate worth?" I asked him.

"Upwards of two million. Of course, the bulk of that is in property and other non-liquid assets."

"How much cash?"

"Something better than five hundred thousand."

"The three primary beneficiaries are his widow, his daughter, and his brother Leonard, is that right?"

"Yes."

"Divided how?"

"The cash into equal thirds," Rossiter said. "Most of the property and other assets go to his widow."

"Including the Moss Beach house?"

"Yes."

"And his collection of antique tobacco items?"

"That too, yes."

"How much is the collection worth?"

"It was appraised at three hundred thousand. The house is valued at half a million at the current market price."

That kind of estate was a hell of a good motive for murder, I thought. Especially so for Alicia Purcell, but also for the daughter, Melanie; people had been given a nudge into the hereafter for a lot less than a couple of hundred grand. Still, as Klein had pointed out, a strong motive didn't mean anything if you couldn't prove a homicide had taken place.

I asked Rossiter, "Did Kenneth make any other bequests?"

"No."

"Nothing to his first wife? Or is she no longer living?"

"Katherine is alive as far as I know. Living in Seattle, I believe. But Kenneth chose not to include her."

"It wasn't an amicable divorce, then?"

"It was not."

"When did they split up?"

"They separated in 'seventy-three; the divorce was final the following year."

"When did he marry Alicia?"

"Immediately after the final decree."

"Was she the reason for the first marriage breaking up?"

Rossiter gave me a look of mild reproach. "I hardly think that's germane to the subject of Kenneth's will," he said.

"I guess not. Were there any unusual stipulations or clauses in the will?"

"As a matter of fact, yes. A proviso that Leonard's bequest not be paid to him until two full years after the closing of probate. And that it not be paid at all if Leonard died in the interim."

"What was the reason for that?"

Rossiter hesitated. Then he shrugged and said, "I see no reason not to tell you. Kenneth disliked his brother's lifestyle and disapproved of the man Leonard was living with."

"Uh-huh, I get it. He couldn't stop Leonard from leaving his own money to Tom Washburn, but he didn't want Washburn to get a piece of *his* money—at least not right away."

"Something like that."

"Nice guy, Kenneth."

Rossiter didn't have any comment.

I said, "Who gets Leonard's third of the estate now?"

"Alicia and Melanie. Evenly divided between them."

Motive for both, I thought, to have shot Leonard as well as to have murdered Kenneth. More so for Melanie, though; when you were getting more than a million, as Alicia was, you'd have to be damned greedy to commit murder for another few hundred thousand.

Rossiter had nothing more to tell me. I thanked him for his time and left him to his work. Downstairs in the lobby, I closed myself inside a public telephone booth and called the Moss Beach number I had got from Ben Klein. A woman I took to be a maid or housekeeper answered. She said Mrs. Purcell was not at home and wasn't expected back until after five. Did I wish to leave a message? I said no, I would call back, and rang off. I would have tried calling Melanie Purcell, too, but she didn't have a phone. Not too many people living on Mission Creek did have one.

Where to next? I asked myself when I came out of the booth. Some of the guests at Kenneth's farewell party had San Francisco addresses; I could start canvassing them, beginning with the gallery owner, Eldon Summerhayes. But I wanted a better handle on the surviving members of the Purcell family first, particularly after

44

Klein's "sweethearts" comment, and now that I knew the details of Kenneth's will. Alicia Purcell wasn't home; maybe Melanie was.

I picked up my car and went to find out.

SIX

M ission Creek is a narrow body of water that leads inland from China Basin, a dead-end canal spanned by the Third and Fourth Street drawbridges—all that is left of old Mission Bay, landfill having claimed the rest. The creek is flanked on one side by warehouses, freight consolidators, and industrial outfits that line parallel Channel Street; on another side by part of the Southern Pacific freight yards; on another by empty storage lots. And over it all loom the curving ramps and overpasses of Highway 280's city terminus. Standing down there along the canal, you can hear the steady thrum of traffic, the air horns on the commuter trains that move in and out of the SP Depot at Third and Townsend, the throb and roar of trucks and heavy machinery. And yet there is something about Mission Creek itself, a kind of timeless solitude, that seems to keep it aloof from its hectic surroundings.

Up until about ten years ago, the canal had harbored a rotting pier and pilings, a lot of sea birds, schools of anchovies and perch, and several squatters who lived on and fished from ragamuffin barges, hay scows, converted Navy landing craft, cabin cruisers, and houseboats. When the Port Authority threatened to evict the boat people in the mid-seventies, with the idea of turning the channel into a modern landscaped marina, the waterfolk had got their act together, formed the Mission Creek Harbor Association, and hired a lawyer to intercede on their behalf with the Bay

Conservation and Development Commission. The result was that they had not only been allowed to stay, but had received a kind of official sanction—the only stipulation being that they clean up the area and maintain it in an acceptable fashion.

The boat people had been scrupulous about keeping their part of the bargain: Mission Creek was a pretty decent place these days, a haven for boat lovers, artists, artisans, and average citizens who disliked conventional city living. There were more than fifty authorized slips, all of them occupied, extending in a nice orderly row up the middle of the creek, with several security-gated ramps giving access to them from the Channel Street embankment. Most of the craft in there now were houseboats of one type or another, sailboats, and cabin cruisers; and most of them were well cared for, if a little on the funky side.

I parked in one of the slots down toward Fourth Street, walked past a gaggle of geese and one of the Port-O-Johns that were strategically placed along the embankment—most of the berthed craft would have chemical toilets, but that kind of waste disposal can be a problem—and went to the nearest access ramp. The security gate there was standing open; it was probably kept locked only at night. I descended onto a narrow board float set almost flush with the murky water of the creek, bordered on one side by the slips and on the other by horizontally arranged logs along which were strung electrical cables and water hookups. The first person I saw was a bearded guy in his thirties, doing some work on the deck of a green cabin cruiser; the smell of creosote coming off him and the boat was strong in the thin cold air. I asked him where I could find the boat belonging to Melanie Purcell, and he pointed back toward Fourth Street and said, "Eight slips that way. Houseboat with the decals."

I moved along in that direction. Gulls and something I took to be a heron wheeled overhead; the water made little slapping sounds against the float and the moored boats. The sounds of the freeway traffic and the SP trains seemed remote, as if they were coming from some dimension or continuum once removed. The houseboat in the eighth slip down had decals all over the front of it—big flower things made out of wood and painted different pastel colors. It also had a peaked roof, some odd angles, varnished wood siding, a pair of bubble skylights, and a round stained-glass window high up under the eaves of its roof.

I didn't see a door anywhere; it had to be around on the aft side. I stepped on board and started that way along a narrow starboard walkway. But I got only as far as a shuttered window halfway along before the noises coming from inside stopped me. Two people were having sex in there, and they weren't being quiet about it. For that matter, they weren't even being civilized about it.

Voyeurism isn't one of my vices; I backed away in a hurry and disembarked onto the board float. Once, several months ago, Kerry had rented an X-rated videotape and played it for us on the new VCR she'd bought, just so we could see what one of those things was all about. What it was all about embarrassed the hell out of me, as old as I am. I quit watching after about five minutes, but Kerry stuck with it for another twenty or so. It wasn't because it made her hot, she said; it was because she thought all those moans and groans and gyrations were funny—in a perverse way, of course. I hadn't believed her for a minute, not before she half dragged me into the bedroom and definitely not afterward.

I climbed up to the embankment and walked along it a ways, killing time. Down where Channel Street right-angles into Sixth, in the shadow of the freeway looming high overhead, some of the Mission Creek residents had turned an acre or so of ground into a surprisingly impressive vegetable garden. Corn, beans, zucchini, strawberries, some other things. It really was a whole different world down here, a little self-contained community that continued to flourish outside the mainstream of city life. Somehow, in a way that I couldn't quite define, it gave me a feeling of hope.

After about ten minutes I went back down to the float, along it to Melanie Purcell's houseboat. This time, when I got as far as the starboard window, nobody was making any noise inside. So I kept moving aft. Around back there was a little oblong deck floored in green Astro-turf and, in the middle of the decal-decorated superstructure, a door that I proceeded to bang on. Nothing happened, so I banged on it again.

It opened abruptly and I was looking at a bulky guy in his early twenties, naked except for a pair of Levi's. He had sandy hair puffed out in one of those frizzes, and judging from the scowl on his face, he also had a lousy disposition. He looked me over, decided I was nobody he knew or wanted to know, and said, "What is it?"

"Richard Dessault?" That was the name of the guy Melanie was living with. His occupation, according to Ben Klein, was "poet." Some occupation.

"So?" he said. "You want something?"

"Not from you. I'd like to talk to Melanie."

"What for?"

"To ask her some questions about her uncle's death."

"Ah, Christ," he said disgustedly, "*another* cop."

"I'm a detective, that's right, but not a—"

He shut the door in my face.

It would have made me mad, except that he didn't shut it all the way; the wind blew it open again. He was moving away across the room inside, toward another door at the opposite end, and when he felt the cold air against his bare skin he said without looking back at me, "Come on in then. I'll get her."

I went in and closed the door, making sure it latched this time, and had a look around. There wasn't much to see. The basic furnishings were a couple of low-slung teakwood tables, a pair of Oriental-style lamps, and a bunch of big pillows—shiny material in a variety of colors and exotic designs, most of them with tassels and fringe—scattered around on the floor. On one of the tables was a fancy water pipe—a hookah, I think they're called—that you use to smoke tobacco, among other substances. It was all supposed to create a sultan's harem effect. But the color TV and stereo equipment along one wall spoiled it; so did the overblown wall poster of some weird rock group called the Aluminum Dandruff.

I waited about two minutes. I could hear voices from one of the other rooms, but not what was being said. It was a little chilly in there, but then maybe they depended on body heat to keep them warm; they had been generating enough of it a few minutes ago. Another of their heating devices, no doubt, was marijuana. The sweetish, acrid smell of it was sharp in the air.

The table nearest me had a note pad and pencil on it. There was some writing on the pad; nosily I moved over a couple of steps and bent down to look at it. Nine lines, almost illegibly printed, under the title "Acapulco Gold":

> gold, gold
> can't feel blue with the gold—
> gold in the sunset,
> gold in the hills
> and valleys of my mind—
> the big gold rush
> gold, gold
> digging the gold—
> the big gold rush

I straightened up again. Poet, my ass, I thought.

The voices stopped finally, and the door across the room opened, and a girl came in. Dessault came in, too, but he hung back by the far wall while she moved forward to where I was. I don't know what I expected her to be like—beautiful and dripping sex appeal, maybe, like heiresses in bad Hollywood movies—but she was a surprise in any case. Not much past twenty-one, skinny, flat-chested, with mouse-brown hair frizzed up like Dessault's and bright vulpine eyes, one of which was slightly cocked. On both cheeks, which were still flushed from her recent exertion, little patches of acne flourished. She wore Levi's and a tank top that made her chest look even flatter. Her feet were bare and dirty and the toenails were painted black.

Sugar and spice and everything nice, I thought sourly.

I said, "Melanie Purcell?"

"That's right. Who're you?"

I told her my name.

"Cop, huh?" she said.

"No. Private investigator."

A frown pinched her forehead and pulled her thin little mouth out of shape; the one cockeye seemed to be looking a couple of inches to my left. "You told Richie you were a cop."

"No I didn't. He jumped to that conclusion."

Dessault pushed away from the wall. "You don't have to talk to him, Mel," he said to her. "What's he snooping around for anyway?"

I looked at him. He looked back at me for a while, not too long; then he said, "Ah, shit," and made a production out of lighting a cigarette—the legal kind that only give you lung cancer.

"What do you want?" Melanie asked me. She sounded sullen and distracted, as if her thoughts were on something else. More fun and games, probably. "Who sent you here?"

"Nobody sent me. I'm investigating your uncle's death."

"Leonard? What for?"

She was a sweetheart, all right. "He was murdered," I said. "Or didn't anybody tell you?"

"You don't have to be a smart-ass," she said, as if she were talking to somebody her own age. "All I've done lately is talk to cops. I'm tired of it."

"You sound real broken up about Leonard's death."

"We weren't close. Besides, he was a damn fag."

"Uh-huh. And you don't like fags, right?"

"Right."

"What would you say if I told you I'm working for Tom Washburn?"

"Him," she said. "You a fag too?"

"That's what I thought you'd say. Look, Miss Purcell, I don't want to be here any more than you want me here, believe me. Just answer a few questions and I'll go away."

"What questions?"

"About your father and the night he died."

"Christ," Dessault said, "not *that* trip again."

I looked his way. "What trip is that?"

"That somebody killed Mel's old man too. Nobody killed him. The old bastard drank too much Scotch and forgot to watch where he was walking, that's all."

"You share that opinion, Miss Purcell?"

She shrugged. "Nobody liked Kenneth; he was a prick. I suppose somebody could've pushed him but I don't think so."

A prick, I thought. Her own father. "You didn't like him much, I take it."

"I had plenty of reason not to. The only nice thing he ever did for me was die and leave me some money."

"A third of his estate."

"Yeah," she said. "But that bitch Alicia got the choicest chunk."

"Probably use it to buy a company that makes dildos," Dessault said, and they both laughed.

"What does that mean?" I asked him.

He didn't answer. So I asked Melanie the same question.

"She collects men," the girl said. "She'll fuck anything in pants."

"Or out of pants," Dessault said. They both laughed again.

"Was that the case while your father was alive?"

"Well, sure," she said. "What'd you think, she was a faithful wife or something?"

"Did your father know about her affairs?"

"Sure. He didn't care. Had plenty of his own."

"His own affairs?"

"That's right."

Nice family. The more I found out about them, the more all-American they looked. "Any woman in particular?"

"Not that I knew about."

"How about Alicia? Any particular man?"

"Why don't you ask her?"

"I probably will. You were at the party the night your father died, weren't you?"

"For a while. I left about eight."

"Why so early?"

"Those friends of his, those rich pigs, bore me out of my skull."

"Then why go in the first place?"

"I needed some bread so Richie and I could split for Hawaii. We know some people on the Big Island." Dessault smirked when she said that. Which probably meant that they had been planning some kind of drug buy; a lot of marijuana is grown in the back-country of Hawaii's Big Island. "Kenneth wanted me to come to the party, see some snuff box he'd bought, so I went. He wasn't too hard to deal with when he was in a good mood and you did what he wanted."

"Why didn't he invite your boyfriend here?" Dessault's name had not been on the guest list.

"He didn't like Richie," she said. "Didn't understand him or his poetry."

Score one for Kenneth.

I said, "You get your money that night?"

"Damn right."

"So he was in good spirits."

"Sure he was," Dessault said. "Kind that come out of a bottle."

Melanie snickered. I didn't say anything.

The girl said, "I told you, he'd got this snuff box. One of a kind or something, worth a lot of money. Crap like that made him happy."

"Did he say where he got the box?"

"No."

"Do you know anybody who speaks with a Latin accent?"

The abrupt shift in questions seemed to confuse her, throw her off balance. "Latin? You mean Mexican?"

"Mexican, South American—like that."

Dessault had come away from the wall again and was scowling at me. "How come you want to know that? What does that have to do with anything?"

I ignored him. "Well?" I asked Melanie. "Anybody?"

"No," she said. "The only person I know with an accent is Alex Ozimas."

"Who's he?"

"Filipino fag. He and Kenneth had some business deals."

"What kind of business?"

"Who knows? I never asked."

"I thought your father didn't like homosexuals."

"He didn't. But he'd do business with anybody. Alex was at the house a couple of times while I was there. He was there that night, come to think of it."

"The night Kenneth died?"

"Yeah."

"His name isn't on the guest list."

"Well, he was just leaving when I got there."

"What time was that?"

"After five. Five-thirty, about."

"Did you talk to him?"

"No."

"Your father mention him?"

"No."

"So you don't know why he was there."

"No."

"You have any idea where he lives?"

"In the city someplace, I think."

"Anything else you can tell me about him?"

"No."

Dessault punched out his cigarette in an abalone shell ashtray and moved up to stand alongside the girl. He put one hand on the back of her neck, began to rub it, and she shivered visibly and leaned against him. She had it bad, all right. But then, maybe he was what she deserved.

He said, "Listen, we've had about enough of this. We've got things to do. Haven't we, Mel?"

She looked up at him; but with the cockeye, it seemed as if she were still looking at me. "Yes," she said. "*Lots* of things to do."

"So why don't you just get out of here," he said to me. "Right now."

I could have pushed it; I felt like pushing it. These two had put me in a foul mood. But I had run out of questions to ask, and besides, the atmosphere of the place was oppressive and I was as sick of them as they were of me.

"Okay," I said. "But maybe I'll be back."

"You'll talk to yourself if you do. You won't get in."

There was nothing more to say. I put my back to them and went to the door. But Dessault followed me, so that when I turned coming out on deck, he was about two feet away.

I couldn't resist the impulse; I said, " 'Gold in the hills and valleys of my mind, the big gold rush.' That's real good stuff, Richie. Ferlinghetti would love it."

"Fuck you," he said, like the poet he wasn't, and for the second time in twenty minutes he shut the door in my face.

SEVEN

B ack in the car, I used my new mobile phone to call Directory Assistance. No listing for Alex Ozimas or anybody named Ozimas. I called the office, to ask Eberhardt to check our copy of the reverse directory of city addresses—but all I got was the answering machine. So then I rang up the Hall of Justice, to see if Ben Klein was familiar with Ozimas—and he was out, too, and there wasn't anybody else around who knew anything about the Purcell case.

I made a U-turn and drove across the Fourth Street drawbridge and uptown to Union Square, where I deposited the car in the underground garage. Powell Street was jammed with tourists, as it almost always was these days: there are several good hotels along its length and it contains the main cable car line between

54

downtown and Fisherman's Wharf. I made my way up to Post Street, and along there until I found the Summerhayes Gallery— one of dozens of art galleries of different types in the area.

It didn't look like much from outside, just a narrow storefront with drapery covering its one window and discreet gold lettering on the glass; but you only needed one good look around the interior to know that this was a high-class place. The floor was parquet, polished to a high gloss, and there was nothing on it except half a dozen Plexiglas cubes, a couple of the smaller ones on pedestals, and glass-fronted and -topped display cases along two walls. The other wall, on my right, had a closed door in its middle. The only decoration was a big tapestry—Turkish, maybe —that hung above the display case directly opposite the entrance. There weren't any paintings in sight; it was not that kind of gallery. There weren't any people in sight, either, but I doubted if I would be allowed to remain alone for very long. A little tinkly bell had announced my arrival.

I wandered a little, looking at what was in the cubes and display cases. Antique boxes, some enameled and some bejeweled and some fashioned of mother-of-pearl. Carved ivory flower arrangements. Exotic paperweights made out of crystal, ivory, intricate patterned glass. Porcelain eggs. A small selection of snuff bottles and boxes, all of curious design, some that looked hand-painted and some that had scenes engraved on their surfaces. Much of the stuff appeared to be Oriental or Far Eastern in origin, with China being the predominant supplier.

I was peering at something I took to be an incense burner—a big bronze elephant that seemed to have a camel's hump on its back and that also seemed to be trying to goose itself with its trunk —when the woman's voice said, "May I help you?" about two feet away.

It made me jump a little because I hadn't heard her approach; she walked softly for a big woman. And big she was: a fiftyish gray-blonde at least six feet tall, with wide hips and a substantial chest encased in a cream-colored designer suit and a mauve blouse. She was smiling politely, but there was a wariness in her

55

gray eyes. I was not the sort of person she was used to seeing in here.

I said, "Yes, thanks. I'd like to see Eldon Summerhayes."

"I am Mrs. Summerhayes," she said. She had a faint accent—Scandinavian, I thought, maybe Norwegian. "My husband is busy at the moment. Is there something I can do?"

"Well, yes and no. I'd prefer to talk to both of you at the same time, if you wouldn't mind. It's about the Purcell family tragedies."

Her nostrils pinched a little and the smile went away. She said, "Are you a policeman?"

"Not exactly. A private investigator."

"I see. For whom are you investigating?"

"Tom Washburn."

"I'm afraid I don't . . . oh. Leonard's friend."

"Yes."

"But why do you come to us?"

"You were at Kenneth's party the night of the accident," I said. "Mr. Washburn believes there's some sort of connection between Kenneth's death and Leonard's murder."

She sighed the way she walked: so softly you could barely hear her. "I'll speak to my husband," she said. "Please wait here."

I watched her move off toward the inner door and disappear through it. When nothing happened after about thirty seconds I took another look at the bronze incense burner. Definitely trying to goose himself, I thought. But the hump was what really intrigued me. Why would an elephant have a hump? What artist in his right mind would give an elephant a hump? Well, I thought then, there's your answer. The artist wasn't *in* his right mind; like most artists in one way or another, he was screwy. But the hump still bothered me. It was one of life's little mysteries, and I don't like unsolved mysteries, little or otherwise.

I was looking over at the inner door when it opened again, after a good three minutes. Mrs. Summerhayes appeared and gestured to me, not without some evident reluctance. I went over there, and she backed up and let me walk into a smallish office with two desks set facing each other in its center. The office would have been larger except that a good-sized vault took up most of one wall—a Mosler, one of the best and most expensive.

The man standing behind the far desk, between it and the vault, was somewhere between fifty-five and sixty, ruddy-faced and white-maned. The ambassadorial type. He wore a pin-striped suit, a bow tie, and a scarab ring on his right hand that was so oversized it caught my attention immediately. He looked sleek and well-fed and self-assured and on the snooty side. I thought that I was not going to like him very much.

He said as the woman closed the door, "I am Eldon Summerhayes." He waited until I had introduced myself and then said, "May I see your identification, please," making it sound like an order rather than a request.

Uh-huh, I thought. She'd forgot to ask for an ID, and he'd let her hear about it, too. I got my wallet out, opened it to the photostat of my investigator's license, and handed it to him. He studied it carefully for about thirty seconds, as if he were examining one of the Dead Sea scrolls for authenticity. Then, with a vaguely martyred expression, he shut the wallet and gave it back to me.

"Very well," he said. "I would ask you to sit down but as you can see, there are only two chairs."

"I don't mind standing."

"Elisabeth tells me you're working for Leonard's . . . friend, Washburn."

"That's right."

"Well, I'm afraid you're wasting your time. Leonard's murder was unfortunate, but I don't see how it could possibly have anything to do with poor Kenneth's accident."

A man is murdered, a man dies in agony crawling through his own blood, and it's "unfortunate." I was not going to like Summerhayes one damned bit, I decided.

I said, "So you're convinced that Kenneth couldn't have met with foul play."

"Of course we're convinced. We have told everything we know to the authorities—several times, I might add."

"I understand he wasn't very well liked. Are you one of those who disliked him, Mr. Summerhayes?"

He scowled at me. "I find that question impertinent."

Impertinent, yet. I said, "Were you a personal friend of his? Or was your relationship business-oriented?"

"He was a very good customer of ours."

"Antique snuff containers?"

"Among other items, yes."

"Did you sell him the one he was showing off at the party?"

"The Hainelin? No."

"Do you know who did?"

"No. He wouldn't say."

"Did he say how much he paid for it?"

"Twenty-five thousand," Summerhayes said. His voice had a pinched quality to it that might have come from jealousy or resentment.

"I've been told it was worth fifty thousand."

"Roughly, yes. If he actually paid twenty-five thousand, it was a bargain."

"You think he might have paid more?"

"It's possible. Kenneth was prone to exaggeration."

"Uh-huh. You said the box was a . . . what was it? Hainelin?"

"That's correct. From the early eighteen hundreds."

"Made out of gold?"

"Yes. With a bas-relief of a Napoleonic battle scene on its hinged side. Napoleon at Toulon."

"Is that what made it so valuable?"

"The fact that it was one of a kind, yes. Plus its age, its fine condition, and of course the fact that it was originated by Hainelin —a master craftsman of the period."

"Kenneth show it to you before that day?"

"No," he said. "I gathered he'd only received it that same afternoon."

I remembered what Melanie had told me about Alex Ozimas— that he'd just been leaving the Purcell house when she arrived between five and five-thirty. "Do you know a man named Ozimas, a business acquaintance of Kenneth's?"

"Ozimas? What nationality is that?"

"Filipino."

"I'm not familiar with the name," Summerhayes said. "I'm sure I never met a Filipino in connection with Kenneth."

There was something in his tone that made me doubt he was telling the truth. I glanced over at where Elizabeth Summerhayes was standing stiffly in front of the door. "Is the name familiar to you, Mrs. Summerhayes?"

She blinked once, as if I'd startled her, glanced at her husband, and said, "No. No, it isn't."

Summerhayes was frowning at me. I asked him, "You just deal in snuff containers? Or do you collect them, too?"

"I sell them. Strictly."

"So the Hainelin box had no special appeal for you."

His frown got darker. "Just what do you mean to imply?"

"What do you think I meant to imply?"

He didn't answer that. Just looked at me in the same dark and disapproving way.

I said, "The two other collectors at the party—George Collins and Margaret Prine. What can you tell me about them?"

"Collins owns several businesses in the South Bay—restaurant supplies and catering services. He has been a serious collector of Oriental and European miniatures for several years."

"One of your customers?"

"Occasionally, yes."

"And the Prine woman?"

"Yes, we've sold to her, too."

"I meant, who is she?"

"Leland Prine's widow," Summerhayes said, as if I should know who Leland Prine had been. "He began collecting snuff containers while in the foreign service in Shanghai in the thirties; Margaret has carried on with the collection since his death. If anything, she is an even more avid enthusiast than he was."

"How avid was her interest in the Hainelin box?"

"My God, man, do you suspect *her* of murdering Kenneth? The woman is seventy-one and frail. Don't be absurd."

"Asking questions that seem absurd is part of my job."

"Yes, well, I'm sure. And I suppose you suspect me as well. Or Elisabeth."

"I don't suspect anyone of anything. I'm just asking questions, like I said."

"If any of us wanted a Hainelin box, or any other rare and valuable miniature, we would not have to resort to murder to obtain it. We are all quite well-to-do, thank you."

"All right. So you agree that the Hainelin went into the sea with Kenneth?"

"Of course I agree. It wasn't found on his body or anywhere in the house or on the grounds; there is no other possible explanation."

There were at least two other possible explanations, but I saw no point in mentioning them. Summerhayes would only have scoffed. He was an ace scoffer, Eldon was.

He said, "A tragedy, a genuine tragedy. A great loss."

"You mean the box?"

"I do. It was an irreplaceable work of art. . . ." He shook his head. "A great loss," he said again.

He was something, this bird. He didn't much give a damn that two men were dead, but he got all sad-eyed and mournful over an antique snuff box.

"Let's talk about Leonard Purcell," I said. "How well did you know him?"

"Hardly at all."

I looked over at the wife. "Mrs. Summerhayes?"

Before she could answer he said testily, "I spoke for Elisabeth as well. How could she possibly have known Leonard any better than I?"

I kept my eyes on her, but she wasn't having any; she shifted position and did some concentrated staring at the open-toed sandals she was wearing. He had her buffaloed good. Or did he? There was something about her, a suggestion of strength and will held in check, that made me wonder if he really dominated her or if she only let him think he did.

"The night of the party," I said, "what was Leonard's mood?"

"Festive," he said. "It was a festive occasion. At least it was supposed to be."

"Lots of liquor?"

"Champagne, mostly."

"Did anybody get drunk?"

"Only Kenneth. The rest of us are civilized people."

"Meaning Kenneth wasn't?"

"At times he could be. At other times . . . no."

"When did you last see him?"

"Shortly before nine-thirty."

"What was he doing?"

"Showing off his collection to Margaret Prine."

"Mrs. Summerhayes? When did you last see him?"

"At the same time," she said. "My husband and I were together."

"The entire evening," he added pointedly. "We weren't out of each other's sight."

I felt like asking him if they'd gone potty together, too. Instead, still looking at her, I said, "Was there trouble of any kind before Kenneth disappeared?"

Summerhayes answered for her again. "Trouble? What do you mean by that?"

"Harsh words, arguments, shoving matches, fistfights. Trouble, Mr. Summerhayes."

"No. I told you—"

"Yes, right, all the guests are civilized people. Were you one of the search party that found Kenneth's body?"

"No. Neither of us was."

"Was Leonard?"

"I don't recall. Possibly. I do remember that he was beside himself afterward. Half hysterical."

"That's understandable, isn't it?"

"I suppose so," Summerhayes said. But there was a hint of distaste in his voice, as if he considered males becoming half hysterical under any circumstances an unmanly thing to do. "He and Kenneth *were* close."

I nodded. "Did you or your wife have any contact with Leonard after that night?"

"No. We hardly move in the same circles."

"Who do you think shot him?"

"I'm sure I have no idea. A burglar, I suppose. Or someone in the gay community. God knows, those people can be violent sometimes. Look what they did to City Hall after the Dan White trial."

"Look what Dan White did to the mayor and Harvey Milk. Look what the jury did for Dan White."

He didn't say anything.

I said, "What can you tell me about Kenneth's daughter?"

"Tell you about her? Why?"

"I'd like your opinion."

"Very well. Melanie is irresponsible, not terribly bright, and a drug freak. She'll waste away her entire inheritance in a few years."

"The kid she's living with, Richard Dessault—you know him?"

"No. And I wouldn't want to."

"Alicia Purcell?"

The scowl again. "What about her?"

"What's your opinion of her?"

"She's a fine woman. Elisabeth and I have always thought so, haven't we, Elisabeth?"

"Yes," she said.

Summerhayes made an impatient gesture and a show of looking at his watch. "We've answered enough of your questions, I think —let you take up enough of our time. We have business to attend to."

"I'm sure you do," I said. "Lots of customers lined up out there, clamoring for attention."

He curled his lip to let me know what he thought of my sarcasm. "Please leave," he said.

I didn't argue with him. I nodded and said that I appreciated his help, even though I didn't, and put my back to him and went out. I made a point of looking at Mrs. Summerhayes as I passed her, but she still wasn't having any. Even with her eyes averted, though, I saw enough of her face to read its expression: she was worried about something. I wondered what it was.

I wondered, too, why her husband had cut me off short when I asked him about Alicia Purcell. And why Elisabeth's voice had been so cold and flat when she agreed that the widow was a fine woman.

EIGHT

O utside the gallery I took another look at the guest list. George Collins lived in Atherton, an affluent community down near Palo Alto, so seeing him would have to wait for another day. Margaret Prine, however, lived on top of Nob Hill—not far away at all. I walked back to Powell and down to the St. Francis Hotel, and went in there to consult one of their public telephone directories. No listing for Margaret Prine. I decided to go ahead and make the short trip anyway, take a chance on her being home. Maybe she could tell me some enlightening things about Eldon and Elisabeth Summerhayes, if nothing else.

I caught a cable car out front, the first time I'd been on one in a couple of years. It was overflowing with tourists, as usual—the main reason why San Franciscans don't ride the cable cars much any more—and I had to hang on outside with what Kerry calls my "ample duff" exposed to pedestrians and passing traffic. I got off at California Street and panted my way uphill past the Stanford Court and the Mark Hopkins and the Fairmont, three of the city's posher hotels, and then over past the Pacific Union Club and Huntington Park to a fancy old apartment building on Sacramento.

There were a couple of doormen in full livery, a species you seldom see anywhere in San Francisco these days except on Nob Hill; one of them took my card and the message that I was here about Kenneth and Leonard Purcell, and said he would see if Mrs. Prine was in. He used a house phone ten feet away, keeping an eye on me all the while. She was home, all right, because he was on there a good minute and a half, but when he hung up and came back to where I was he said, "Mrs. Prine isn't available, sir."

"I saw you talking to her."

"I'm sorry, sir. She doesn't wish to see you."

"Did she say why?"

"No, sir. I'll have to ask you to leave, please."

I was getting tired of people asking me to leave places. But it wasn't his fault—he was only doing his job—so I didn't pick on him about it. I left with something else to wonder about now: Why had Margaret Prine refused to see me?

I hoofed it all the way back to Union Square, not bothering with a cable car because there wasn't one in sight when I got to California and Powell and because it was an easy walk downhill from there. I ransomed the car, drove over to the Civic Center, and stopped in at the main library, where I checked out a couple of books on the history of snuff and snuff containers. I knew next to nothing about the subject and I figured it would be a good idea if I boned up a little. The more you know about something, the better off you are—in my business especially.

When I got back to the office it was locked up tight. But there was a note on my desk from Eberhardt, typed because his handwriting is so bad you needed a cryptographer to decipher it. The note said:

3:15 P.M.
    Ed Berg called. He got the dope on the Church of
the Holy Mission and the Moral Crusade. Too involved
to put down here, I'll tell you when I see you. Back
around five.

Thanks a lot, Eb, I thought. I crumpled the note, threw it into the wastebasket, and checked the answering machine. Two calls,

one for Eberhardt, one for me that didn't require immediate attention. So I dragged the reverse city directory out of my file cabinet
and found an A. Ozimas in the index. He was a resident of one
of those big, new high-rise apartment buildings in Pacific Heights.
I knew the building—Pacific Heights is my neighborhood; my flat,
in fact, was only a few blocks away, on the other side of the hill
—and if Ozimas lived there, he was even wealthier than Melanie
Purcell had led me to believe. All of the units were condos, and
the cheapest would go for something around $250,000.

I considered driving over there, but it was after four and Eberhardt was due back pretty soon. I stayed put and rang up the Hall
of Justice. Ben Klein and his partner, Walt Tucker, were still out;
the cop I talked to didn't know when they would be back. I would
have to wait until tomorrow to find out what, if anything, the
police knew about Alex Ozimas.

My second call was to Tom Washburn at his friend's place.
When I got him on the line I asked if he'd ever heard Leonard
speak of Ozimas. He said, "No, I don't think so. Who's he?"

"Business acquaintance of Kenneth's. The man you talked to on
the phone—could his accent have been Filipino instead of Latin?"

He thought about that. "I'm not sure," he said at length. "I
don't know any Filipinos, I don't know what their accent sounds
like."

"Could sound Spanish, depending on the person speaking."

"Do you think this man Ozimas might be the caller?"

"Not really. He seems to have quite a bit of money; he wouldn't
need to shake anybody down for a couple of thousand. But I don't
want to overlook any possibilities."

Washburn wanted to know what I'd found out so far; he
sounded pretty low, so I told him in detail how the day had gone.
It didn't do much to cheer him up, but then I wasn't trying to
cheer him up. I'm a detective, not a professional candy-striper. I
asked him some questions about the Summerhayeses, but he had
never met either of them and couldn't remember Leonard ever
saying much about them. He didn't know anything about George
Collins or Margaret Prine, either.

Directory Assistance gave me a telephone number for George

Collins at the address I had in Atherton. I called the number, and a male voice informed me that Mr. Collins was out of town. I asked when he'd be back. The voice said it was not permitted to divulge that information. Thanks a lot, voice, I thought. I left my name and number and asked that Mr. Collins get in touch with me as soon as he returned.

So much for the telephone. I leaned back, put my feet up, and opened one of the books I'd got from the library. After half an hour and some fairly thorough spot-reading, I knew more about snuff and snuff containers than I would ever need to know. Not that the subject matter was dull; it was pretty absorbing stuff, in fact, once you got into it. I knew, for instance, that it had been neither Caucasians nor Orientals who had discovered snuff, but New World Indians; and that tobacco in general had been unknown in Europe until Columbus made his second voyage to the Americas at the end of the fifteenth century. I knew that by the last quarter of the sixteenth century tobacco was used in one form or another in all the countries of the world, and "snuffing" was so popular throughout Europe that two Popes found it necessary to ban the practice during church services. I also knew that, according to legend, the first time Sir Walter Raleigh's manservant saw tobacco smoke pouring out of his master's mouth and nostrils, he chucked a jug of beer into his face because he feared Raleigh's brains were on fire.

As for snuff bottles and boxes, I knew that they had been painstakingly handmade from any number of substances, the most popular of which were gold, silver, ivory, horn, wood, glass, and tortoise shell; that they were sometimes decorated with precious and semi-precious stones; that they came in myriad sizes and shapes (miniature caskets, for one shape; Napoleon's hat, for another); that the most valuable ones from an artistic point of view, and therefore the most sought after by collectors, were those created by notable artists that had *repoussé* or raised patterns engraved or incised on their surfaces, or which were festooned with intricate hand-enameled scenes, or which had been made of plane-tree wood in the Laurancekirk region of Scotland. I knew that the prize creations were bottles done in China by Yip Chung

San, who had plied his craft during the Manchu dynasty and whose specialty involved painting scenes on the *inside* of the bottles, somewhat like mirror writing; and gold, silver, and ivory boxes by such European (and in particular, French) artists as Hainelin, Petitot, Watteau, Fragonard, and the von Blarenberghes, father and son. And most interestingly of all, from my point of view, I knew that in 1904 a British collector, Sir Joseph Duveen, had paid the equivalent of thirty thousand dollars for what was said to be the rarest of all gold boxes by Hainelin, reputedly made as a special gift from Bonaparte to one of his lieutenants.

I was just starting on the second library book, to see if it contained any information not covered in the first, when Eberhardt shouldered in. He saw me sitting there with my feet up, reading, and pulled a face. "Look at this," he said. "I'm out all day busting my hump and here you are, sitting on yours reading a book."

"I'm working, Eb."

"Yeah. Sure you are." He sailed his hat on top of one of the hideous mustard-yellow file cabinets and sat down at his desk.

"How goes the insurance thing?" I asked him.

"No sweat. Have it wrapped up tomorrow. You got my message, I guess."

"Non-message, you mean."

"Yeah, well, the whole thing's kind of involved. You know I'm no good putting words down on paper."

"So put 'em out in the air. What did Ed Berg say?"

He settled back and put his own feet up. "Man, I'm bushed. What say we close up early and go get a beer?"

"Not tonight, I've got things to do. Come on, Eb, talk to me."

"Okay, okay." He got out his little pocket notebook and flipped a few pages. "The Church of the Holy Mission is one of those fundamentalist Christian cults, but not your standard kind; this one's got some organization and power. Couple of hundred people in the congregation and more joining all the time. They're starting to make a few waves."

"What kind of waves?"

"This Moral Crusade. Moral Majority stuff, like we figured, only even more hardline—strictly Old Testament, or so they claim. Pro-censorship, anti-freedom of choice, anti-sex, that kind of crap."

"Who's behind it?"

"Let's see. . . . Guy named Dogbreath—"

"Named *what?*"

"Wait a minute." He squinted more closely at his notebook, turning it a little from side to side. "Can't even read my own writing."

"No kidding," I said.

"Daybreak, that's it. Clyde T. Daybreak."

"That's not much better, Eb. Are you sure?"

"Positive. I remember now."

"What kind of name is Clyde T. Daybreak?"

"You're asking me? I'm only relaying information here."

"Well, who is he? Where'd he come from?"

"Used to be one of those traveling evangelists somewhere down South. Tennessee or somewhere. Came out here about ten years ago, got himself hooked up with the Holy Mission—Ed didn't know the details—and eventually turned it upside down."

"How so?"

"Church was founded about thirty years ago," Eberhardt said, "by a dropout from the Rosicrucians. Doctrine back then was half Old Testament and half mysticism, not too appetizing to most people, so they struggled along on a membership of twenty or thirty until this guy Daybreak came along. He took over when the founder died, revamped the doctrine by getting rid of the mystical angle and going the authoritarian route."

"Meaning strict obedience to him and his dictates."

"Right. It cost him most of the old followers, but it didn't take him long to line up plenty of new ones—enough so he was able to buy a big Victorian on Lanford Street, not far from downtown San Jose. He and his assistants live there now. They used to hold services in the basement; now they hold 'em in a new wing they built last year."

"What's this about assistants?"

"Ed didn't know much about that part of it. Three or four guys that call themselves 'Reverend' and no doubt do what Daybreak tells them. *He* calls himself 'the Right Reverend.' Which makes the other guys 'the Wrong Reverends'?"

"So Dunston is one of the assistants."

"Seems that way. Name wasn't familiar to Ed."

"I wonder how he got involved with Daybreak and the church, coming out of that commune the way he did."

Eberhardt shrugged. "Who knows how these types find each other? They just do."

"Yeah," I said. "Anything else I ought to know?"

"Just that Daybreak has been sucking around a couple of those religious cable-TV channels in the Bay Area, trying to go public with the Moral Crusade. Looks like he's pushing to turn himself into another Falwell. Big noise with a big following."

"Not to mention a big bank account."

"Well," Eberhardt said wryly, "that's God's work, too. Ask any capitalist."

We sat there for a time, not saying anything. Pretty soon I thought to look at my watch, and it was a couple of minutes after five. I got on my feet.

"Quitting time," I said to Eberhardt.

"So it is. You sure you don't want a beer?"

"I do want one, but I've got to make a stop on the way home. And Kerry's coming around six-thirty."

We put the telephones on the answering machine and closed up. On the way downstairs Eberhardt said, "So what are you going to do? About Dunston, I mean."

"I don't know yet. Kerry and I have to talk it over."

"Maybe you ought to go down to San Jose, have a talk with the big cheese himself."

"Daybreak? Maybe. I'll think about it."

We split up at the garage down the street, where we had a monthly parking deal worked out, and I drove up to California and then over and up into Pacific Heights. The building where

Alex Ozimas lived was on Laguna, across from Lafayette Park—one of the nicest parks in the city. It was newish and not half as attractive, to my taste, as some of the older apartment buildings in the area; but then, a lot of people prefer new to old. I parked illegally in a bus zone—legal parking in that area after five o'clock is next to impossible—and went into the building vestibule to look at the mailboxes.

Ozimas, I discovered, had the twenty-first and top floor all to himself—the penthouse, no less. The penthouse in a building like this had to go for at least three-quarters of a million. Some Alex Ozimas. Or Alejandro Ozimas, as he was listed on the brass nameplate above his mailbox.

But I was going to have to wait to get a look at him. I rang his bell three times, the last time for a good fifteen seconds, and nobody answered. Which figured. It had been that kind of day.

NINE

I made one business call when I got home. The maid or housekeeper at the Moss Beach house had told me Alicia Purcell would be back "after five"; it was after six when I hauled the phone out of the bedroom on its long cord, sat down with it on the living room couch, and rang up the Purcell number. A different woman answered this time: the servant apparently didn't live in and was gone for the day. When I asked for Mrs. Purcell the voice said, "Yes? This is Alicia Purcell."

I identified myself and my profession and said that I was investigating the death of her brother-in-law.

There was a pause. Then she said, "May I ask who is employing you?"

"Tom Washburn."

"Oh, I see. Well, I don't know how I can help you. I hadn't seen Leonard for at least two months before he was ... before he died. I told that to the police."

"Yes, ma'am. But I'm following a particular line of inquiry, at Mr. Washburn's request. I wonder if I could—"

"What line of inquiry is that?"

"That there is a connection between what happened to your husband and Leonard's murder. That maybe your husband's death wasn't an accident after all."

Silence for about five seconds. "That's absurd," she said finally.

"Maybe so. Mr. Washburn doesn't think so."

"There is no basis for such a supposition. None at all except for a ghastly coincidence—two brothers dying under tragic circumstances six months apart."

"Yes, ma'am," I said patiently. "But Mr. Washburn wants the possibility checked out. I'd appreciate it if I could count on your cooperation."

"I've already told you, the idea is preposterous. There is nothing I can do for you."

"Well, that's not quite true. I have some questions—a few details you might help me clear up. If you wouldn't mind I'd like to stop by sometime tomorrow—"

"Can't you ask your questions now?"

"I'd prefer to ask them in person, Mrs. Purcell." I also wanted a look at the house and grounds, but I wasn't about to tell her that over the phone. "What time would be convenient for you?".

More silence. It could go either way; if she told me to go diddle myself, there wasn't much I could do about it. But she didn't tell me to go diddle myself. After about ten seconds she said in a wintry voice, "Oh, all right. I'll be here all morning. Come when you like."

"Thank you. Could you tell me how to get to your house?"

"Are you familiar with Moss Beach?"

"A little."

"I live on the hill next to the Marine Reserve."

"The beach with the tidepools?"

"Yes. You have the address, I suppose?"

She gave me just enough time to say, "Yes," before she hung up on me.

The Purcells were *some* family. I wondered if Kenneth's widow was going to be as unpleasant in person as his daughter had been. Could be. If my luck was running good, though, she wouldn't have her own version of Richie Dessault to make things even more unpleasant.

I took the phone back into the bedroom and myself into the kitchen. There were some packaged chicken parts in the refrigerator—I'd taken them out of the freezer that morning—and a couple of zucchini that weren't too fresh but not shriveled up so badly you wouldn't want to eat them. I opened a can of Bud Light, then put the chicken on a broiler pan and sprinkled some spices on each piece. Then I cut the zucchini in half lengthwise, scooped out the innards of each half to form little green-and-white boats, and filled them up with grated parmesan cheese and a couple of dabs of margarine. Not exactly a gourmet feast, but Kerry wouldn't mind; she didn't care that I was not the culinary type. If she had wanted gourmet cooking she would have taken up with a male equivalent of Julia Child.

I put the chicken in the oven to broil, took my beer into the living room, and picked up the 1939 copy of *Popular Detective* that I had started reading last night. *Popular* had not been a top-of-the-line pulp, but occasionally you found an issue that contained a diamond in the rough—a "Diamondstone" in the rough, in this case, that being the name of a suave, wealthy magician sleuth created by one of the better pulpsters, G. T. Fleming-Roberts. The Diamondstone story in this issue, "Three Wise Apes," was pretty good and I got absorbed in it—so absorbed that I almost forgot about the chicken. I remembered just in time to hurry in and turn the pieces over before they started to burn.

The kitchen clock said 7:20, which startled me somewhat; I hadn't realized it was that late. I might have begun worrying about Kerry—she was supposed to have gotten there at 6:30—except that I had no sooner gone back into the living room when I heard her key in the lock. She came in looking windblown and wilted at the edges, and trailing wine fumes. She wasn't drunk, but then again she wasn't quite sober either. Which started me worrying in a different direction, because she seemed to be drinking a good deal lately: white wine, for the most part, not that that made me any less concerned. The pressures of her job, she said, but I wondered if maybe that was turning into a convenient excuse.

Ray Dunston had provided her with another good excuse for boozing it up tonight. The first thing she said was, "He came by the agency this morning. Ray. Right after he left your office."

"You talk to him?"

"No. But Donna—the receptionist—said he seemed weird. He left his card and asked her to have me call him."

"Did you?"

"God, no."

She shrugged out of her trenchcoat and sank down on the couch next to me. A big curl of her copper-colored hair hung over one eye; the rest of it had been roughed up by the wind. Some other time I would have felt like putting my hands all over her. Not right now, though.

I said, "Cop friend of Eberhardt's checked up on the Church of the Holy Mission and the Moral Crusade," and went on to tell her what Eb had told me.

She didn't interrupt or offer any comments; she just sat there looking pained. When I was done she laid her head back, exposing the slim white column of her throat, and closed her eyes and said, "Oh Lord, what am I going to do?"

"What are *we* going to do, you mean."

"All right, we."

"He showed up on my doorstep this morning, remember?"

"I said all right."

"And getting looped isn't going to help, you know."

She opened one eye. "I'm not looped."

"Close to it."

"Nonsense. You're not going to start in on me, are you?"

I didn't say anything.

"I only had four glasses of wine," she said.

"*Only* four glasses? That's a lot of wine."

"No, it isn't. I'm a big girl; I go potty by myself and everything. Besides, I needed it. I had a rotten day. And Jim Carpenter was nice enough to invite me out to MacArthur Park for drinks."

"Him, huh?" I said. "Good old Jim."

She had both eyes open now and she rolled them in one of those martyred expressions women put on now and then. "We're not going to start *that* again, too?"

"What again?"

"You being jealous of Jim Carpenter."

"Why the hell should I be jealous of him?"

"That's a good question. You sure act like you are."

"Well I'm not."

"I can't even go out for a couple of glasses of wine—"

"*Four* glasses of wine."

"—without you getting jealous, for God's sake."

"I told you, I'm not jealous. Screw Jim Carpenter."

"Isn't that what you're afraid I'm doing? Or will do?"

"Goddamn it," I said, and then I couldn't think of anything else to say. So I sat there with my mouth shut, feeling impotent.

She was silent, too, for a time. Then she made a face and sniffed the air like a poodle and said, "What's burning?"

"Nothing's burning. That's the chicken for dinner."

"Smells like it's burning."

Kerry got up and went into the kitchen. I followed her. She opened the oven, looked inside, made a face, and shut the thing off. "Charcoal," she said.

I took a look for myself. It wasn't that bad—some of the pieces showed a little black around the edges, that was all. I said as much to her. She said, "Then you eat it," and closed the oven door and went to the refrigerator.

"What are you looking for in there?"

"Some wine," she said. "Isn't there any damn wine here?"

"No. You drank it all up two nights ago."

"Well, why didn't you buy some more?"

"Why didn't you? I don't drink that stuff."

"Stuff? You make it sound like poison."

"It is if you guzzle enough of it."

"Here we go again. Guzzle. Hoo boy."

"You can't deny you've been drinking a lot lately."

"I've had a lot of problems lately."

"Sure, I know. Pressures at work."

"That's right."

"And now there's your Looney Tunes ex."

"That's right. And then there's *you.* "

"Me?"

"You. I hate it when you moralize at me."

"I don't moralize—"

"Yes you do. You act like a prig sometimes."

". . . Did you say prick?"

"I said *prig.* But the other applies just as well."

"Now listen, Kerry—"

"Oh shut up. God, you can be stuffy sometimes."

"If it's too stuffy for you here why don't you go home?"

"That's a good idea. At least I can have a glass of wine at home without a male Carrie Nation looking over my shoulder."

"Male Carrie Nation. That's very funny."

"Pretty soon you'll start quoting the Bible at me. You're about one long step from joining the Moral Crusade yourself, you know that?"

"Quit shouting, will you?"

"I'm not shouting!"

"You're being hysterical—"

"And you're being an *asshole!*"

She stormed out of the kitchen, hurling the swing door after her with such force that it came back through the frame and almost whacked me in the face. I clawed at it, cussing, and went on through into the living room. She had her coat and her purse and was heading for the door.

"Where the hell are you going?"

"Home. You told me to go home."

"I didn't tell you to go home—"

"Goodbye, you jerk," she said, and out she went, slamming the door behind her.

I stood there shaking. I wanted to hit something, but the only object handy was me. Fifteen seconds passed, and I was still standing in the same place, and there was a scraping sound in the latch and the door opened again and she came back in.

"I don't want to go home," she said in a small, tired voice. And she started to cry.

All the anger went out of me at once; in its place, also at once, came feelings of awkwardness and inadequacy. I do not deal well with crying women. Crying women, especially if I happen to be the one who made them cry in the first place, give me the craven urge to slink off somewhere and hide. Instead, I kept standing there. She kept standing there too, bawling her head off.

Nothing happened to change the tableau for maybe half a minute. Then we sort of groped toward each other at the same time, and clung together mumbling apologies, and a couple of minutes after that we were in bed making love. And a couple of minutes after *that,* she sighed and said, as if nothing at all had happened and she had just walked in the door, "God, what are we going to do about Ray?"

Sometimes I think I lead a strange life. And then there were times when I knew damned well I did.

TEN

We left the flat together at nine on Friday morning. I usually leave earlier—eight-thirty or so, in order to get to the office and have it open for business at nine; but today, for two good reasons, I waited for Kerry, who didn't have to be at Bates and

Carpenter until 9:30. One reason was that I wasn't going to the office first thing. (So I had called Eberhardt, waking him up, and asked *him* to go in early for a change and open up.) The second reason was that I liked to sit around with Kerry in the morning, lingering over coffee and indulging in the mild fantasy that we were old married folks. The mild fantasy was all mine, unfortunately, and likely to remain just that. She wasn't having any more of marriage after her experience with Ray Dunston—not that I could blame her much. She also kept refusing to move in with me. She didn't want to give up her apartment on Diamond Heights, she said, even though it cost her a thousand dollars a month; and she liked the feeling of independence living alone gave her. This in spite of the facts that we already shared some expenses, we each kept part of our wardrobe at the other's, and we slept together—either at her place or mine—an average of four times a week.

There was no discussing the subject with her; she got defensive and angry whenever I tried, which usually led to a fight. I hoped the same thing wasn't going to happen with the subject of her alcohol consumption. It was a matter we hadn't discussed any further last night. What we *had* discussed, at great length and to no conclusion whatsoever, was the Reverend Dunston and his relationship with the Right Reverend Clyde T. Daybreak. I think we both had the same fantasy on that score: that he would just disappear again, as magically as he had appeared yesterday morning, and we would never have to deal with him again.

I got my old clunker started and drove up over Laguna and down to the high-rise where Alex—excuse me, Alejandro—Ozimas had his penthouse. Parking isn't so bad around there after nine A.M.; most of the neighborhood drones (of which I was one) had left for work by then. I found a place for the car around the corner, and walked back and rang Ozimas's bell.

There was an answer this time, after about ten seconds. A young, unaccented male voice, of the type that can only be described as fruity, yelled through the speaker in angry tones, "Yes? What is it?" If I had had my ear down there I might have suffered damage to the eardrum. I pushed the talk button and gave my name and occupation and said I wanted to discuss an important business matter with Mr. Ozimas, one relating to Kenneth Purcell. The voice snapped, "I'll see if he's receiving," and clicked off.

I waited. And I thought: So it's late in the fourth quarter of a crucial game for the 'Forty-Niners, they're trailing by six points, they've got the ball and eighty yards to go for a touchdown. Joe Montana calls time out and goes over to the sidelines to talk to coach Bill Walsh. Walsh says, "What I think we should do, Joe, I think we should throw deep to Dwight Clark down the left sidelines." And Montana says, "Good idea, Coach, but I'd better check with Dwight first. I'll see if he's receiving."

I laughed aloud at my own wit and made a mental note to share it with Kerry and Eberhardt. It made me feel like kicking my heels a little, like Snoopy on top of his doghouse when he gets off a good one. Maybe this was going to be one of my better days.

At least three minutes went by. I was getting ready to ring the bell again when the electronic locking system made its wounded-fly sound. I pushed inside and got into the elevator and rode it up to the twenty-first floor, where it deposited me in a kind of foyer with a couple of chairs in it, in case anybody needed to sit down while waiting. I didn't need to sit down or wait: the door opened five seconds after I used the ornate knocker in the middle of it.

The kid who materialized in front of me was about twenty, dressed in a white housecoat and dark slacks. He had clear, pale skin, curly brown hair, and features like those on a classic Greek statue. He was very pretty; you couldn't describe him any other way. He was also furious about something. His dark eyes glittered and snapped, his mouth was so pinched at the corners you could see little white knots of muscle there, and his fruity voice was shrill with rage when he said, "Follow me. He'll see you in the breakfast room."

I followed him through some demented interior decorator's idea of elegant living. Everything was in white and silver, with little touches of glossy black; it made me feel as though I were walking through rooms full of snow and silver frost. There was also a lot of nude statuary, mostly male, none of it as pretty as the kid. Eventually we ended up in a glassed-in nook that overlooked a jungle of potted plants on the penthouse terrace. When the weather was clear, as it was today, you also had a sweeping view of the city. Even the towers of the Golden Gate Bridge were visible to the north, above the wooded hills of the Presidio.

There were two people sitting in the nook, facing each other across a table laden with expensive silver and china and the remains of breakfast. One of them was a diminutive platinum-blond woman of about twenty-five, her sleek little body draped in a lacy peignoir; she was attractive, vapidly so, and her eyes had a dull, bombed-out look. She was picking a cinnamon roll apart into crumbs, as if she were trying to make confetti out of it. The man across from her wore a silver robe with black piping. He was twice her age—small, brown, lots of black hair combed into waves, handsome in a dissipated way. I would probably have taken him for a Filipino even if I hadn't known who he was.

He smiled at me and said, "I am Alex Ozimas. Please sit down." His voice carried an accent, but it was very faint. He struck me as an intelligent and educated man.

I sat on the table's third chair. The girl continued to pick the roll apart; she didn't look at me or at Ozimas or at the furious kid in the white coat. She might not have known any of us were there.

Ozimas said to the kid, "Ted, bring another cup and pour our guest some of your excellent coffee."

Ted was standing a little behind him, so that Ozimas didn't see him mouth the words *Fuck you* before he turned and stalked off. Or maybe Ozimas did see it. He said to me, "I must apologize for Ted. He is very angry with me this morning."

"Oh?"

"He doesn't like it when I entertain young women."

I got it then. Ted was more than just a servant; he probably lived here and he probably also shared Ozimas's bed on a more or less regular basis. Melanie Purcell had called Ozimas a "fag," and this place and the kid pretty much confirmed his sexual orientation. Or rather, it confirmed his primary sexual orientation. It was plain that he liked a woman now and then, maybe as a change of pace.

That was why the bombed-out blonde was here this morning. "Ted is a good boy," Ozimas said, "despite his jealous nature. I don't know what I would do without him." Then he laughed abruptly and said, "Don't you find it amusing?"

"Find what amusing?"

"The fact that Ted is Caucasian and I am Filipino. For many years it was a status symbol for rich white Americans to have Filipino houseboys. Surely you remember. I have reversed the trend. I am a rich Filipino who has a white American houseboy."

It hadn't occurred to me to look at it that way. I said, "Good for you," because I couldn't think of anything else to say.

"You don't approve?"

"I have no opinion either way. It's your business."

"Ah yes, business. You are a private detective?"

"That's right."

I gave him one of my cards. He looked at it and nodded slowly and then put it down beside his plate. "Please tell me who gave you my name in connection with Kenneth Purcell."

"His daughter, Melanie."

"Yes, a lovely girl."

I looked at him.

"Actually," he said, "a despicable little bitch. Kenneth despised her, too, of course."

"He left her a lot of money in his will."

"She was his daughter," Ozimas said, and shrugged. "He believed in providing for his family."

"Did you know his brother?"

"Yes."

"What was your relationship with him?"

"Relationship? Ah, of course. Leonard was a homosexual and I am a bisexual; therefore you think we might have been lovers."

"I don't think anything," I said. "I'm only asking a question."

"Let me ask *you* a question before I answer yours. Do you dislike homosexuals?"

"No. The man I'm working for is gay."

"Ah?"

"Leonard's housemate, Tom Washburn."

"I see. I'm afraid I have never met the man."

"About Leonard," I said. "How well did you know him?"

"Not well at all. I saw him two or three times at Kenneth's home."

"Nowhere else?"

"No."

"You do know he was murdered last week?"

"Of course. And are you investigating his murder?"

"Yes. Washburn believes it's connected with Kenneth's death."

"Really? In what way?"

"His theory is that Kenneth didn't fall accidentally—that he was murdered too."

Ozimas raised an eyebrow. But he had time to think about what he was going to say in response because the houseboy, Ted, reappeared just then. The kid took a fancy china cup and saucer off the silver tray he was carrying, banged them down on the table —not quite hard enough to break or chip either one—and poured me some coffee, most but not all of which wound up in the cup.

"Now, Ted," Ozimas said reprovingly, "if you keep this up I won't take you to Big Sur this weekend."

The kid didn't answer, didn't even look at him. He backed up, glaring over our heads, and stalked off again.

For a time it was silent in the nook. Ozimas was still thinking; he had his mouth open slightly and he kept tapping his forefinger against his front teeth. The blond woman had finished shredding the cinnamon roll and was also making use of a forefinger: wetting it and then blotting up the crumbs one by one.

I got tired of the quiet and said, "So what do you think, Mr. Ozimas? *Could* Kenneth have been murdered?"

"I hadn't considered the possibility until now," he said. "But, yes, I suppose he might have inspired someone to an act of violence. He could be . . . abrasive, shall we say."

"Anyone in particular?"

"Are you suggesting *I* might have killed him?"

"No," I said. Then I said, "Did you?"

He liked that; it made him laugh. "Hardly. I was not at his home that evening."

"No, but you were there earlier that day. Around five."

"How did— Ah. Melanie. Yes, I was there. I left at about five-thirty. I drove straight home, as I remember, and spent the evening here; I expect Ted can vouch for that, if it becomes necessary."

"Would you mind telling me why you went to see Kenneth?"

"It was a business matter."

"What sort of business? Foreign interests buying up American real estate?"

He had been open up to now, urbane and faintly self-mocking; now I watched him close off—like watching something soft turn hard and unpleasant. This was the real Alex Ozimas. This was a shrewd and thoroughly corrupt son of a bitch who had got to where he was right now, twenty-one stories above the rest of us mortals, by manipulation, bribery, deceit, and general villainy. I looked at him right then and knew he was capable of anything to get what he wanted, or to protect what he already had. Anything at all.

He said in a flat voice, "My business dealings with Kenneth Purcell were of a private and confidential nature. I will not discuss them with you or anyone else."

"Does that include the federal government?"

He drank coffee instead of answering—and pulled an annoyed face because it was cold.

I said, "All right, I won't ask about your real estate deals. My hunch is that you and Kenneth had different business that day."

He studied me for a while; it was like being scrutinized by a rock. Then he said, "Yes?"

"A snuff box," I said. "An early eighteen hundreds snuff box made by Hainelin, with a Napoleonic battle scene engraved on the lid. Napoleon at Toulon."

Nothing changed in his face—and then it did, all at once. The hardness went out of it and a smile formed in the waxy brown softness that remained. I took this to mean he considered the conversation back on safe ground.

"You believe I gave this snuff box to Kenneth?" he said.

"Not gave it to him. Sold it to him. I'm sure you're a generous man, Mr. Ozimas, but fifty thousand dollars is a hell of a lot of generosity."

He laughed. "Yes, so it is."

"*Did* you sell him the Hainelin box?"

"I see no reason not to be frank with you. Yes, I sold the box to Kenneth."

"For how much?"

"Twenty-five thousand dollars."

"Why so little, if it was worth fifty thousand?"

"Why not? I might have sold it to a certain other collector for its full value, but Kenneth was my good friend. And he had recently done a substantial favor for me . . . no, I will not tell you what that favor was. Also, I confess I paid less for the box than the twenty-five thousand Kenneth paid me."

"Where did you get it?"

"In Manila."

"Who did you buy it from?"

Ozimas smiled and shook his head.

"This certain other collector you mentioned," I said. "Someone here in San Francisco?"

"Yes."

"Who?"

He hesitated, but only briefly. "Margaret Prine."

"Oh? So you know her, then."

"I have sold her a few items in the past. Items Kenneth already had or was not interested in owning."

"She's an avid collector, I've been told."

"Quite avid. I am sure she would have been eager to have the Hainelin box if I had approached her with it."

"But you didn't."

"No."

"So she didn't know before the party that you had sold it to Kenneth?"

"Not unless Kenneth himself told her."

"How long before the party did *he* know you had it?"

"Perhaps a week."

"And you gave it to him that night, around five o'clock?"

"Yes." Amusement decorated his face again. "Do you think Margaret Prine might have murdered poor Kenneth? Because she wanted the box for her own collection?"

"Stranger things have happened, Mr. Ozimas."

"Yes, but Margaret Prine? No, no, the idea is too amusing."

"Hilarious," I said. "Would you like to suggest a better candidate?"

"I believe I will leave such speculation to you."

"How about Kenneth's widow? What's your opinion of her?"

"A very attractive woman. Very clever. She propositioned me once, you know."

"Did she?"

"Do you find that difficult to believe?"

"No. Should I?"

"*I* don't think so. Not that I'm irresistible, of course; it was merely that she considered seducing a man of my tastes a stimulating challenge."

"Uh-huh. Where did this happen?"

"Here in my home. Kenneth asked her to drop off some papers while she was in the city shopping."

"Did you take her up on the offer?"

"I was severely tempted, I admit," Ozimas said. "But I have certain scruples; I do not make love to the husbands or wives of business associates."

"You're a gentleman, you are."

Another of his laughs. He was a guy who liked to laugh; he had a terrific sense of humor for a crook and a satyr.

I asked him, "Would you say Mrs. Purcell is capable of murder?"

"Aren't we all, given the proper circumstances?"

"Would Kenneth's money be her proper circumstances?"

"I hardly think so. He gave her as much as she wanted while he was alive, allowed her to go and do as she pleased."

"Does that include affairs with other men?"

84

"Oh yes. Kenneth had affairs, too. Theirs was an open marriage."

I asked bluntly, "Did he have an affair with you?"

The laugh again. "No, no. He was a confirmed heterosexual. He considered homosexuality an aberration and a sickness."

"But you and he still got along?"

"Yes. Ours was a business relationship. One does not have to like one's business associates to have a mutually satisfactory arrangement."

"You mentioned that he had affairs. Any woman in particular?"

"I don't know. He seldom discussed his female friends."

"How about Mrs. Purcell? Any man in particular?"

"Not to my knowledge."

"Eldon Summerhayes, maybe? You know who he is?"

"Of course. Was he one of Alicia's conquests, you mean?"

"Yes. Was he?"

"I really couldn't say. You might ask her."

"Would she tell me?"

"I wouldn't be surprised."

"How well do you know Summerhayes?"

"Mostly by reputation. He despises me, I've been told."

"Is that so? Why?"

"Because I am wealthy, and a bisexual, and a Filipino."

"Have you ever had any business dealings with him?"

"None. I despise him as much as he despises me."

"Would you say he's honest or dishonest?"

"A little of both. Aren't we all?"

"Not necessarily. How did he and Kenneth get along, do you know?"

"If you are asking if I consider Summerhayes capable of murder," Ozimas said, "the answer is yes. My candid opinion is that the man is capable of anything."

Birds of a feather, I thought.

I asked him a few more questions, mainly about Melanie Purcell. None of his answers told me anything new, or gave me any fresh insights. As for the boyfriend, Richie Dessault, Ozimas claimed to know nothing about him, to have never met him. He seemed willing to sit there talking to me all morning, if that was what I wanted. It was the last thing I wanted; he and his apartment and his pretty, jealous, pouting houseboy and his spaced-out platinum blonde made me want to go home and take another shower. I hadn't even touched the coffee the kid had poured for me. I did not want to drink Ozimas's coffee and I did not want to put my mouth on one of his cups.

I stood up finally, and thanked him for his time, and he said, "Not at all. It was my pleasure. If Kenneth was also murdered I certainly want to see the person responsible brought to justice."

"You believe in justice, do you?"

"Naturally."

"Sure you do," I said, and I left him laughing and showed myself out.

Eberhardt was still at the office when I got there. But he had nothing to tell me—there hadn't been any calls or visitors—and he left after five minutes for San Rafael, to finish up the insurance investigation for Barney Rivera.

I called the Hall of Justice. Ben Klein was in but not very helpful. He didn't know anything about Alejandro Ozimas; Ozimas's name had not come up during his investigation into the Leonard Purcell homicide. He said he would run the name through the city, state, and FBI computers, and let me know if he turned up anything. He hadn't talked to Margaret Prine—no need to, he said, considering her stature in the community—and he had no idea why she should have refused to see me. Unless, he said, she just didn't want to be bothered by a private detective.

My second call was to Joe DeFalco, a *Chronicle* reporter and another poker buddy. He was away from his desk, but I left a message and he called back within five minutes. He didn't know much offhand about Margaret Prine—just that she was a wealthy society matron whose late husband had been ambassador to China before the Communist takeover, and later on, in the fifties and sixties, a presidential advisor on Chinese affairs. But he said he would run a computer printout of her file for me and have it ready by mid-afternoon, if I wanted to stop by and pick it up. I said I would, and when I hung up I found myself thinking about how newspapers keep a file on everybody who has ever made news of any kind, so it'll be handy for the obit writers when the person trundles off to his reward. Gives you a morbid little shiver when you think about things like that—or it does me, anyhow. I wondered what *my* file consisted of. Well, maybe I would ask DeFalco to run a printout one of these days. And maybe I wouldn't; I was not sure I wanted to see it.

There wasn't much else to do at the office. I locked up and got the car out of the garage and went to interview Kenneth Purcell's horny widow.

ELEVEN

M oss Beach is a little town on the coast halfway between Pacifica and Half Moon Bay, some twenty-five miles south of San Francisco. There isn't much to it: a few dozen homes on both sides of Highway 1, some stores, a couple of restaurants, a somewhat dilapidated motel, and a year-round population of about four hundred. Some of the oceanfront and near-oceanfront homes are pretty nice, surrounded by wooded acreage and with easy access to the highway. The weather isn't the best down along there—the fog likes to come in often and hang around for a while —or else Moss Beach would be prime Bay Area real estate. Even as it is, you needed to make a very comfortable living wage to afford property on the ocean side of the highway.

The weather wasn't bad today: sunny, with those thin streaky cloud swirls that make the sky look as if it had been stirred by a giant stick. There was a sign where California Avenue intersected Highway 1 that told you to turn there to get to the James V. Fitzgerald Marine Reserve. I turned there and drove maybe a fifth of a mile, at which point California Avenue dead-ended at an unpaved road mysteriously called North Lake Street. If you turned right you ended up at the Marine Reserve—a long beach above which towered high sandstone bluffs and wooded parkland, and along which were rocky tidepools where you could take a close-up look at tiny mollusks, crustaceans, anemones, and other marine life. I went the other way on North Lake, south past some nice-looking houses on one side and the thickly wooded slopes of the park on the other.

Why *Lake* Street? I thought as I drove. There wasn't any lake around here; just the ocean and the trees and the highway not far away. And why *North* Lake when there wasn't any *South* Lake in the vicinity? Another of life's little mysteries to annoy hell out of people like me, people with trivial minds, people who did too much thinking for their own good.

I came around a bend in the road, and on the right a narrow private drive, also unpaved, angled up through the growth of cypress and fir trees on the hillside. There was no name on the postbox at the drive's entrance, but the number was the one I wanted; I swung past it, onto the narrow roadbed. After about a hundred yards, the drive leveled off into a gravel parking area big enough for maybe a dozen cars. The far end of it was bordered by a whitewashed stucco wall that curved away into the woods on both sides. The wall was about eight feet high, so that you couldn't see over it, but the double-doored gate in the middle was made out of filigreed wrought iron and gave you a clear view of what lay within: a garden dominated by rosebushes and big ferns and a modernistic two-story house. The house, as far as I could tell, was all the same whitewashed stucco as the wall, with roofing that was part redwood shake and part Spanish tile. There was a squat, tower-like thing on the far side, and some odd angles here and there—as if its architect had begun taking hallucinogenic drugs halfway through the drafting of the plans.

I put the car up next to the gate and got out. Two other cars were parked there—a dust-streaked but new BMW and an elderly Fiat that needed body work and that may or may not have belonged to the maid/housekeeper. Set into the wall on one side was a bell-button and one of those speaker things. I pushed the button. Pretty soon a woman's voice—the housekeeper's, I thought—came through the speaker, asking me who I was and what I wanted. I told her. Nothing happened for maybe thirty seconds; then there was a buzzing and a click and the gate parted inward in the middle, an odd effect like something solid and substantial breaking open. Before I could take a step, the woman's voice said imperiously, "Please close the gate again when you come through."

I went in and closed the gate. A crushed-shell path bisected the garden to the front entrance. On both sides of the house, I saw as I followed the path, more cypress and fir trees rose up to give the place an even more secluded feel. But there were no trees to the rear; the ones that had grown there had been cleared off so as not to spoil the sea view. The other thing I noted was that the path branched near the front door, with the branch leading around on the north side to a kind of covered porch. Another path led away from the porch at right angles, into the woods.

The door opened just before I got to it and the housekeeper looked out. You'd have known she was a housekeeper anywhere you saw her; she was about fifty, she was dumpy, she had fat ankles and gray hair and the kind of mouth that seems always to be on the verge of shaping the words "Wipe your feet," and she was wearing the kind of shapeless, nondescript dress nobody but a domestic would wear. She said, "Come in, please," in the same imperious way she'd told me to close the gate. I went in, smiling at her on the way as a sort of experiment. It proved out, too: she didn't smile back.

She led me down a hall to the back of the house, into the sort of room people like Alicia Purcell would call the "sun room." There was no sun in it now, but there would be plenty later in the day, splashing in through a wide set of sliding glass doors. Outside the doors was a cobblestone terrace with a swimming pool at the far end and, closer in, some funny-looking tubular outdoor furniture—the umbrella over one of the tables had an artistically crooked pole and was made out of sparkly cloth the color of a loaded diaper. Nobody was on the terrace. Nobody was in the sun room, either, except the housekeeper and me.

Just me five seconds later. She said, "Mrs. Purcell will see you shortly," and went away without waiting for a response.

I crossed to the glass doors and looked out. Fishing boats on the ocean, the tip of a point to the south—that was about all you could see of the surroundings from in there. Beyond the terrace were some scrub cypress and then the cliff that fell away to the sea. The land bellied out to the north, though, where the woods were thickest, to provide another hundred yards or so of clifftop in that direction.

It was quiet in there; whatever Alicia Purcell and the housekeeper were doing, they weren't making any noise in the process. When I turned from the window my shoes made faint hollow thumps on the hardwood floor.

The furniture was all modernistic, and for my taste just as weird-looking as the outdoor stuff. The paintings on the walls were modernistic, too—abstracts or whatever. One of them caught my eye. Smacked my eye might be a better term. It was of a being with two heads. One of the heads was human enough and had red squiggles splashed down over the nose and mouth and chin; what the squiggles looked like was blood dripping from a wound on his forehead. The other head was that of a green horse. The name Chagall was painted in big childish blue letters across the bottom. If the two-headed thing was supposed to signify something profound, I couldn't even begin to figure out what it was. And if this was great art you could have it and welcome. I'll take vanilla.

I was still studying this monstrosity, with some of the same awe a little boy feels at the sight of his first potato bug, when the footsteps sounded in the hall. The woman who came in was in her early thirties, dressed in a black suede skirt and jacket, a white frilly blouse, and knee-high black boots. I could understand why some men would find her seductive. She was tall and leggy and on the regal side. Coal-black hair, eyes like black olives, pale skin, lipstick the color of blood. Sexy as hell, all right, if you liked your women looking as though they'd just crawled out of a coffin after a hard night of biting necks. She didn't do much of anything for me, which was a good thing for several reasons. One of them being that I never did like having my neck bitten.

She came forward with her hand extended and a smile on her bright crimson mouth. "I'm sorry to have kept you waiting," she said as we clasped hands. Hers was soft, almost silky, and tipped by blunt nails stained the same crimson color as her mouth; the pressure of her fingers was somehow intimate, sensual. "I was attending to some personal business."

"Quite all right, Mrs. Purcell."

"I'm afraid I was a bit snappish on the phone last night and I'd like to apologize."

"Apology accepted." Evidently she had decided to be civil and cooperative—a point in her favor.

"It's just that everything has been such a strain the past six months. My husband's accident, the period of readjustment, and now the terrible thing that happened to Leonard . . . I'm sure you understand."

"Yes."

"Well. Would you like some coffee? Tea?"

"Nothing, thanks."

"Shall we sit down, then?"

We sat on the weird-looking furniture. She got what looked to be a couch; I got a chair that appeared to have been made out of a bunch of twisted-up coat hangers and had a funny off-color orange cushion that seemed to massage my rear end as I lowered into it, as if it were something sentient and perverted bent on playing grab-ass. I almost came up out of the thing in reaction.

91

As it was I managed to curb my imagination and stay put—but I sat gingerly, with no squirming around. I did not want to give the chair any ideas.

Mrs. Purcell crossed one leg over the other. They were nice legs, and she was letting me see plenty of them under the short hem of the skirt. I wondered if the free show was deliberate—if she just naturally came on to every man she encountered—or if she just didn't give a damn.

She said, "I suppose it's that call Tom Washburn received?"

"Ma'am?"

"The reason he believes Kenneth was murdered. The call he took that was meant for Leonard."

"How did you know about the call?"

"The police told me when they were here—the San Francisco police, last week. He was a crank, of course. The caller."

"Was he? Why are you so sure?"

"If he did know something . . . sinister about Kenneth's death—and I don't believe that for a minute—why would he have waited six months to contact Leonard?"

That was the sticking point, all right. But I said, "He might have had his reasons."

"What reasons, for heaven's sake?"

"I don't know, Mrs. Purcell."

"Well," she said, and waved a hand as if to wave away the entire issue. She probed in the slash pocket of her skirt, drawing the hem even higher on her thighs, and came out with a package of cigarettes and a platinum-and-gold lighter. I watched her light up and blow smoke off to one side. Marlene Dietrich, I thought. She didn't smoke a cigarette; she made love to it.

I waited, not saying anything, to see what she would do with the conversation. Pretty soon she said, "Last night you mentioned some details you wanted to clear up. What are they?"

"They have to do with the night your husband died."

"Yes?"

"According to the newspaper accounts, he disappeared at around nine-thirty—"

"Approximately, yes. That was the last any of us saw him."

"Who saw him then?"

"Lina. He went out through the kitchen."

I said, "Who would Lina be?"

"My housekeeper. She let you in."

"Did your husband go out alone or with someone?"

"Alone."

"When did you last see him?"

"Not long before that. In his hobby room."

"May I ask what you talked about?"

"His drinking," she said. "He'd had several Scotches and he was rather drunk. He had a tendency to make a spectacle of himself when he drank too much, so I—"

"How do you mean, make a spectacle of himself?"

"Oh, you know: he became obnoxiously loud, argumentative, sometimes insulting to guests."

"But he hadn't reached that state when you spoke to him?"

"No. But I knew it wouldn't be long before one of his mood swings. I asked him to please not drink any more."

"What did he say?"

"He said he wouldn't."

"Was he always that accommodating?"

"Not always, no. He was that night—I suppose because it was an occasion for him. He'd just bought a valuable French snuff box . . . you know about that, I'm sure."

"Yes."

"Well, that must be why he went out on the cliffs," she said. "To accomodate me, I mean. To sober up."

"What did you do after you left him in the hobby room?"

"I don't remember exactly. It was such a hectic evening— parties are always hectic for the hostess—and I'd had a fair amount to drink myself. Champagne, at least that wears off after a while. I think I went to the kitchen to see how Lina was doing."

"And after that?"

"Let's see . . . That was when Leonard and I talked in the library."

"Talked privately, you mean?"

"Yes."

"What did you talk about?"

She reached over to crush out her cigarette in an ashtray that looked like the cross-section of a stomach in the Pepto-Bismol commercial. "It was girl-talk," she said, and smiled.

"How do you mean, Mrs. Purcell?"

"Well, you know Leonard was gay . . ."

"Yes."

"And that he and Tom Washburn had been living together for some time . . ."

"Yes."

"Well, they were thinking seriously about getting married. Did you know *that?*"

"Washburn mentioned it, yes."

"Leonard wanted my opinion," she said. "He knew I wouldn't laugh at him; he knew I would understand. That was what we discussed."

"You and Leonard were close, then?"

"Close? No, I wouldn't say that. We only saw each other a few times a year. But we *could* talk to each other; we had a kind of sisterly rapport. And I don't mean that to sound facetious."

I nodded and said nothing.

"I was shocked when I heard he'd been murdered," she said, "but after Kenneth's death . . . well, I couldn't feel any deep sense of loss. I still can't. Can you understand that?"

"Yes, ma'am."

"Please don't call me ma'am," she said. "It makes me feel like an old lady. Do I look like an old lady?"

"Not from where I sit."

She smiled again and recrossed her legs and tugged the skirt down a little. Not much.

I said, "Do you feel a deep loss at your husband's death?"

Her eyes moved over my face, as if trying to find a way inside my head so she could read my thoughts. Then she shrugged and smiled self-deprecatingly and said, "To be honest, no. Kenneth

94

and I were no longer in love; we seldom even slept together any more. He led his life and I led mine."

"Then why did you stay married?"

"He liked having me around, and I like this house." The self-deprecating smile again. "He was a very wealthy man," she said. "And if that sounds mercenary, so be it. I would much rather be rich than poor."

"Did you know you were one of the principal beneficiaries of his will?"

"Of course. Kenneth had no financial secrets from me. Do you think *I* murdered him? For his money?"

"Money is a primary motive for murder," I said.

"Not in my case. I never wanted for anything the entire time we were married. And I was here in the house when he fell; others have already vouched for that. Not that I or anyone else *needs* an alibi. My husband's death was an accident; I believe that with all my heart."

I said, "Let's go back to you and Leonard in the library. How long were you together?"

"Fifteen or twenty minutes."

"Did you leave at the same time?"

"Yes."

"And then?"

"Someone, I don't remember who, asked me where Kenneth was. No one had seen him in a while. I thought perhaps he'd passed out in his bedroom—he'd done that more than once at a party—but he wasn't there. He wasn't anywhere in the house."

"What did you do then?"

"I knew he must have gone out on the cliffs," she said. "He'd done that before, too, even though I warned him not to; it's dangerous out there at night. I didn't want to go alone for that reason, so I asked Leonard and one of the other guests, George Collins, to come with me. We took a flashlight and when we reached the edge . . . there was a moon that night and we could see Kenneth down below—" She broke off, sighed, and lighted another cigarette. "Well, it was an ugly scene and I'd rather not talk about it. I've been trying to forget that night for the past six months."

I watched her do her Marlene Dietrich number with the fresh coffin nail. "I understand he had the Hainelin box on his person," I said, "and that it was lost when he fell."

"Yes. It wasn't among his collection or anywhere else in the house when I looked for it later. And the pocket of his jacket was torn in the fall, the pocket he'd put the box in."

"Is there any chance he set the box down somewhere before he went outside? That it was picked up by one of the guests?"

"You mean stolen? Good God, no. None of those people is a thief."

"Uh-huh. They're all too civilized, right?"

"Yes. Exactly."

"But some of them are also dealers and collectors," I said. "And the box was worth a lot of money."

She was shaking her head. "No. Theft is out of the question."

Not as far as I was concerned, it wasn't. But I said, "I don't know much about that type of antique art. Do you mind if I have a look at the rest of your husband's collection?"

"I don't mind, but I'm afraid that's impossible."

"Oh? Why?"

"I've had it unmounted and crated," she said. "Antiques of that sort mean nothing at all to me; frankly I don't even find them aesthetic. I intend to sell the entire collection as soon as Kenneth's will clears probate."

"I see. Do you have a buyer yet?"

"As a matter of fact, I do."

"It wouldn't be Eldon Summerhayes, would it?"

One of her finely penciled eyebrows formed an arch. She said slowly, "You're quite a detective."

"I've been one a long time."

"Yes, well, Eldon is an old friend. He is also a dealer in that type of art . . . but then you already know that, I'm sure."

"May I ask how much he's paying you?"

"Really, that is none of your business."

"No, it isn't. But I'm curious."

She ran her eyes over my face again in that same probing way, and then took one last drag off her cigarette and scrubbed out the butt. "It's no secret," she said. "Eldon is paying three hundred thousand for the collection."

"Cash on the barrelhead?"

"We've arranged a deal," she said noncommittally. "He has several buyers."

"Is Margaret Prine one of them?"

"I'm sure I don't know. Why do you ask about her?"

"Curiosity again. Did you know your husband got quite a few pieces in the collection from Alex Ozimas?"

The abrupt shift from Summerhayes to Margaret Prine hadn't phased her; neither did the one from Prine to Ozimas. She said, "Yes, I knew that."

"The Hainelin box was one of them," I said.

"Was it? He didn't mention where he'd got it, just that it had been a bargain. Kenneth could be close-mouthed at times."

"Also about his business dealings?"

"Yes."

"What sort of business did your husband and Ozimas transact together? Other than antique art, I mean."

"Something to do with real estate. I was never particularly interested in the details of Kenneth's business."

Nothing changed in her expression as she spoke, but I sensed she was lying. She knew exactly the sort of quasi-legal dealings her husband had been involved in—and hadn't given a damn as long as the money kept rolling in.

I asked her, "How well do you know Ozimas?"

"Not well at all."

"I spoke to him earlier today. He indicated otherwise."

"Did he?"

"He said you propositioned him once. At his penthouse."

Her smile, this time, was sardonic. "I'm not surprised," she said.

"Not surprised at what?"

"That he would tell you a thing like that."

"Then it isn't true?"

"Of course it isn't true. A man like Alex? Good God, I hope I never have to stoop that low!"

"Why would he lie, Mrs. Purcell?"

"Vanity. Ego. He considers himself irresistible to men and women both, no matter what he might say to the contrary. He's really a disgusting little shit."

"Unlike Eldon Summerhayes?" I said.

The eyebrow formed another arch. "What does that mean? Are you asking if I've had an affair with Eldon?"

"Have you?"

"If I have it's none of your concern. My sex life and partners are my business, no one else's."

"Ozimas says differently. So does your stepdaughter."

"Oh, I see, you've talked to her, too." The coldness of last night was back in her voice; I had pushed her just a little too far. "Well, my stepdaughter is a selfish, nasty-minded little drug freak, and if you talk to her again you can tell her I said so." She got to her feet and smoothed her skirt down over her thighs. "End of interview," she said. "I have nothing more to say to you and I've things to do. Please show yourself out."

I stood too. "If you don't mind, Mrs. Purcell, I'd like to take a look at where the accident happened."

"Go right ahead," she said icily. "Stay there as long as you like. Once you leave you won't be allowed back on my property again. Good morning."

I watched her walk out of the room. Funny thing about sexy women like her: their hips hardly sway at all when they're angry. When she was gone I went to the sliding glass doors and let myself out that way. A short distance beyond the side porch, I could see the path angling away through the woods. I pointed myself in that direction.

Some Alicia Purcell, I was thinking. I just didn't know what to make of her. On the surface she had been open and frank with me about everything including her sexual freedom and her greed—a

98

product of the permissive eighties, straightforward and up-front all the way. And yet there was something secretive and calculating about her, a kind of feral cunning that belied her candor and her casual seductiveness. Maybe she was both types of woman at once: one of those complex personalities made up of conflicting elements. I couldn't shake the feeling that there were things she had concealed from me, but it could be that those things had nothing to do with her husband's death or the murder of his brother.

I simply could not get a proper handle on her. And it bothered me, made me uneasy, that I couldn't.

TWELVE

The path leading out to the cliffs was fairly wide, full of jogs, and littered with twigs and pine needles. The fir and cypress trees that hemmed it in grew close together, their branches interlacing high overhead to shut out all but random shafts of sunlight. It was gloomy enough now, during the day; at night it would be a vault of blackness. You'd have to know the path pretty well to want to come out here after dark. And even then—and especially if you'd been drinking heavily—you would have to be a damned fool to do it.

After eighty or ninety yards the path curved and the trees thinned out, letting me see a patch of barren, sunlit ground and the ocean stretching away beyond. Another dozen yards and I was out of the trees, onto the barren patch. But I didn't stay on it for long; it was no more than ten yards wide and the edge of the cliff was right there, no guard rail or any other protective barrier, just a more or less sheer drop-off. My stomach did a little flip-flop— I've never dealt well with heights—and I scooted sideways to where a gnarled old cypress grew from the cliff wall, bent backward by the force of high winds so that some of its branches extended well inland from the edge. I caught hold of one of the larger branches and hung on.

The view from up here was impressive, if you liked that sort of high-lonesome perspective. To the south a slender, white-sand beach curved into a jutting peninsula a quarter of a mile away; a couple of houses had been built on high ground along the beach and a third was perched on the tip of the peninsula. To the north there was another, much longer stretch of beach and the Marine Reserve's tidepools; I could see half a dozen people wandering among the low rocks, peering at the sea creatures that lived among their ribs and hollows. And down below, a hundred feet from where I stood, there was maybe twenty yards of sand and at the base of the cliff, a jumble of big jagged rocks. The tide was out now; when it was in, as it apparently had been on the night Kenneth took his dive into eternity, the beach would be covered and the surf would boil up over those rocks with considerable force. Even if he'd survived the fall itself, he'd have had nowhere to go. And the sea would have battered him to death within minutes.

Looking down at the rocks made me shiver involuntarily and take a tighter grip on the cypress branch. I transferred my attention to the cliff wall. It was eroded sandstone and not completely sheer; there were little outcroppings out there, a ledge farther down with one live stunted cypress growing on it and the bony sun-bleached skeletons of a couple of others: a deadfall. If Kenneth had fallen over that way, he might have survived. But he must have fallen instead from the middle of the open patch of ground, straight down onto the rocks.

You'd have to have a death wish, I thought, to stand out on this cliff on a dark, windy night. Or be so liquored up your judgment was impaired and you were oblivious to the danger. Kenneth's death could easily enough have been an accident; you couldn't fault the local authorities for calling it that way.

There were kelp beds lying offshore and the smell of them was strong on the cool air. Ordinarily I don't mind the odor of kelp; but now it only added to my feeling of discomfort. I decided I had had enough of the cliffs, thank you. I let go of the branch and backed away to the inner edge of the clearing. Briefly I thought of prowling around a little, checking the ground under the trees. But if there had been anything unusual to find, the San Mateo County cops would already have found it. Or else it had been removed before they were able to search the area. I turned onto the path and made my way back through the trees.

When I got to the house there was no sign of Alicia Purcell, but over under the side portico the housekeeper was wrestling with the lid on a big metal garbage can. I walked over and put on one of my best smiles for the lady.

"Help you with that?"

No answering smile, but the look she gave me wasn't hostile. "The lid's stuck. Does that sometimes for no reason I can tell."

"Let's see if I can unstick it." I gave it a hefty yank and it came off in my hand. "There you go."

"Thank you."

"Glad to do it."

I stood holding the lid until she had emptied the contents of a kitchen garbage pail into the larger container; then I put the lid back on for her.

"Push it down tight, even if it sticks," she said. "Neighbor's dog gets in here sometimes and forages."

I pushed the lid down tight and gave it a little twist. It stayed put when I tugged on it.

"That's fine," she said. "I hate dogs."

"I'm not too crazy about them myself . . . Lina, is it?"

"Yes."

"Lina, I'd like to ask you a few questions."

"Questions? About what?"

"The night of Mr. Purcell's accident. Mrs. Purcell said it was all right," I lied. "Check with her, if you like."

She hesitated, looking dubious, and I thought she was going to call my little bluff. But she stood her ground; and pretty soon she said, "Ask your questions, then. But I don't have much time. I'm a busy woman."

"I'm sure you are. I won't keep you long. That afternoon, before the party, Mr. Purcell had visits from his business associate, Mr. Ozimas, and from his daughter."

Lina made a sniffing sound; I took it to mean she didn't approve of either Ozimas or Melanie. "That's right," she said.

"Were they the only two? Or did he have other callers?"

"No. No one else came until the party started at seven."

"Mr. Ozimas left around five-thirty?"

"Yes. Just as the girl arrived."

"Did he come back that night? While the party was going on?"

"He did not."

"Do you have any idea what he and Mr. Purcell talked about during his visit?"

"No," she said, and glowered at me. "Eavesdropping is *not* part of my duties here."

"I didn't mean to imply that it was."

"Well, I don't know anything about Mr. Purcell's business, or Mr. Ozimas's business, or anybody's business but my own. I have my duties and I see to them, that's all. I know my place."

I smiled to show her I understood and that I had intended no offense. The smile got rid of her glower, but it didn't do much to melt the layer of frost in her eyes. She had about as much good humor as a hanging judge.

I said, "What time did Melanie leave?"

"I don't remember exactly. I didn't see her go."

"Would you say it was around eight or so?"

"I told you, I didn't see her go."

"But she wasn't here at nine-thirty, was she?"

"No. I had the buffet ready at half past eight. She was gone by then."

"What was her mood that evening?"

"Her mood? Same as always."

"And that is?"

"Sassy," Lina said, and let me have another sniff. "No respect for her elders, that girl. Mrs. Purcell won't have her in the house anymore."

"They don't get along, then?"

"Never have. That girl would try a saint's patience."

"Did she get along with her father?"

"Sometimes."

"When he gave her money?"

"I don't know anything about that."

"Were she and Mr. Purcell getting along that night?"

"Seemed to be. He was in a mood to get along with everyone."

The way she said that, I took it as a reference to the fact he'd been drinking. I said, "Do you remember what time you last saw him?"

"About nine-thirty."

"Where was this?"

"In the kitchen. I was fixing another tray of canapés."

"Were you alone?"

"I was."

"Did he speak to you?"

"No. He went right on outside."

"How did he seem? Was he steady on his feet?"

"Well, he'd had quite a bit." Another sniff. "But the way he stalked out, he was navigating all right."

"Why do you say 'stalked out'?"

"Because that's what he did."

"You mean he was upset? Angry?"

"Seemed like."

"Any idea why?"

"No."

"Did you mention this to Mrs. Purcell?"

"Not right away. Not until later."

"After he was found, you mean?"

"Yes."

"What did she say?"

"Said she couldn't imagine what he'd been upset about. Unless it was just that he'd had too much. Things upset him easy when he took too much."

"After he went outside, did anyone else go out through the kitchen?"

"Not that I saw. But I took the canapés in right afterward."

"How long were you gone from the kitchen?"

"Couple of minutes."

"Then you came back."

"I did."

"Did you stay in the kitchen after that?"

"Yes. Well, except for half a minute when I went to buzz open the front gate."

"Buzz open the— You mean someone else arrived between nine-thirty and ten?"

"Just the deliveryman."

"*What* deliveryman?"

"From Cabrillo Market. They stay open until eleven most nights and they deliver. We were almost out of champagne, so I—"

"How long after Mr. Purcell went outside did this deliveryman arrive?"

"Well . . . ten minutes or so."

"Did he bring the champagne around here, to this door?"

"He did."

"But Mr. Purcell wasn't anywhere around by then."

"I didn't see him if he was."

"Did you tell anyone else about the deliveryman? The police when they were here?"

"Don't think so, no. I'd forgotten all about him until just now. I don't see what a deliveryman—"

"Do you know his name?"

"Danny."

"His *last* name?"

"No. He never said it."

"Does he still work for Cabrillo Market?"

"He did the last time I called for a delivery."

"When was that?"

"Three weeks ago."

"Would he be Latin, this Danny? Speaks with a slight accent?"

"Why . . . yes. He's Mexican. Now how did you know—?"

"Thanks, Lina. Thanks very much."

I left her standing there with her mouth open. I didn't rush around to the front gate, but then I didn't take my time either. This was the first break I'd had, and it might just be a big one.

What better candidate for Tom Washburn's mysterious caller than a Mexican deliveryman nobody had seen except the forgetful Lina?

What better witness to murder than an "invisible" man?

THIRTEEN

The Cabrillo Market was a fifth of a mile south on Highway 1, or Cabrillo Highway as it was called through here. It was a cavernous place with an old-fashioned oiled, black-wood floor —a combination market, deli, butcher shop, and liquor store. The woman behind the grocery check-out counter was busy with a line of customers; I didn't want to incur anybody's anger by interrupting, so I wandered into the back to the customerless deli counter.

The guy behind the counter was about my age, lean and sinewy inside one of those white full-length aprons that look like bleached-out overalls. I asked him if Danny was working today and where I might find him.

"Danny Martinez, you mean?"

"If he's the deliveryman here."

"Well, he used to be. Not any more."

"Oh? As of when?"

"Two weeks ago. I had to let him go." There was a note of regret in his voice. "I'm Gene Fuller, I own this place."

I introduced myself, letting him have one of my cards at the same time, and said I wanted to talk to Danny as part of a confidential investigation I was conducting. To forestall questions I didn't tell him the investigation had to do with the Purcell family. But he wasn't the nosy type, as it turned out.

When he was done looking at my card I asked him, "Would you mind telling me why you let Danny go?"

"Well . . . he's had it rough the past month and I can sympathize with that. But I got a business to run here, I got my customers to think about. Not to mention insurance on the truck—last thing I need is to get sued. People can do that, I guess maybe you know —sue an employer for negligence if one of his employees has a drunk-driving accident."

"Danny was drinking on the job?"

"Yeah. Damn shame, all the way around."

"Had he done that kind of thing before?"

"No, no. Up until last month he was always sober, a good worker."

"What happened to change that?"

"His wife left him," Fuller said. "Well, his common-law wife, I guess you'd call her. Took their kid, five-year-old boy, cute little guy—took him and all their savings and went back to Mexico."

"What was her reason?"

He shrugged. "They didn't get along too well, always fighting. Just one of those things, I guess. But Danny's crazy about the kid. That's what tore him up, her taking the kid."

"Couldn't he do anything about getting the boy back?"

"He didn't have any money for a lawyer. Besides, Eva was . . . well . . ."

"An illegal alien?"

"I don't want to say."

"My investigation has nothing to do with immigration matters,

Mr. Fuller. I'm not interested in the resident status of Danny or his woman. And I have no intention of repeating anything you tell me."

He nodded slowly, but he said, "I still don't want to say. I'll tell you this, though: Danny was born in the Salinas Valley. I know that for a fact."

"How long did he work for you?"

"Three years, about."

"You said he was a good worker. Honest, too?"

"Oh, yeah. Never any problem with that."

"I'd appreciate it if you'd tell me where he lives," I said. "It would save me some time."

"I'll tell you," Fuller said, "but you won't find him there."

"Why not?"

"He's gone. Lit out somewhere—Mexico, I figure."

Damn! I said, "When?"

"I dunno. Sometime after I fired him. I got to worrying about him, the way he'd been drinking, I wanted to see how he was, if he had another job or maybe he needed a few bucks . . ." Fuller let his gaze slide away from mine; like a lot of compassionate men in the macho eighties, he was embarrassed to let his compassion show because he was afraid it would be mistaken for weakness. "Anyhow, I drove out to his place last Sunday. Most of his stuff is gone. Packed everything into his beat-up old Chevy truck and took it with him. Nothing much left but the furniture, cheap stuff from the Salvation Army."

"And you think he went to Mexico?"

"To look for his son," Fuller said, nodding. "Better that than moping around here, getting drunk and feeling sorry for himself."

"Whereabouts in Mexico?"

"Search me. He never said where Eva was from."

"Did he live here in Moss Beach?"

"Yep. Back in the hills a couple of miles."

"Private house?"

"An old farm. Lived there ever since he came here."

"Rented?"

Fuller nodded again. "Danny had a lease. Some fellow down in L.A. owns the property."

"How do I get there?"

He gave me directions. Then he said, "This investigation of yours . . . Danny's not in any trouble, is he?"

"I hope not, Mr. Fuller."

"Me too. He's a good man, believe me. It's just he's had a run of lousy luck, you know?"

"Yeah," I said, "I know."

I thanked him for talking to me—and then, because there didn't seem to be any hurry now, and because disappointment and frustration sometimes make me hungry, I gave him an order for a poor-boy sandwich to go. I was eating too many sandwiches these days, which was one of the reasons my weight had crept up another few pounds. But how were you supposed to eat balanced, non-fattening meals when you were out on a job like this? And I was damned if I was going to eat any more yogurt and cottage cheese and carrot sticks; Kerry had had me on that kind of starvation diet once and it had been pure torture. Russian peasants and Basque sheepherders, she'd said, lived to be a hundred eating yogurt and soft cheese and vegetables. Well, so what? What was the use of living to the century mark if you weren't enjoying life? I was willing to bet that when those ancient Russian peasants and Basque sheepherders finally did croak, not one of them had a smile on his face.

I bought a Bud Light to go with my sandwich and had my lunch sitting in the car. I did some ruminating while I ate. Despite what Fuller had told me about Danny Martinez's honesty, it seemed pretty clear—at least to me—that Martinez was the man Tom Washburn had talked to on the phone. He was of Mexican descent and he spoke with a slight accent. He had been at the Purcell house the night of the party, at the approximate time of Kenneth's death; he could easily enough have seen or heard something incriminating. And he had had a run of bad luck that might have made him bitter enough to throw up a life of honesty in favor of one big grab at a tarnished brass ring. The run of bad luck also explained the six-month hiatus between Kenneth's death and the phone call to Leonard's home: Martinez hadn't needed money back then, had had a job and a family. As for why he hadn't gone to the police with what he'd seen or heard—maybe it wasn't all that incriminating or maybe he just hadn't wanted to get involved.

And now he was gone, probably somewhere in Mexico by this time. If Leonard had paid him the missing two thousand dollars, as it seemed likely he had, that would explain the sudden departure.

But there were still questions. Had he actually seen or heard anything that night? It was conceivable he had pulled the whole thing out of his imagination, although that struck me as improbable for a simple-living deliveryman whose life was crumbling around him. If Kenneth *had* been murdered, and if Martinez *did* know who was responsible, had he given the name to Leonard? Had he confided it to anyone else—his wife, maybe, or a close friend? And exactly where was he now?

Well, maybe there was something at his farm, something he'd left behind, that would give me a clue. I finished the last of my sandwich and the last of the Bud Light, got the car started, drove back into the village proper, and hunted up Sunshine Valley Road.

It was a winding, two-lane country road that led back into the foothills to the east, past scattered homes—some new and well-maintained, some not so new and not so well maintained; past a couple of sprawling ranches that specialized in the breeding of quarter horses. After a couple of miles, the road made a sharp loop to the north and took me across a bridge that spanned a vegetation-choked creek. Just beyond the bridge a dirt road cut back to the east, up into another series of low hills thickly wooded with eucalyptus, madrone, and fir trees. Fuller had told me this would be Elm Street and a sign at the intersection confirmed it.

I turned up the dirt road, past the only visible house around and through more trees, none of which was an elm. Another of those irritating little mysteries: Why Elm Street if there weren't any elms on it? Moss Beach seemed to be full of enigmas, large and small. Beyond the trees to the south, where the land fell away into a tiny valley, I could see different kinds of flowers blooming in cultivated fields. They would belong to one of several ranches down there that specialized in growing flowers for sale to various nursery suppliers in the area.

When I had gone a fifth of a mile, a green wooden mailbox appeared on the south side of the road. Directly opposite on the north side, a pair of ruts that passed for a lane angled up through the trees. Those ruts, Fuller had said, would take me to Danny Martinez's farm. But I didn't make the turn right away. Instead I stopped alongside the mailbox—Martinez's, presumably, since it was the only one in the vicinity—and got out and poked inside. There were two pieces of mail, both addressed to Daniel Martinez, but neither was worth tampering with: a PG&E bill and a mail-order catalogue. I put them back into the box and got into the car again.

The ruts took me along the shoulder of a hill and then around and down into a good-sized clearing flanked on three sides by woods. The fourth side was a field that had been planted with vegetables and melons and that contained a couple of fruit trees. There were two buildings in the clearing—a sagging barn and an old farmhouse set back against the wooded slope to the east. A chicken coop stood adjacent to the barn but there weren't any chickens in it.

I stopped the car in the middle of the dusty yard and hauled myself out of it again. It was quiet; the only sound was a jay scolding something in the fir trees behind the house. I walked over that way, up a slight incline to where a child's battered wagon was lying upside down near the stairs. The stairs had a newish look and the white paint on them was fresher than on the rest of the house; some of the roof's shingles also looked new. Until the events of the past month, Martinez had evidently kept the place up pretty well.

At the top of the stairs was a shallow porch with a geriatric swing and a rickety table on it. There was a screen door into the house, and a regular door behind it that stood ajar; the screen door wobbled open when I tugged on it. I called out, "Hello, inside," and waited a while, just to be safe. Nobody answered me, so finally I went on in.

Tiny front hall, with a kitchen opening on one side and a living room or parlor on the other. I turned into the parlor first. Salvation Army furniture, all right—sofa, two chairs, three tables, an old desk with papers strewn over its surface, some of which had fallen or been tossed on the worn carpet. One of the inner walls had been decorated with crayon marks, red and green, in a kid's nonsense pattern that seemed more aesthetic to me than the Chagall painting in the Purcell house. A crucifix made out of dark wood and a painting of a Mexican village adorned the other inner wall. The two outer walls were mostly windows with cheap chintz curtains drawn back from the glass; the set to the north looked out on the open field and the set to the west gave you a view of the yard, of the barn—

I was looking that way, toward the barn, when the man came out of it. His sudden appearance brought me up short; he was moving in a furtive way, his face and eyes turned toward the house. Bulky guy, sandy hair done up in a frizz—familiar even at this distance.

Richie Dessault.

What the hell? I thought. I ran back into the hall and out onto the porch. He was no longer by the barn and no longer moving furtively; he had started to run up into the woods on the far slope, being more or less quiet about it. I thought about yelling at him, but it wouldn't have done any good: he was building a good head of steam, dodging this way and that through the trees, and he wasn't looking back. I pounded down the stairs and across the yard in front of the barn. But by the time I got to the foot of the slope he had vanished near the crest.

I didn't see any point in chasing after him; he had thirty years on me and a lot more wind and stamina. And I couldn't have caught him anyway because after a minute or so there was the distant sound of a car engine revving up, over on the other side of the hill. Another road, probably, invisible from here.

What the *hell?* I thought again. What was Dessault doing here?

What was his connection with Danny Martinez? And why hadn't he driven his car into the yard, as I had, instead of leaving it out of sight and skulking over here through the woods?

I swung around and went into the barn, to see if I could tell what he'd been doing in there. The interior was gloomy and nurtured a sour smell composed of dust, dry rot, manure, and other things I couldn't define. On the packed-earth floor just inside the doors was a large stack of lumber, a couple of sawhorses, a scatter of carpentering tools; it looked as though Martinez had bought the lumber with the idea of making additional repairs on both the house and the barn. Along one wall was a workbench cluttered with all sorts of junk, from spools of wire to a radio in a cracked plastic case; propped against another wall were a hand plow and some gardening tools. At the rear were three horse stalls, two of them empty, the one in the far corner containing another, smaller stack of plywood sheets and two-by-fours. A ladder gave access to a hayloft; it looked sturdy, so I climbed it far enough for a look into the loft. The only things up there were a rusty pitchfork and some remnants of old hay.

Dessault hadn't been doing anything in here, the way it looked. Except hiding, maybe. Caught here, or out in the open nearby, when he heard my car; so he'd waited, watching, until I entered the house, and then made his escape through the trees.

But I still couldn't figure a reason for him being here. Did he know Martinez? The way he'd reacted yesterday morning, when I'd asked Melanie if she knew anyone who spoke with a Latin accent . . . now that I thought about it, his reaction had been a little too sharp and edged with surprise. Maybe he *did* know Martinez. But that still didn't explain his presence here today, or his furtiveness.

The barn was oppressive, somehow; I went back out into the sunshine and took a look at the chicken coop. Nothing there. I crossed to the house again. And prowled through its five rooms and bath, starting with the parlor.

The loose papers on and around the desk weren't particularly interesting. Old bills, some paid and some not; a couple of personal letters written in Spanish to "Eva cara mia" and signed "Mama," but with no address or envelope to tell me where they'd come from; some crayon drawings similar to the one on the wall, the kind of stuff proud parents save. What *was* interesting was the way the papers were strewn around, as if they had been pawed through by somebody in a hurry. Martinez? Or Dessault? And if it had been Dessault, why? What was he looking for?

The kitchen was next. Pots and pans, a few dishes, some packaged and canned foodstuffs in the cupboards—Martinez hadn't bothered to take any of that. Or clean out the refrigerator, either: a couple of things in there wore greenish fur coats. But again, there was evidence here of haste either in packing for departure or in a rapid search. Cupboard doors stood open, drawers had been pulled out and left that way, the shards from a broken vodka bottle were scattered across the drainboard and among a tier of dirty crockery and utensils in the sink.

A dining area opened off the kitchen, but there wasn't anything in it except a table and some chairs and a sideboard. Nothing in the little boy's bedroom, either, except a bunk-style bed; the closet was empty except for a couple of dropped coat hangers, a toy soldier with its head twisted off, and the remains of a balsa-wood model airplane. I moved into the bath that separated that bedroom from the one where Martinez and his common-law wife had slept. The medicine cabinet door was open, revealing two empty shelves and one containing some used razor blades. A vial of cheap men's cologne had been dropped and broken in the sink; but there was not much odor from it, even when I poked my nose down there, which meant that the vial hadn't been broken recently.

The closet in the master bedroom was empty, too. So were the bureau and the two nightstands flanking the bed. The bed still had its sheets and pillows and blankets, all of them rumpled and not very clean. On the wall above it was another crucifix, this one made out of bronze with silver ornamentation. An oval mirror in a dark-wood frame hung on another wall, and what drew me to it were two color snapshots wedged between the glass and the frame on one side. One of the snaps was of a laughing little boy with huge brown eyes, like a child in a portrait by Keane. Danny Martinez's son. I wondered, for no particular reason, what his name was. The other photo was of a man and a woman and the same little boy, the man holding the child in one arm, all three of them grinning. It had been taken at a beach somewhere; the ocean, spattered with sunlight, was visible behind them.

I took that one off the mirror and looked at it more closely. The woman was slim and attractive in a narrow-faced way, with shiny black hair that fell almost to her waist. The man—Danny Martinez, no doubt—was tall, heavy through the chest and shoulders, and sported a bandit's mustache. They had made a nice-looking family, the three of them, back when this photo was taken. It gave me an odd, sad feeling, being here in the house they'd shared, a house emptied of all but the residue, the ghosts, of their years together. No more outings on the beach, no more closeness, no more laughter. Nothing left now but bitterness and pain and the wreckage of a man's self-respect.

I stood for a time holding the snapshot, staring at it. Then, on impulse, I slipped it into the inside pocket of my jacket and turned and left the bedroom, left the house. Nothing more for me there either. Like the barn, it too had become oppressive.

FOURTEEN

I drove around the area for a while after I left the Martinez farm. It took me all of five minutes to find the road and the gravel turnaround where Richie Dessault had parked his car. So he wouldn't have had to know the area any better than I did in order to find the road himself and figure out that it was a short trek through the woods and over the hill to the Martinez place. And he hadn't had to worry about anybody noticing him or the car because there weren't any other houses within sight.

On the way back along Elm Street I stopped at the only neighboring house I'd seen in the immediate vicinity, the one I'd passed coming in. A middle-aged woman greeted me cordially and told me nothing useful. She knew Danny Martinez—"a nice young man," she said—but she hadn't seen him since his wife and son went away to Mexico, and expressed surprise to learn that he was gone too. She didn't know any of his friends; and when I described Dessault she gave me a blank smile and shook her head. The only thing of any interest I got from her was the little boy's name: Roberto.

From there I drove over to Highway 1 and headed up the coast over Devil's Slide; there wasn't anything more for me to do in Moss Beach today. I picked up the 180 freeway beyond Pacifica and followed it all the way downtown to the Fourth Street exit, where I got off and looped back around to Mission Creek. But that was a waste of time, too: if Dessault and/or Melanie were inside their houseboat, they were not opening the door for the likes of me.

I drove up Fifth, put the car briefly into the Fifth and Mission garage, and went across the street to the *Chronicle* building to collect the package on Margaret Prine. DeFalco had left it with the lobby guard, so I didn't have to go upstairs; I was back in the car in three minutes, and on my way to the office three minutes after that.

Eberhardt was there when I came in, polluting the air with one of his smelly pipes. I don't know where he gets his tobacco, but the stuff is as black as tar and smells like tar. It must be contraband, made in somebody's basement; no reputable tobacco manufacturer would inflict crap like that on the public. Or was "reputable tobacco manufacturer" a contradiction in terms? I thought. They kept right on putting cigarettes on the market, didn't they? Pre-fab cancer, all wrapped in nice bright packages, with sexy ads to entice teen-agers into the carcinoma fold. I wondered how many tobacco company executives had quit smoking, or never started in the first place, because they themselves were afraid the health warnings the government forced them to put on their product might be true.

I asked Eb, "What are you mulling over? Something profound, I trust."

"I was thinking about getting laid," he said.

"A very deep philosophical subject. You got any prospects?"

"Might have."

"Yeah? Anybody I know?"

"Not yet. Maybe you will, though, if things work out."

"What's her name?"

"Barbara Jean. She's from the South."

Uh-oh, I thought, here we go again.

"South Carolina," he said. "Charleston."

"Where'd you meet her?"

"She works in Henderson's office in San Rafael."

"Whose office?"

"Henderson. The guy who wants the double-indemnity policy with Great Western. She's a secretary."

"And you've got a date with her, huh?"

"Might have. She gave me her number."

"I'll bet she did."

"No wisecracks. She's a lady."

"Sure. That's why you're already thinking about getting laid."

"Men *always* think about getting laid," he said. "We're just a bunch of animals."

"Ain't we though. She have a big chest?"

He gave me an injured look. "No. She's no Wanda, if that's what you're thinking."

That was exactly what I was thinking. Wanda was his most recent passion, an unlovely lady with an enormous chest, three brain cells, and an irritating personality (or lack of one). They had been engaged for a while, until Kerry—leave it to Kerry—had got sloshed on wine during a dinner foursome at a place called Il Roccaforte, the worst Italian restaurant in the world, and dumped a bowl of spaghetti over Wanda's dyed blond head. The con-

116

voluted repercussions of that had opened Eberhardt's eyes, or at least had removed them from their blind fastenings on Wanda's chest, and allowed him to see her for what she was. He had been down-in-the-mouth ever since the break-up, bemoaning the fact that he was getting old and women didn't find him attractive anymore—all of which I took to be sexual frustration. A woman was just what he needed, as long as she was a good woman who was good for him. But ever since his wife Dana had left him a few years ago, he had had a knack for picking losers. Barbara Jean, from Charleston, South Carolina. Oh boy.

I said, "Well, good luck. I hope it works out."

"Me too. I'll let you know."

"I can hardly wait. So did you wrap up the insurance thing?"

"Everything except the paperwork. I already called Barney."

"Why aren't you doing the paperwork now?"

"I hate that crap."

"Who doesn't? Hop to it. We don't get paid until the report is delivered, remember?"

I went over and sat at my desk. There was a piece of paper on the blotter with a name scrawled on it—Ruth something—and a telephone number. I held it up. "What's this, Eb?"

"Oh, yeah, right. Woman called a little while ago, said she wanted to talk to you about Leonard Purcell."

"What's her last name? You write like a monkey on LSD."

"Mitchell. Ruth Mitchell."

"I don't know any Ruth Mitchell."

"She said she's his ex-wife. Leonard's."

"She tell you why she wants to talk to me?"

"No. Just call her back."

Well, she could wait; I had other calls to make. The first one was to Tom Washburn. I told him what I'd found out about Danny Martinez, and it got him excited and I had to calm him down. The information was positive, apparently corroborating his theory, but we were still a long way from any conclusive answers.

I asked him, "Does Martinez's name mean anything to you?"

"No. This is the first I've heard it."

"You're sure Leonard never mentioned it?"

"Positive. I'd remember a name like that."

"How about Richard or Richie Dessault? Did Leonard ever mention him?"

"I don't think so. Who's he?"

"The kid Melanie is living with. He calls himself a poet."

"No, I'm sure he never said anything about a poet."

"Are you up to going back to your house?"

"I . . . suppose so. Why?"

"You might check through Leonard's papers, see if there's anything on Martinez, Dessault, or Alex Ozimas."

"All right. If you feel it's a good idea."

"Worth the effort, anyway. Call me if you find anything."

We rang off, and I dialed the Hall of Justice. Klein was in. And not a little surprised at what I had to tell him. "I don't know how you do it," he said. "We didn't even get a smell of this guy Martinez."

"I get lucky sometimes. You'll check him out, Ben?"

"Right away."

"What have you got on Dessault?"

"Not much. He's got a record, but it's small-time stuff; I'll dig deeper, see if I can turn up a link to Martinez." He paused. "By the way, I ran Ozimas through the computers. Nothing on him state or local. I'm still waiting for the FBI report."

"Thanks, Ben."

"I'm the one who should be thanking you," he said. "Maybe apologizing, too. If this Martinez angle pans out, you and Washburn were right and we just blew it."

"It happens. No apologies necessary. I've blown a few in my time, too, God knows."

When I cradled the receiver Eberhardt's piece of paper caught my eye again; I picked it up and squinted at it again. "What's the last digit of Ruth Mitchell's number?" I asked him. "A two or a three? I can't read that, either."

He quit pecking at his old Smith-Corona, got up, and came over and looked at the paper. "That's a three. Can't you tell a three from a two?"

118

"Not the way you write it."

I dialed the number. And a recorded voice came on and said it was sorry, that number was no longer in service. I disconnected and said to Eberhardt, who was back at his desk, "A three, huh? Damn number's out of service, with a three."

"So maybe it's a two. Try it with a two."

I said a couple of words under my breath and tried it with a two. This time the line buzzed emptily. I hung up on the tenth ring and got the directory out and looked up Ruth Mitchell. No listing. I said some more words under my breath and thought: The hell with it. Let her call me back, if it's that important.

I opened the envelope from Joe DeFalco and read the *Chronicle*'s file on Margaret Prine. It told me nothing I didn't already know, except that her husband, Leland Prine, had died of heart failure in 1974, that she was chairperson of a couple of local charity drives, and that she had been hit by a car and suffered a broken hip while crossing the street in front of her building in 1981. The only item of interest wasn't part of the file at all; it was Mrs. Prine's unlisted telephone number, which DeFalco had dug up somewhere. Newspaper people, for some reason, seem to have better resources than detectives when it comes to ferreting out unlisted numbers.

Mrs. Prine could wait a while longer, though. There was somebody else I wanted to see first—more specific information I needed. I put the file away, got on my feet, asked Eberhardt to take care of locking up, and left him smoking his pipe and looking thoughtful while he pecked out the Henderson report.

Barbara Jean, from Charleston, South Carolina. Well, shut my mouth. Y'all want some pecan pie, Ebbie, dahlin?

I couldn't wait to see the expression on Kerry's face when I told her.

It was twenty of five when I walked into the Summerhayes Gallery. There weren't any customers today, either—just Elisabeth Summerhayes standing behind one of the display counters, using a soft cloth to polish one of the patterned glass paperweights. She did not look very pleased to see me. Her mouth turned down at the corners and her back got stiff; she put the cloth and the paperweight down carefully and folded her hands together at her waist as I approached.

"My husband is not here," she said when I reached her.

"Do you expect him back?"

"No. I will be closing myself, very soon."

"When can I see him?"

"On Monday, if he chooses to talk to you."

"Meaning you think he won't?"

"He does not like to be bothered by detectives."

"I'll bet he doesn't. Is that how you feel, too?"

"Yes. Why don't you leave us alone? We know nothing about what happened to Kenneth or Leonard Purcell."

"I think you do," I said. "For instance, when I was here yesterday why didn't you or your husband mention the purchase of Kenneth's collection?"

She blinked at me. "The . . . what?"

"Kenneth's collection of antique tobacco art. Mrs. Purcell told me you and your husband are buying it."

"But I don't—" She broke off, and her downturned mouth got tight at the corners. Something hot showed in her eyes, something I took to be a combination of sudden understanding and sudden anger. "How much did Mrs. Purcell say we are paying for the collection?"

"Three hundred thousand."

"*How* much?"

"Three hundred—"

"Yes, all right, I understand."

I thought: So that's the way it is. But I said, "This the first time you've heard about it, Mrs. Summerhayes? I'm surprised your husband didn't tell you."

She didn't answer the question. "When are we to take possession, according to Mrs. Purcell?"

"As soon as Kenneth's will clears probate. Not too much longer now."

"And the money? Has any of it been paid as yet?"

"I don't know," I said. "Why don't you ask your husband?"

Silence. But she was thinking of a confrontation with him; you could see it in those angry eyes, in the hard set of her jaw and the stiffness of her body. She was a bundle of thinly contained rage. And of hurt, too, maybe; she struck me as the kind of woman who would hide her pain more deeply than any other emotion.

Just the same I thought: Go ahead, push her a little more. Be a bastard. That's the kind of business you're in, isn't it? "Evidently your husband has a buyer or two lined up for some of the pieces," I said. "I suppose it depends on whether or not *he's* been paid."

"What does?"

"Whether or not he's paid Mrs. Purcell."

"Yes," she said, "yes, I suppose so."

"I'd be interested to know who those buyers are. And which pieces they're buying."

Silence again.

I said, still pushing her, "I understand from Mrs. Purcell that she and your husband are close friends. Have they known each other long?"

More silence.

"Mrs. Summerhayes?"

"Go away," she said abruptly.

"Ma'am?"

"You heard me. I have nothing more to say to you."

"All right, we won't discuss your husband. Suppose we talk about Danny Martinez instead."

Blank stare. "Who?"

"Mexican fellow who delivers for one of the markets in Moss Beach. He was at the Purcell house the night Kenneth died."

"I don't know what you are talking about," she said. "Go away. Will you please go away?"

"Just a few more questions—"

"Go away!"

She half yelled it this time—and then, contrarily, she went away herself, without waiting to see what I would do. I watched her come out from behind the counter in a stiff, angry stride, cross to the office door, open it, and disappear inside. She didn't slam it behind her; she was not the door-slamming type. But I had the feeling that if I went over there and tried the knob I would find she had locked herself in.

I went out to the street instead, not liking myself too much at the moment. Hurting people is a thing you have to do sometimes, to get at the truth of something, to ease a greater hurt or right a serious wrong. But it's never easy and never pleasant, no matter who the person happens to be. And I had nothing against Elisabeth Summerhayes; as far as I could tell, her only major flaw was that she allowed herself to remain married to an asshole.

So I had hurt her for a purpose, and maybe it would help me get at the truth. Heating and stirring things up usually made *something* happen. If I was lucky, it wouldn't all blow up in my face.

FIFTEEN

The telephone was ringing when I let myself into my flat. I thought it might be Kerry, even though she had a dinner date tonight with one of her lady friends, so I made a run for the bedroom and hauled up the receiver in the middle of another ring.

But it wasn't Kerry; surprisingly enough, the caller was Alicia Purcell. "I hope you don't mind my calling you at home," she said. "But I tried your office and I don't particularly like talking to answering machines."

"Quite all right. What can I do for you?"

"Well, I've been thinking about this morning . . . the way our interview ended. I've decided I behaved rather badly."

"Maybe we both did," I said.

"Yes, maybe. But I don't want you to have the wrong impression of me. If there's any chance at all of a connection between Leonard's murder and Kenneth's death I really would like to help."

"I appreciate that, Mrs. Purcell."

"Won't you call me Alicia? I don't care for formality."

"If you like."

"I thought . . . well, I plan to be home this evening and I thought that if you have any more questions, and if you're not busy, you might like to come by for another talk. I promise to be much more cooperative this time."

Uh-huh, I thought cynically, I'll just bet. She *might* be sincere, of course, but more likely she was after something—and my flabby middle-aged body wasn't it. Probably looking to find out what *I'd* found out so far, for whatever reason, and going about it in the way she knew best. What was it her stepdaughter had called her? A collector of men? Not this man, lady. Even if I was the type to play games, which I wasn't, I was too old and too jungle-wise to become another hide in a female hunter's trophy case. I also didn't happen to believe in sex on the barter system—the old you-pump-me-for-information-and-then-I-pump-you tradeoff. And if all of that wasn't enough, the woman did nothing whatsoever for me physically. The thought of spending an intimate evening with her, of her maybe biting my neck with that bloody red mouth of hers, gave me a case of the shudders.

I said, "Thanks for the offer, Mrs. Purcell, but I've made other plans for the evening."

"Alicia," she said. "You're sure you couldn't break them?"

"Positive. My fiancée wouldn't like it."

"Oh, I see. Perhaps another time, then."

"If it becomes necessary. I do have a few questions I could ask you now, though, since you're eager to help."

There was a pause. I imagined her gritting her teeth, holding herself in check—a nice little fantasy image, true or not. But she had left herself wide open for this and there wasn't any way for her to refuse me without making herself look bad.

123

When she came to the same conclusion she said, "Go right ahead."

"Do you know a man named Danny Martinez?"

"Who?"

"Danny Martinez. A former deliveryman for Cabrillo Market."

"Hardly. Lina takes care of deliveries. Why are you asking me about a deliveryman?"

"He was at your house the night of the party. He made a delivery at about the time your husband disappeared."

"Yes?"

"He's the man who contacted Leonard two weeks ago. The man who claimed your husband was murdered."

"I see. Have you talked to him, then?"

"Not yet. He disappeared a couple of weeks ago."

"Disappeared?"

"Packed up his belongings and left the area—probably for Mexico. The authorities are looking for him now."

"You've told the police about him?"

"Any reason I shouldn't have?"

"No, of course not. Have you uncovered any other proof Kenneth was murdered?"

"I'm working on it," I said.

"I still find the idea incredible. If it's true, I can't imagine who could have done it."

"I'm working on that, too."

"Do you suspect someone?"

"No one specifically. Not just yet."

"Do you think the same person murdered Leonard?"

"That's the way it looks."

"Will you let me know if you find out anything else? I'm very concerned about this, naturally."

"Naturally. You'll be one of the first to know."

"Thank you," she said. "Good night."

"Good night, Mrs. Purcell."

I put the handset down, thinking, Brrr! Hot stuff, hell; underneath that sexy exterior she's a chilly piece of goods. Going to bed with her would be like going to bed with a block of ice. You'd wake up in the morning with some of your parts frozen solid.

I took off my suit and put on my old chenille bathrobe, the one Kerry hated and was always threatening to throw out—grounds for break-up of our relationship if she did. A Bud Light and a 1937 issue of *Strange Detective Mysteries* helped me unwind. Paul Ernst's "Madame Murder—and the Corpse Brigade" made me hungry, for some reason; at least my stomach was growling when I finished it. There was some chicken left over from last night. Most of it, in fact, since Kerry had refused to eat more than one wing, saying, "I *hate* burnt chicken." Well, it wasn't burnt, not too badly anyhow. All you had to do was scrape off the black crap here and there and the rest of it went down just fine. I gobbled four pieces and some cold zucchini-with-parmesan, opened another beer, and returned to the living room and *Strange Detective Mysteries.*

The damn telephone rang again just as I was entering the bang-up finale of "Idiot's Coffin Keepsake" by Norbert Davis.

Grumbling, I put the magazine down and went to answer it. And this time it wasn't anybody I wanted to talk to—the *last* person I wanted to talk to, as a matter of fact. It was the Reverend Raymond P. Dunston, and the first thing he said was, "I would like to speak to my wife. Please put her on the line."

I swallowed the first two words that came to me and held my tongue and my temper for a good ten seconds. When I felt I could speak in a rational and reasonable tone I said, "In the first place, Dunston, you don't have a wife; you have an ex-wife. And in the second place, she isn't here."

"I called her apartment," he said. "She isn't there. She isn't working late at her office, either."

"She's gone out to dinner with a friend."

"What friend?"

"A lady friend."

"What is the friend's name?"

"That's none of your business."

"Is she coming there afterward?"

She wasn't, but I said, "Well? What if she is?"

" 'Can a man take fire in his bosom, and his clothes not be burned?' " he said. " 'Can one go upon hot coals, and his feet not be burned? So he that goeth in to his neighbor's wife; whosoever toucheth her shall not be innocent.' Proverbs, six: twenty-seven through twenty-nine."

"Now listen, Dunston—"

"It is you who should listen," he said. "Not to me but to the word of God. Kerry Anne is my wife. She is my *wife*. 'Bone of my bones, and flesh of my flesh. Therefore shall a man leave his father and his mother, and shall cleave unto his wife: and they shall be one flesh.' Genesis, two: twenty-three and twenty-four."

"Quote the Bible all you want," I said, "it doesn't make any difference. Kerry *isn't* your wife, she doesn't want to be your wife, she'll never be your wife again. That's the way it is, so you might as well face—"

He hung up on me.

I strangled the receiver for a time and then slammed it down. But my aim wasn't very good: it hit the base unit glancingly and knocked the thing off the nightstand, and when it fell it landed on my right instep. I hopped around on the other foot, cussing, and tripped on a corner of the bedspread and sprawled sideways across the bottom of the bed and cracked my funny bone on the frame. When I recoiled from that I slid off onto the floor and banged down on both knees. I heaved myself up raging, feeling like a fool, and the phone was lying there in two parts and a beeping noise was coming out of it. I wanted to kick it to shut it up, but I had enough sense to know that if I did I would probably break a toe or my whole damn foot. I sat on the bed—let the thing beep, the hell with it—and alternately rubbed my elbow and my instep, the two places that hurt the most, while I thought dark thoughts.

Dunston, I thought, this is not going to go on much longer. It is going to be resolved, Dunston, one way or another, even if I have to put in a long-distance call to God myself.

After a while the dark thoughts went away, leaving the feeling of foolishness behind. I sighed, got up, made the phone whole again, and limped into the living room. And crawled back into "Idiot's Coffin Keepsake," which was right where I belonged.

SIXTEEN

S aturday morning, early, I drove down to Mission Creek again.

It was another sunny day, cool and cloudless, and some of the boat people were out and about, doing various things to their crafts. Richie Dessault wasn't among them and neither was Melanie; and I didn't get an answer when I boarded their houseboat and banged on the door astern. I walked around on both sides of the superstructure, trying not to act like a suspicious character as I looked at each of the four windows—*at* them, not through them, because all four were either shuttered or draped. If anybody was inside, he or she wasn't making a sound.

I stepped off onto the board float, and a voice said nearby, "Looking for somebody?" It was a guy on the boat adjacent to the east, an ancient but freshly painted sloop with the name *Wanderer* painted on the bow. He was about seventy and wore a sailor's hat, a sweatshirt, and a pair of faded denims—one of those crusty types who have spent so many years on or around the sea they look as if they've been preserved in salt-cake. He also looked wary, which told me my non-suspicious-character act needed some work.

I said, "Richie Dessault or Melanie Purcell, either one. Have you seen them?"

"Her this morning. Not him."

"How long ago did you see her?"

"Twenty minutes, maybe."

"Leaving here?"

"Yep. On her way to Blanche's."

Blanche's was a waterfront café down near the Fourth Street drawbridge. I said, "How do you know she was going there?"

"She was on foot. No place to walk to down that way except Blanche's."

"Was she alone?"

"Yep."

"You wouldn't have any idea where Dessault is, would you?"

"Nope. You a policeman?"

"Why do you ask?"

"Look like one. Wouldn't mind it if you busted Dessault. Her too, for that matter."

"Sounds as though you don't like them much."

"Don't like 'em at all." He made a disgusted noise. "Drugs—all the time, drugs. What's the matter with kids nowadays, you tell me that? Smoke that crap, suck it up their nose, shoot it in their veins. Don't make any sense to me."

"Me neither," I said.

"So you gonna bust 'em?"

"No. I'm not a policeman."

"What are you, then?"

"Just a guy who's having some trouble with God, among other things."

"Huh?" he said. Then he said, "Oh, one of *those,*" and turned away and moved quickly astern, to escape any attempt I might make at pamphlet distribution, proselytizing, and/or money-begging.

I sighed and walked to the nearest ramp and climbed up to the embankment. I was not having a good day so far, probably because I had not had a good night. Alicia Purcell. Dunston's phone call. Sleeping alone and not sleeping very well. Dreams again: Leonard Purcell crawling through his own blood, me down on my knees holding something alive and wiggling in my hands, something I knew was his soul. And now it was Saturday, the first day of the weekend, a day to enjoy life a little—except that Kerry had some shopping she wanted to do, and there wasn't anything pleasurable or relaxing I felt like doing alone. All I felt like doing was working. This Purcell business—Leonard and Kenneth both—kept tumbling around inside my head, frustrating me because there were so damned many angles to it. I was convinced that Tom Washburn was right, there was a definite link between the two deaths; but *what* link? I couldn't make the angles fit the right pattern without more information, without a clearer idea of the common denominators, and until I did make them fit I was not going to have much peace.

Blue Saturday. Blah Saturday. But maybe not, you never know; maybe the day would turn out to be a good one after all. You just have to plug away and hope for the best.

It was not far down to Blanche's—I could see it clearly from where I stood, a weathered, rust-red building with a long pier behind it jutting out perpendicularly into the creek—but I didn't feel much like walking. I got into the car and drove down there and parked among a scattering of other cars. The place didn't seem crowded, judging from the number of cars, and it wasn't. There was one customer at an inside table, another picking up his breakfast from a woman behind an order counter; neither of them was Melanie Purcell. I went out through a side door, onto the pier. Seven or eight people were sitting out there, at wooden tables set among a jungley profusion of potted plants and trees, and dozens of green gallon wine jugs that served as vases for a variety of flowers.

Melanie was there, sitting alone at a table next to the pier's picket-fence railing. She wore shorts and a baggy T-shirt; her legs were so thin they were like white stalks. She was drinking coffee and fiddling with a mostly uneaten blueberry muffin, and she didn't look happy. She looked even less happy when I came up to her and said, "Hello, Melanie. Nice day, isn't it?"

"Oh, shit, *you* again. What do you want now?"

"A few minutes of your time. Mind if I sit down?"

"I don't have to talk to you," she said.

"That's right, you don't. Where's Richie today?"

Some sharp emotion—I took it to be pain—darkened her eyes

and pulled her mouth out of shape. She looked away from me before she said, "None of your business where he is."

"Don't you know?"

"Sure I know. Why wouldn't I know?"

"What's the secret, then?"

"There's no secret." I sat down across from her as she spoke. She looked at me again, but the one cockeye made it seem as though her gaze was still somewhere else. Her expression had changed to one of bluff and anger. "What do you care where Richie is?"

"I want to ask him some questions," I said.

"What questions?"

"About Danny Martinez."

"Who?"

"Danny Martinez."

"I don't know anybody named Danny Martinez."

"No? Well, Richie does."

"Am I supposed to care about that?"

"You should. Danny Martinez knows who murdered your father."

Her mouth opened, closed again; the surprise seemed genuine. "You're crazy," she said. "You're full of shit."

I didn't say anything.

"Kenneth wasn't murdered," she said.

I still didn't say anything.

"You're making it up," she said. "There's nobody named Danny Martinez."

"Yes there is. He used to work for Cabrillo Market in Moss Beach, delivering groceries and liquor. He made a delivery to your father's house the night he died, right about the time he died. He saw or heard what happened. A couple of weeks ago he contacted your Uncle Leonard and tried to sell him the name of the person who pushed Kenneth. Maybe he did sell him the name; maybe that's why Leonard was shot. I don't know yet. I won't know until I find Martinez."

She was shaking her mouse-brown head. "I don't believe you," she said. "I don't believe any of that."

"It's true, Melanie."

"No," she said. Then she said, "Even if it is, what does Richie have to do with this Martinez?"

"That's what I'd like to know. He was at the Martinez farm in Moss Beach yesterday afternoon. I saw him there. The place is deserted now; Martinez split for Mexico a couple of weeks ago. I think Richie was searching the house."

"You're lying," she said.

"Why would I lie to you?"

"You're trying to get something on Richie—"

"Melanie," I said, "where is he?"

"I'm not going to tell you!"

"Did he come home last night? Has he been home since yesterday afternoon?"

She got up fast, so fast she almost upset her chair. "You son of a bitch!" she said, loud enough so that her voice carried to everyone on the pier. They all turned to look at us. "I don't have to listen to any more of this! You hear me? No more of this!"

Her face had gotten red and she was trembling; she had worked herself into a state, and quickly. I stood up, too, and just as I did a brawny guy in a sheepskin vest came over from one of the nearby tables. He said to Melanie, "Some trouble here, kid?"

I said, "No trouble," but she said, "He tried to pick me up. He offered me money to go to a motel with him, the goddamn creep."

Ah Christ, I thought, that's all I need.

The guy put his eyes on me. He was one of these macho types, the kind that see themselves as champions of law, order, and virtue —the kind to whom violence is the answer to every problem and Stallone's Rambo is the great American hero. This attitude of blind-leap heroism and distorted patriotism was rampant in the country these days. Nobody seemed to be *thinking* much anymore, including the politicians; it was all might makes right, action and reaction, and never mind how many innocent people might get hurt in the process.

True to form, the guy balled up his fists and said, "That right, asshole? You try to molest her?"

"No, it's not right."

"She says it is."

"She's playing games. Look at her."

"Pervert," Melanie said between her teeth. She was backing away now, fading into the small crowd that had gathered from the other tables. "Lousy goddamn pervert."

"I ought to break your face," the guy said to me.

"Lay a hand on me, you're in big trouble. Melanie, come back here!"

But she was moving away now, not looking back. I wanted to go after her, but if I made a move the brawny guy would jump me. The rest of them were liable to jump me, too; it was that kind of potentially ugly scene. I stayed where I was and let her go.

"You're the one who's in trouble, pal," the guy said. "Hey, somebody go call the cops."

"I *am* a cop," I said, making it sound tough. "How about that, asshole?"

It was the only way to handle the situation, the only way to keep it from turning any uglier; I was not about to get myself manhandled on little Melanie's account if I could help it. And it worked, too: it took the edge off their righteous anger, made them uncertain and suddenly uneasy.

"Cop?" the brawny guy said.

"You got it. That girl is a suspect in a murder case. Her name is Melanie Purcell, she lives down on the creek. Maybe one of you knows her. Her uncle was murdered last week."

One of them did know her, one of the other men. He said, "Yeah, that's right. He's right."

The brawny guy said in a backing-down voice, "Then why'd she say you tried to pick her up?"

"Why the hell do you think? So she could get away. Now do we break this up and let me get on with my job or do you people want some hassle for obstructing justice?"

They broke it up, muttering among themselves. All except the brawny guy; he was reluctant to let go of his chance to play Rambo. Before it could occur to him to ask for my ID, I shoved past him and went off the pier and alongside the café and out

132

through a side gate. There was no sign of Melanie, and I hadn't seen which way she'd gone—not that I gave much of a damn right then. Even if I caught up with her again I wasn't going to get anything more out of her, not today.

I got into the car. The brawny guy had come out of Blanche's and was standing by the gate watching me. And as I swung out onto Fourth Street I saw him writing on a piece of paper—my license number, probably, just in case he'd let a dangerous sex offender escape after all.

Do-gooders and damn fools, I thought. World's full of both nowadays, and the problem is you can't tell one from the other anymore. I wasn't even sure which one I was, not on most days and definitely not on this true blue Saturday.

I went to the office, something I try to avoid doing on weekends because I really don't like the place much, thanks to the fine greedy hand of Sam Crawford. The air was stale from the smoke from Eberhardt's cheap tobacco, and I wanted to open a window; but the night chill still lingered and it wasn't warm enough outside to let in fresh air, not unless I wanted to sit around shivering. Something was going to have to be done about Crawford, too, but not right now. Right now he was at the bottom of the list.

I filled the coffee pot from the bottle of Alhambra water, put it on to heat, and sat at my desk. The piece of paper with Ruth Mitchell's name and telephone number—*apparent* telephone number—was still lying on my blotter. I picked it up and squinted again at the last digit in Eberhardt's scrawl. Then I scooped up the phone and dialed the number that hadn't been answered yesterday, the one with a two as the final digit.

Five rings, and a woman's voice said hello.

"Ruth Mitchell?"

"No, she's not here right now. This is her sister Claudia. May I help you?"

"Well, I don't know," I said. "She called my office yesterday and left a message." I added my name and the fact that I was a private investigator.

"Oh yes," the woman said. She sounded disapproving, as if she thought contacting a private detective, no matter what the reason, was a lapse of good judgment. "She told me about that."

"Do you know why she called?"

"Well, about Leonard, of course. She was married to him once, after all."

"Yes, ma'am."

"She heard you were investigating his murder. She wants to know if you're making any progress."

"How did she hear about me?"

"She called the police again. They told her."

"Again? She's been in touch with them before?"

"Yes. But I just don't know why she should care." The disapproval was sharper now. "The way he treated her, cheating on her with *men* . . . my God!"

"Yes, ma'am."

"If I told her once after the divorce I told her a hundred times —good riddance. I warned her. Once bitten, twice shy, but she never listens to me."

I could understand why. But I said, "When do you expect her back?"

"Not until tonight sometime. She had to go to Sacramento. They're having a seminar today. A motivational seminar, whatever *that* is."

"They?"

"Her company. She works for Avon Cosmetics, didn't you know that?"

"No, ma'am, I didn't. Will you please tell her I returned her call?"

"Yes, I'll tell her. What else should I tell her?"

"Ma'am?"

"About your investigation. *Are* you making progress?"

"I'm doing my best."

"That doesn't tell me anything."

"I'm afraid it's all I *can* tell you, Mrs. Mitchell."

"Miss Mitchell. I'm not married."

I could understand that, too. I said, "Goodbye, Miss Mitchell," and put the receiver down before she could say anything else.

The coffee water was boiling. I made a cup of instant and sat down again. The building was quiet—the real estate office and the Slim-Taper Shirt Company were both closed today—and that made this a good place to do some more thinking.

But it was another exercise in futility. Assume Kenneth Purcell was murdered; assume Danny Martinez had seen or heard enough to identify the person responsible; assume Martinez had sold that person's name to Leonard and that Leonard had been murdered by that person. All right. But where did Richie Dessault fit in? It was possible, even though he hadn't been at the party the night of Kenneth's death, that he had snuck onto the grounds some time after it got under way. But why? Not with the intention of murdering Kenneth; he couldn't have known Purcell would decide to go outside alone at any time during the evening. I couldn't think of another reason he might have gone there on the sly that night, long after Melanie had left. And yet if he hadn't had a hand in either Kenneth's or Leonard's demise, what was his connection with Danny Martinez? And if I had read Melanie right this morning, where had Dessault been since yesterday afternoon? Why hadn't he come back to the houseboat?

More questions: What had upset Kenneth just before he stalked out of the house? Did it have a bearing on his death? Did the missing Hainelin snuff box fit in anywhere? Did Alex Ozimas and his carnal appetites? Alicia Purcell and *her* carnal appetites? Her evident affair with Eldon Summerhayes? Summerhayes's secret purchase of Kenneth's antique collection? Elisabeth Summerhayes? Margaret Prine?

All the questions, all the names, seemed to run around bumping into each other inside my skull; they were giving me a headache. I remembered the photograph of Danny Martinez and his family that I'd confiscated, and took it out and looked at it—I wasn't quite sure why. It made me feel a little sad again, the way it had in the farmhouse. But that wasn't all. Something about it bothered me vaguely, something that seemed lodged in my memory—

The telephone bell went off. It made me jump and I came close to upsetting my cup of coffee; I wasn't expecting it to ring on a Saturday morning. I picked up and said, "Detective agency," and Eberhardt's voice said, "I figured I'd find you there. Don't you know it's Saturday?"

"Too damn well. What's up, Eb?"

"Nothing much. Ben Klein tried calling you at home; when he didn't get an answer he called me. He's another one working on his day off."

"What did he have to say?"

"He ran the check on Danny Martinez. Nada—not even a traffic violation. He's got somebody looking into Martinez's background, to get a line on where in Mexico the common-law wife came from. But it'll probably take some time."

"Most things do nowadays. Did he say anything about Richie Dessault?"

"No connection with Martinez that he could find," Eberhardt said. "Dessault has a record of two arrests, both in San Mateo County. One six years ago, when he was eighteen—suspicion of grand theft, auto. The second last year—possession and attempted sale of cocaine. Both charges eventually dropped for insufficient evidence. Translation: the D.A.'s office doesn't bother going to trial on small-potatoes cases unless they've got a lock on a conviction."

"Don't be so hard on them. All D.A.s have a tough row to hoe these days."

"Yeah," he said. "Thanks to the shysters."

"Let's not get started on the shysters," I said, even though I agreed with him. "Anything else I should know?"

"Ben says no."

"Okay, thanks. So what are you up to today?"

"I dunno yet. Maybe I'll drive over to Berkeley, take in the Cal game. You want to come along?"

"I don't think so." But then I thought about it, and I said, "Hell, maybe I will. What time'll you leave?"

"Before noon. One-thirty kickoff."

"Let me make a few calls, see how the day shapes up."

136

"You're a workaholic, you know that? Drop dead of a heart attack one of these days, you don't start taking it easy. All right. Give me a buzz by eleven-thirty if you want to go."

I said I would and rang off. He was probably right about my needing to take it easy; Kerry kept telling me the same thing. It was a nice day, perfect football weather; why not take the afternoon off, go to the Cal game, soak up some sun and a few beers? I had no leads that needed immediate attention. Except for Richie Dessault—but I didn't have any idea where he was and I was not about to hang around Mission Creek all day, waiting for him to show up. I thought about calling Tom Washburn, but he hadn't got in touch with me and that meant he either hadn't gone back to Leonard's house yet, or if he had, hadn't found anything among Leonard's papers worth telling me about. I could drive down to Moss Beach again, try to find somebody who knew Danny Martinez, maybe knew where Eva's family lived in Mexico; but Klein already had somebody working on that. No point in duplication of effort. I still wanted a talk with Margaret Prine, and one with Eldon Summerhayes, but they could both wait until Monday. Besides, to get either of them to see me on their home turf today, I would need ammunition—and I wasn't exactly loaded at the moment.

I fidgeted around for a time, while I drank the rest of my coffee. I wanted to go to the game with Eberhardt and yet I kept having mind's-eye flashbacks to that bloody night in Leonard's house— little messages of guilt. I told myself I was being obsessive. I reminded myself that I had been working plenty hard on this case, that I had already made some headway by ferreting out Danny Martinez's name. And I just about had myself convinced to go ahead and call Eberhardt, take the rest of the day off, when the telephone rang again.

"This is Elisabeth Summerhayes," the voice on the other end of the line said, surprising me. "I am glad I reached you. I didn't know if you would be available today and I want to do this before I change my mind."

"Do what, Mrs. Summerhayes?"

"Talk to you about what you told me yesterday," she said. Her voice was flat but I thought I detected an undercurrent of anger. "About Kenneth Purcell's collection."

"I see."

"But not on the telephone. Can we meet?"

"Of course. Would you like to come here?"

"No, I can't. My husband is out and my car is being repaired."

"I could come to your home . . ."

"No. He might return." She paused and then said, "Do you know Sutro Heights Park?"

"Yes."

"The parapet above the Great Highway?"

"Yes."

"I can be there in one hour."

"So can I. No problem."

"In one hour, then."

She hung up and I did the same, feeling relieved in spite of myself. Partly because the stirring up I had done yesterday seemed to have produced results, and partly because now I could spend the afternoon working instead of loafing at the Cal game, even though the Cal game was where I really wanted to be.

A bundle of ambivalences and inconsistencies, that was me. A living, breathing paradox, groping through a Saturday that might not turn out to be so blue after all.

SEVENTEEN

There is an old superstition among San Franciscans that Sutro Heights is either haunted or cursed (nobody seems able to decide which). Not the park itself, which stretches for a couple of blocks south and west from Point Lobos Avenue, above Cliff

House. Just the part along the rim of the promontory that contains the ruins of Adolph Sutro's once-palatial estate.

Sutro was a German tobacco merchant and mining engineer who made his fortune in the Comstock Lode silver mines, and who became mayor of San Francisco in the 1890s. He bought the Heights ten years before that, after returning from Nevada; renovated and built additions on the cottage that already stood on the property, forested the land with cypress and pine and eucalyptus to act as windbreaks, and constructed elaborate gardens full of fountains, gazebos, and a hundred plaster statues of wood nymphs and Greek gods and goddesses cleverly painted to look like marble. But Sutro hadn't much enjoyed his life on the Heights; things had begun to go wrong for him soon after he moved there—"as if something was exerting calamitous influences," according to the legend. The cottage was badly damaged when a schooner carrying a cargo of gunpowder went aground on Seal Rocks and exploded. Sutro's wife died unexpectedly. Cliff House, which he had bought for his own amusement, burned to the ground. His term as mayor was marred by infighting and corruption beyond his control. He contracted diabetes and his mind went on him. His daughter, the last member of the Sutro family to live on the Heights, also went insane before she died in the late thirties. And as if all that wasn't enough to foment the superstition, a well-known local ballerina had plunged to her death off the crumbling parapet above the Great Highway in 1940, under circumstances that were still shrouded in mystery.

I didn't buy the "haunted or cursed" business myself; the only ghosts I believe in are those that haunt the human mind, and the only curses I give much credence to are the profane ones people hurl at me during the course of my work. Still, there *is* something vaguely eerie about the Sutro ruins—a sense of loneliness and despair that seems to pervade the place. Not too many people go out there on days when the fog comes roiling in off the Pacific, when the wind blows in gusts and moans among the trees and rocks. I had been out there once on a day like that. It hadn't bothered me at the time, except to stir my imagination and my sense of history, as places like that always do; but then, I hadn't been back since. Not until today—and I surprised myself by thinking, as I curbed the car on Forty-eighth Avenue, that I was glad it was a nice sunny day without too much wind.

I walked into the park, thinking about the superstition and about the fact that there were not a lot of expensive homes in this neighborhood. Back a ways on Clement, across from the Lincoln Park Golf Course, there were some; maybe that was where the Summerhayeses lived. Either there, or all the way over on the other side of Lincoln Park, in Sea Cliff, and she'd taken a bus to get here. Not that it mattered. If I needed to know their address I could find it without too much trouble.

The look of Sutro Heights did little to belie its legendary status. It was weedy and generally unkempt, with a lot of gopher holes and earth mounds pocking the grassy areas and a few pieces of disreputable statuary and urns here and there that may or may not have dated back to Adolph's time. It was neither crowded nor deserted today: a few careless dog owners and their squatting, leg-lifting pets, some kids playing frisbee, a young couple sitting cross-legged on a blanket toasting each other with red wine in plastic glasses. I followed the old carriage road past the last remaining gazebo—it was decorated with graffiti, these being creative and enlightened times—and toward the high ground at the outer end.

When I got there I turned onto a sandy path that took me up to a flight of crumbling stone stairs. At the top of the stairs was what had once been a grand terrace, roughly circular and enclosed by low stone walls; now it contained a few wind-sculpted cypress trees and a profusion of weeds, high grass, and litter. Near the westward parapet, where the ground was bare and gravelly, were some low backless benches. Elisabeth Summerhayes was sitting on the middle one, looking out to sea. There wasn't anybody else around.

She sensed my presence as I approached, glanced my way, and then looked back toward the ocean. She was wearing a knee-length leather coat with a fur collar and her blond hair was tied down

140

with a scarf. She looked small and huddled at a distance, and oddly, considering her stature, the impression didn't change much even when I reached her side.

She still wouldn't look at me, so I sat down on the other end of the bench and took in the view myself. From up here you could see a good portion of the south rim of the city, the full two-mile sweep of Ocean Beach in that direction. The other way and down below, the area in front of the new Cliff House was clogged with tour buses, sidewalk vendors, tourists. Seaward, lying just offshore beyond Cliff House, gulls and pelicans swarmed over Seal Rocks; and much farther out—thirty-two miles—the Farallone Islands were like an irregular blot of shadow on the horizon. Impressive, all in all, but I couldn't enjoy it. Directly below the parapet, the cliff wall fell away to an extension of the carriage road and then, steeply, to the Great Highway; looking down there made me think of the promontory at Moss Beach—it made me think of death.

It was quiet here, almost too quiet; the noisy activity around Cliff House and the stream of Saturday afternoon afternoon traffic on the Great Highway seemed muted. I could feel the odd pervasiveness of the place, even on a day like this, and I would have broken the silence myself if Mrs. Summerhayes hadn't done it first.

She said without preamble, and still without looking at me, "My husband has been having an affair with Alicia Purcell. For at least a year now."

I couldn't think of a response.

"He came home one night with scratches on his neck, after he'd been to see her. He said he was seeing Kenneth but I knew Kenneth was away that night. He was very clever about not letting me see the scratches; I saw them anyway." She paused to watch a gull that came winging up over the cypress beyond me. Then she said, with a kind of dull bitter loathing, "I hate women who mark men, the ones with claws like cats."

"Have you confronted her?"

"I wanted to, several times. But I didn't."

"Why not?"

"I don't know. I really don't know."

"You haven't confronted your husband either?"

"No. Eldon is not a man you can confront. He blusters, he denies, he lies, he makes you feel as if you are the one who has done wrong. He would never admit the truth."

"How serious is it between them?"

"Not serious. Very, very casual. Lust is what binds them together, nothing more."

"Did Kenneth also know about the affair?"

"I don't know," she said. "Possibly."

"Would it have bothered him if he had? Would he have had words with your husband about it?"

She shook her head. "He knew the kind of woman Alicia is. He condoned her lust because he understood it. He was filled with lust himself."

"Forgive me for asking this, Mrs. Summerhayes, but did he ever make a pass at you?"

"Yes. Once. I slapped his face."

"When was that?"

"A long time ago. Three years."

"How did you get along with him after that?"

"I had as little to do with him as possible. My husband handled all our business dealings."

"How did he and Kenneth get along?"

"They had no trouble. They are two of a kind, after all." Another pause. "If you're thinking Eldon might have murdered Kenneth, you're mistaken. He had no reason. He doesn't want Alicia; he only wants her body."

"There's Kenneth's money," I said mildly.

"Yes. But I have more than Alicia inherited, you see—much more. My father was a very rich man in Oslo."

Again I couldn't think of anything to say.

"Eldon told you the truth that we were together when Kenneth died," she said. "Not alone together; with some of the other guests. If someone pushed him, it wasn't Eldon. Nor I. I had contempt for Kenneth but I didn't hate him. I couldn't have killed him if I had. I couldn't kill anyone." She seemed to think about something for a time. "Not even Alicia," she said.

I had nothing to say to that, either. Silence rebuilt between us; she still wasn't looking at me—hadn't looked at me the entire time we'd been talking. It was an eerie sort of conversation, as if there were a great distance between us and we were each talking to ourselves. It matched the surroundings, made me even more aware of them.

She had more to say; I sensed it, and I sensed, too, that prodding was not the way to get it out of her. When she was ready to talk she would, not before.

A good three minutes passed, with her looking out to sea and me looking here and there, everywhere but at her. Birds made a racket in the cypress nearby. A dog came bounding up onto the terrace, took a look at us, sniffed around, peed on one of the empty benches, and went away again.

"I examined the gallery records last night, after you left," she said. The words came so abruptly that her voice startled me a little, even though I had been waiting for her to speak. "My husband paid Alicia fifty thousand dollars four months ago, from his private checking account."

"A down payment on Kenneth's collection?"

"I don't know. It was for an unspecified reason. But on the same day he also deposited seventy-five thousand dollars."

"Where did he get it?"

"From one of our better customers."

"For something he'd sold, you mean?"

"Yes."

"Who was the customer?"

"Margaret Prine."

"Uh-huh, I see. Do you have any idea what it was he sold her?"

"It was nothing from our inventory at the time," she said. "I made a careful examination of those records, too."

"Would Mrs. Prine pay that much money for something in Kenneth's collection?"

"She was not impressed with his collection. His best pieces

are ones she already owns or was not interested in. All except one."

"The Hainelin snuff box?"

"Yes."

"Would Mrs. Prine have paid seventy-five thousand for that?"

"I think so. Yes, she would have."

The implications were obvious. If the Hainelin box *was* what Mrs. Prine had bought from Summerhayes, then it followed that the fifty thousand he'd paid Alicia Purcell on the same day was for purchase of the box. But why would she lie about having had it all along? Why the deception? It was legally hers anyway, as part of her husband's collection.

There was only one reason I could think of: Everyone knew Kenneth had been carrying the box on his person that night. If she admitted having it after his death, suspicion might fall on her—suspicion that she'd got it from him out on the cliffs, before she pushed him off—

No, hell, that didn't wash. She was alibied for the time of Kenneth's fall; she *couldn't* have pushed him. So why worry about being suspected, when everybody including the authorities was perfectly willing to call her husband's death an accident? All she'd have to do in any case was to say he'd given her the Hainelin *before* he stalked out of the house.

And that brought me right back to the original question: Why hadn't she admitted she had the box?

I put the question to Mrs. Summerhayes. She said, "I don't know. I don't understand women like Alicia, why they do things."

"Your husband might know."

"Yes, but he won't tell you if he does. He won't tell me."

"Why do you suppose he kept the two transactions secret? Because of his affair with Mrs. Purcell?"

"Yes. And because of the money. He likes to gamble in the stock market and he knows I won't give him money for that any more. He has lost too much in the past."

I wanted to ask her why she put up with a bastard like him, why she stayed married to him. But I already knew the answer. She

144

loved him, and it didn't really matter to her what he was or what he did: she loved him.

She was still sitting in rigid profile, and this time I sensed that she had said all she'd come to say. It had not been easy for her to talk to me as she had; it had been an act of small vengeance, born of bitterness and pain, and I thought that she might regret it later on. But it wouldn't be because of anything I did.

I said, "What you've told me here is in confidence, Mrs. Summerhayes. I won't repeat it to anyone under any circumstances, especially not your husband. You have my word on that."

She nodded as if she didn't care one way or the other; but when I stood up she looked at me full-face for the first time, as if she had not expected a kindness from someone like me. Then she averted her gaze again, without speaking. And I left her there, a big woman sitting small and huddled and alone among the ruins.

I drove back downtown to O'Farrell, parked on the street—the downstreet garage was closed on Saturdays—and went up to the office. The books on snuff bottles and boxes that I'd checked out of the library were still there, on a corner of my desk; I opened the one I'd skimmed through previously, refamiliarized myself with some terms and types, and then got Margaret Prine's telephone number out of the *Chronicle* file and dialed it.

An elderly female voice answered and admitted to being Mrs. Prine. I said I was Charles Eberhardt, from New York; that I was a dealer in antique miniatures; that I understood she was a prominent local collector of rare snuff boxes; and that I had for sale an exceptionally fine and unusual eighteenth-century ivory box bearing a portrait by the famed English miniaturist, Richard Cosway. Was she interested? She was interested, all right. But she was a wily old vixen: she wasn't about to show enthusiasm to a voice on the telephone, to react to such a proposition with anything but coolness and caution.

She said, "May I ask how you obtained my name and telephone number, Mr. Eberhardt?"

"Certainly. They were given to me by Alejandro Ozimas,"

Pause. "I see. And why did you choose to call me about the Cosway piece?"

"Mr. Ozimas said you were a collector of discerning taste. He also said you were both discreet and quite able to pay my price."

"And that price is?"

"Twenty thousand dollars."

"I see," she said again. "Describe the box, please."

"It is made of ivory, as I said; oval-shaped, with delicate gold ornamentation. The Cosway portrait is of the Prince of Wales—an associate of Cosway's, as I'm sure you know. Or at least he was before the scandal that linked him romantically with Cosway's wife."

"You're certain it's authentic?"

"Absolutely certain."

"How did it come into your possession?"

"I purchased it from a collector in Hawaii."

"His name?"

"I'm afraid I can't divulge it."

Another pause. Then she said flatly, "I do not buy stolen or tainted property, Mr. Eberhardt."

I'll just bet you don't, I thought. But I said, feigning indignance, "Nor do I sell stolen or tainted property, Mrs. Prine. Perhaps I've made a mistake in calling you. I'm sure Mr. Ozimas can recommend another local collector . . ."

"Just a moment. If you're from New York, why don't you take the Cosway there and sell it to one of your customers? You *do* have customers in New York?"

"Of course. But I hope to make another purchase while I'm in San Francisco, a very lucrative purchase, and it happens I'm short of cash at the moment. That's why I'm willing to let the Cosway box go for twenty thousand." It sounded phony even to me, but if I was reading her correctly it wouldn't make any difference. "May I show it to you? I could bring it to your home within the hour—"

"I'm afraid that's out of the question. I am expecting guests shortly."

"This evening, then?"

"Also out of the question."

"Tomorrow? It's important that I complete a sale on the Cosway as soon as possible—no later than Monday. I'm sure you understand."

"I'm sure I do," she said. "Very well, Mr. Eberhardt. Shall we say tomorrow afternoon at three?"

"Good. At your home?"

"I'd prefer not. Do you have objections to meeting publicly?"

I didn't, although I would have preferred the chance to look at her collection—at the Hainelin box, if she did have it. I hadn't expected an invitation anyway. She didn't know me from a hole in the wall; she would have had to be a damned fool—and she was hardly that—to let a stranger who knew she had a valuable art collection set foot inside her door.

I said, "None at all. Where do you suggest?"

"The main lobby of the Fairmont Hotel."

"How will I know you?"

"I carry a gold-headed cane," she said. "You'll know me by that. I look forward to seeing the Cosway, Mr. Eberhardt."

"You won't be disappointed when you do."

"I sincerely hope not," she said, and the line clicked, and that was that.

I thought as I cradled the receiver: Even money she's trying Ozimas's number right now, to check up on Charles Eberhardt. But Ozimas had indicated that he and his houseboy were going to Big Sur this weekend; otherwise I wouldn't have taken the calculated risk of using his name. The odds were pretty good that Mrs. Prine would show up at the Fairmont tomorrow afternoon, on schedule.

I hung around the office for a while, making inroads on a written report to Tom Washburn. Nobody telephoned, and I was fresh out of productive ideas. Hunger made me call it quits around two-thirty. I drove home, treated myself to a beer and the last of the leftover chicken, and spent the rest of the afternoon puttering around the flat, making a few minor repairs—damn toilet kept running, even when you jiggled the handle—and listening to the rest of the Cal game. The Bears were down twenty points late in the fourth quarter when I finally shut off the radio. Some game. It was a good thing I hadn't gone with Eberhardt, I thought; I'd have been bored sitting there in the sun guzzling beer. Bored to tears.

I almost believed it, too.

At five I called Kerry. She was in a good mood; she said, "Come on over. I rented us a movie."

"Yeah? Which one?"

"You'll see when you get here."

"Not another of those X-rated jobs?"

"No, but it'll do things for your body temperature."

"I'm too old for that kind of stuff. Think about my heart."

"I've got a different organ in mind," she said.

I said, "That's me you hear knocking on the door."

I took a quick shower, changed clothes, got the car, and drove up to Diamond Heights. Parking on Kerry's street is sometimes as bad as it is on mine; somebody must have been having a party this afternoon because there wasn't a space anywhere closer to her building than a block and a half. I hoofed it uphill, taking it slow so I wouldn't use up all my energy just getting to her.

Even so, I was puffing when I reached the building vestibule. Which is why I had my head down, which is why I didn't see the guy coming out of the door. He didn't see me either; we collided, caromed off each other—and I found myself standing there eye to lunatic eye with the Reverend Raymond P. Dunston.

I said, "What the hell are you doing here?"

He said, and I'll swear to it, "God sent me."

"Dunston, if you don't leave Kerry alone—"

"She is my wife."

"She is *not* your wife!"

" 'Bone of my bones, and flesh of my flesh. Therefore shall a man leave his father and his mother—' "

"You quoted that one before. Try a new one."

"Heathen," he said.

148

"Crackpot," I said.

We glared at each other for about five seconds. Then he turned on his heel and stalked off, and I turned on mine and went inside and upstairs and whacked on Kerry's door so hard I jammed my wrist doing it.

She opened up, took one look at me, and said, "Oh God, you ran into him."

"Literally." I pushed past her, massaging my wrist.

"You didn't do anything to him?"

"No, I didn't do anything to him. But I might have if I'd had a straitjacket handy."

"I didn't let him in," she said.

"Good for you. Did he tell you God sent him?"

"Yes. Among other things."

"Me too. He's driving me as crazy as he is, you know that?"

"You think he's not driving *me* crazy?"

"This is the last straw," I said darkly. "Tomorrow we quit pussyfooting around. Tomorrow we put an end to this one way or another."

"How?"

"By paying a visit to the Church of the Holy Mission," I said. "By having a talk with the Right Reverend Clyde T. Daybreak, with or without God's permission."

EIGHTEEN

I don't much like San Jose.

This is no reflection on the people who live there—not on most of them, anyway. Everybody's got to live somewhere, and in California these days, with the economic situation being what it is, your options are pretty much limited to areas with a reasonably high employment rate. There are some nice little communities near San Jose—Los Gatos, for instance; I have nothing against those. Just San Jose itself. It's like a big overgrown kid who sprouted up too fast, seems bewildered by his sudden wild growth, and doesn't quite know what to make of himself. It can't make up its collective mind if it wants to be a big metropolis or a small city, or if it's really just a little country town at heart. It has no real identity because there are too many opposing components in its makeup: part agricultural, part industrial, part Silicon Valley hype, part Mexican barrio, part Vietnamese refugee resettlement center, and part mindless, tasteless urban and suburban sprawl. It has some cultural attractions downtown, and the local Yuppies have begun renovating and restoring some of the old mid-city Victorians; but the downtown area is just a pocket surrounded by slums, industrial areas, cheap apartment buildings, and seemingly endless strings of tract houses and shopping centers. The city also has a high crime rate and harbors more than a few bizarre institutions, not the least of which are the Winchester Mystery House, a model of lunatic construction built by the widow of the inventor of the Winchester rifle, who believed she would die if the house was ever completed and therefore kept adding on things like doors that open on blank walls and stairways that lead nowhere; the Rosicrucians, a leading candidate for the Weirdest California Cult award; and now the Church of the Holy Mission, not to mention the Moral Crusade, the Reverend Raymond P. Dunston, and the Right Reverend Clyde T. Daybreak.

When Kerry and I got to San Jose a little past noon on Sunday, it was the first time I'd been there in more than a year. It seemed much more sprawling and congested than I remembered it, even on a Sunday—not that that surprised me any. I took the downtown exit off Highway 17, and we drove around for twenty minutes looking for Langford Street; if Kerry were a better mapreader we'd have found it in ten because it was not far from either City Hall or the San Jose State University campus. The neighborhood was neither well-to-do nor shabby: Langford was that vanishing breed, a lower-middle-class inner-city residential street shaded by leafy trees and featuring a dozen different architectural styles, from wood-shingled cottage to big gabled Victorian.

The biggest lot and the biggest Victorian on the fourteen-hundred block belonged to the Church of the Holy Mission, which announced its presence by means of a six-foot, billboard-type sign on its front lawn. It was three lots, actually, on a corner; in addition to the Victorian, freshly painted a sedate white with blue trim, it contained a low modern wing, a separate box-shaped outbuilding, and parking facilities for maybe thirty cars. The parking area was full at the moment, although it wouldn't be for long: services must have just ended because people were streaming out of the modern wing, most of them young, some with small children in tow.

"They look normal enough, don't they," Kerry said as I drove by hunting a place to park.

"You can't tell a fanatic by his appearance."

"They're not all fanatics," she said, and sneezed. She was getting a cold and she'd been snuffling and sneezing all morning. "A lot of them are disillusioned or have emotional problems."

"Yeah," I said. And a lot of them, I thought, will drop out later on even more disillusioned and with even greater emotional problems. There had been an article in the *Sunday Examiner-Chronicle* not too long ago—the Sunday paper is usually the only one I read —that dealt with dropouts from fundamentalist and ultrafundamentalist religious groups. Things were so bad with these people after experiencing a cultist dependency on leaders like Daybreak, authoritarian types who practice a kind of religious mind-control, that an outfit called Fundamentalists Anonymous had been formed to help them deal with the real world again. Maybe the Church of the Holy Mission wasn't quite one of the wild-eyed ultrafundamentalist sects, but like the Southern Baptist Convention and other mainline fundamentalist churches, which Daybreak seemed to be patterning it after, it would bring more harm than good to some of its followers.

A car was pulling out of a space in the next block. I waited patiently while the driver, an elderly lady wearing a hat that looked like the rear end of a rooster, maneuvered her way clear; then I wedged us into the space. We passed several members of the flock as we walked back to the church. None of them was smiling; they all had a solemn mien. Services at the Holy Mission were serious business, no doubt. There aren't many chuckles in fire-and-brimstone religion.

We went along a path toward the wing. Kerry said *sotto voce*, "What do we do if we run into Ray?"

"Ignore him. It's Daybreak we want, not nightfall."

She didn't think that was very amusing; neither did I, for that matter. There was something about the place, now that we were on the grounds and breathing its sanctified atmosphere, that made *me* feel solemn and cheerless.

A middle-aged guy in a dark-blue suit and tie was standing at the entrance to the wing. Beyond him, through an open set of doors, I could see a plain raised altar, a podium with a microphone on it, and a section off to one side that contained an organ and some chairs for the choir. The rest of the space was taken up with rows of unpainted wooden pews. There were a few people in there, none up around the altar; Dunston, happily, wasn't among them.

We stopped alongside the middle-aged guy and I said, feeling a little foolish, "We're looking for the Right Reverend Daybreak. Can you tell us where he is?"

"Of course, brother. He is in the Sanctuary."

"The which?"

"The Sanctuary." He gestured at the boxy-shaped outbuilding. "For his hour of meditation. Perhaps I can help you? I am Reverend Holloway."

"Thanks just the same, but we need to talk to the Right Reverend. It's very important."

"In what way, brother?"

"It has to do with money," I said. "My wife and I are thinking of making a substantial donation to the Moral Crusade."

That perked him right up. He said, "Come with me, please. If the Right Reverend has not yet begun meditating I'm sure he'll be pleased to give you an audience."

Audience, yet. As if he were right up there with the Pope. We went with Holloway to the Sanctuary, and he took my name and disappeared with it inside. When we were alone Kerry said, "Why did you lie to him?"

"Quickest way to get results. If I'd told him the truth, do you think we'd be getting a fast audience? We'd be getting a fast runaround instead."

"You're not going to lie to Daybreak, are you?"

"No. We'll be paragons of indignant virtue. Just let me do the talking."

The Reverend Holloway was back in less than two minutes. He smiled at us gravely and said, "The Right Reverend Daybreak will see you," as if he were announcing a miracle at Lourdes. "This way, please."

We followed him inside. Some sanctuary; it looked like a glorified office building—no doubt this was where the take from the church's various nontaxable enterprises was counted, blessed, and secreted. Through an open door I had a glimpse of one large, mostly bare room that may or may not have been used for meditation; three other doors along the central hallway were closed. We stopped before the last of these. Painted on the panel in dark-blue letters were the words: THE RIGHT REVEREND CLYDE T. DAYBREAK. And below that, in somewhat larger letters: THE MORAL CRUSADE. A hand-lettered sign thumbtacked above the knob told you to *Please Knock Before Entering*.

The Reverend Holloway knocked. A voice inside said, "Come right in," and Holloway opened the door and Kerry and I went in. He stayed out in the hall, shutting the door after us.

It was a large office, done in plain blond-wood paneling, with its dominant feature being a plain blond-wood desk set in front of windows shaded by Venetian blinds. The blinds were open now and sunlight came streaming in. It bathed the Spartan contents of the office in a benign radiance, as if by design: the desk, a group of matching and uncomfortable-looking chairs, a blond-wood file cabinet, a painting of Christ on one wall, a huge cloth banner on another—dark-blue lettering on a snowy white background that said THE MORAL CRUSADE—and the sole occupant coming toward us with both hands outstretched.

Clyde T. Daybreak was something of a surprise. I had half-expected a tall, dour, hot-eyed guy dressed in black—a sort of cult version of Cotton Mather. Or maybe the strong silent type with a gaze that was both penetrating and hypnotic, like Robert Mitchum in *Night of the Hunter*. Clyde T. was neither one. He was short, he was round, he was bald except for a reddish Friar Tuck fringe forming a half-circle around the back of his head. He wore the same kind of conservative dark-blue business suit as the Reverend Holloway, and a skinny tie with a gold clip that, believe it or not, formed the words *The Moral Crusade*. He was smiling, and his cheeks were red and rosy, and his eyes were as bright and blue and serene as a mountain lake on a summer day.

He took hold of my hand and worked it up and down vigorously, as if he were trying to prime a pump. Which, in a manner of speaking, he probably was. He said, "Welcome, brother, welcome!" in a just-perceptible Southern drawl. Then he took Kerry's hand and pumped it and said, "Welcome, sister, welcome!" Through all of this I paid close attention to his eyes. Behind the bright blue serenity there was a shrewdness and something that might have been guile. He had a kind of aura about him, too, that electric quality that makes people respond to religious and political zealots everywhere—a combination of intense will and either deep conviction or the ability to simulate it. He was the type who could lead a crusade, all right, all the more so for his plain looks and deceptively open manner.

He asked me, "Have we met before, brother? I don't seem to recall having the pleasure."

I told him it was our first visit to the church. I didn't tell him I hoped it would be our last.

He invited us to sit down, ushered us to the chairs in front of his desk, held Kerry's for her, and then bounced around behind the desk and sat down himself. His swivel chair must have been wound up high or built up with extra padding; as short as he was, he still seemed to be looking down at us like a little king on his throne.

"Were you with us for services this morning?" he asked.

I said, "No, we missed them. We just got here."

"Too bad, too bad. You're familiar with the teachings of Ezekiel, of course? The resurrection of dry bones?"

I nodded. Kerry took out her handkerchief and sneezed into it.

"Well," Daybreak said, and smiled, and then said, "The Reverend Holloway tells me you've come to offer a donation to the Moral Crusade."

"Actually, no," I said. "That was just a ruse to get in here to see you."

He had terrific poise, you had to give him that; his smile didn't even waver. "Deceit is a sin, brother," he said gently.

"That depends on the magnitude of the deceit. Some kinds are more sinful than others."

"To be sure. But all sin is wicked, brother; those who indulge in it casually are no less apt to be damned than those who embrace it with open arms. The sins of man are the devil's playthings."

"Would you say harassment is among them?"

"I beg your pardon?"

"Harassment. The kind that's done in the name of God."

"I'm afraid I don't understand."

"This lady is Kerry Wade," I said. "Does the name mean anything to you, Reverend?"

"No, brother, it doesn't. Should it?"

"It should if your assistants confide in you. Ms. Wade is your Reverend Dunston's ex-wife."

His smile was gone now; but it seemed to have faded out gradually, rather than to have disappeared all at once. In its place he wore a grave, earnest expression.

"I still don't understand," he said. "Perhaps you'd better explain the purpose of your visit."

"Isn't it obvious? We're here to put a stop to Reverend Dunston's delusion that Ms. Wade is still his wife. She divorced him more than five years ago."

"The Church of the Holy Mission does not recognize divorce," Daybreak said. "In our eyes, divorce is—"

"—a pernicious invention of man," I finished for him. "Uh-huh, so I've been told. But that doesn't change the legality of Ms. Wade's decree. Or her unwillingness to remarry her ex-husband, which is what he keeps pestering her to do."

Kerry blew her nose loudly, as if in emphatic agreement.

Daybreak said, "May I ask the nature of your involvement in the matter, sir?" I seemed to have lost my status as his brother; now I was just plain "sir." "Are you Mrs. Dunston's attorney?"

"It's Ms. Wade, and no, I'm not her attorney. I'm a friend of hers, a close friend. Dunston has been harassing me, too."

"Ah," Daybreak said.

"Ah?"

"Ah."

"All right," I said testily, "I confess: I'm a fornicator. What of it?"

Kerry suppressed a giggle and blew her nose again. It sounded like a goose honking.

"Your confession saddens me," Daybreak said. "It comes without shame. There is so much sin in today's world, so little shame."

"And I suppose the Moral Crusade is going to reverse the trend?"

"We will do our part," he said passionately. "Yes, we will."

"Well, let me tell you this," I said. "Sinners have rights, too, the same as moral crusaders. And one of them is the right to live our lives without interference—"

I broke off because Daybreak was shaking his bald head. He said, "Sinners forfeit their rights until they renounce their wicked ways. God has no patience with those who spurn His teachings, who foul the paths of righteousness."

"Did He tell you that?"

"Sir?"

"Do you talk to God, Reverend?"

"Of course."

"Does He answer you?"

"Of course."

I was starting to get flustered, which in me is one step shy of losing both my patience and my temper. I said, "And I suppose He told you it's okay for a man to hound his ex-wife just because he—"

"A man does not have an *ex*-wife, sir," Daybreak said. "When a man marries it is for his lifetime and that of his wife's; in God's eyes it is for all of eternity. If his wife should leave him he is justified in demanding that she return to his house and his bed."

"No matter what she wants, is that it?"

"It is what God wants that matters."

"There are laws—"

"God's laws are higher."

I could feel myself sliding toward the edge of unreason. And at this point I was not even sure I wanted to stop the slide. I said, "Listen to me, Daybreak. I've had just about enough of—"

"Oh, stop it," Kerry said suddenly. "I've had enough of this myself."

Daybreak and I both looked at her. She sneezed, blew her nose, snuffled, and said to him, "You win, Reverend—you and my ex-husband both. I can't fight it anymore. I'll go back to him."

I gawked in disbelief. Daybreak beamed. "The Reverend Dunston will be pleased to hear that, my dear," he said. "Surely the Almighty will be, too."

I said, "Kerry . . ."

She ignored me. "Does Reverend Dunston live here at the church?" she asked Daybreak.

"Oh yes. He has an apartment in our main house."

"Then that's where I'll be living, too?"

"Yes. You'll find it quite comfortable."

"But you know, I'm not going to remarry him."

"There's no need, my dear. You've never been *un*married."

"Oh, I understand that," she said. "But I wonder if everyone else will."

"Everyone else?"

"Everyone in your flock. And everyone in the Bay Area, not to mention other parts of the country. And especially NOW and the other women's organizations. Oh yes, and let's not forget the American Civil Liberties Union."

"I don't understand . . ."

"Well," she said, "the Church of the Holy Mission may not believe in divorce or the individual freedom of women or the laws of the land, but a lot of people do. I'll bet the newspapers will be delighted to hear from me."

"Newspapers?"

"Yes. As soon as I move in with Ray . . . I mean the Reverend Dunston . . . I'll call half a dozen papers and tell them both your church and your so-called moral crusade sanctions the keeping of women in religious bondage."

"*Bondage?*"

"Exactly. When the women's organizations hear about it they'll come here in droves and picket the church and disrupt your activities. Then there'll be national wire service stories and all sorts of television coverage. The church and the Moral Crusade will get a *lot* of publicity, Reverend Daybreak. Won't that be nice for you?"

He sat there blinking at her. Me too, only my blinks were ones of admiration. She had succeeded in doing with a few well-chosen words what I hadn't even come close to doing with a barrelful: rattling him right out of his sanctimonious self-assurance. He said lamely, "My dear Mrs. Dunston . . ."

"I can see the headlines now," Kerry said. " 'Church Forces Woman to Live with Ex-Husband.' 'Church Condones Bondage of Women in the Name of Religion.' " She let him have a sweet, guileless smile. "The whole thing will probably become a nation-wide *cause célèbre,*" she said. "In fact, I'll make sure it does. I'm in advertising, you know—the Bates and Carpenter agency in San Francisco. We're very good at saturation promo campaigns, the manipulation of public sentiment. Even better than you are." Another sweet smile. "That should help no end when the lawsuit comes to trial."

"Lawsuit?" he said. "Trial?" he said.

"Oh, I forgot to mention that, didn't I? If I can get the right lawyer—and I'm sure I can—we'll ask as much as, oh, ten million dollars in punitive damages. We'll settle for less, of course. It all depends on the church's assets at the time."

Daybreak got jerkily to his feet; the look on his face was one of pure horror. He seemed to realize that, because he wiped it off and then turned his back to us and stood staring out through the venetian blinds, his hands washing each other just above his tailbone.

I looked at Kerry and mouthed the words *You're terrific.* She wrinkled her nose at me, snuffled, and sneezed again.

For about two minutes it was very quiet in there. Then Daybreak turned around, slowly, and looked at Kerry; I might not have been there anymore. He had the mask of serenity in place again. He even managed to work up a faint nervous smile as he said, "You'd go through with it, wouldn't you, Mrs. Dunston—everything you said?"

"Yes, Reverend, I would. And my name is Wade, not Dunston—Kerry *Wade.* Please remember that."

"As you wish."

"As it *is.*"

"What do you want from me, Ms. Wade?"

"I want you to have a nice long talk with my ex-husband. I want you to tell him to leave me *and* my friend alone from now on. I want you to explain to him exactly what will happen if he doesn't."

"Is that all?"

"That's all. I don't think it's too much to ask, do you?"

"I will speak to Reverend Dunston," he said.

"Immediately?"

"Immediately."

"Good." She stood, and I bounced right up alongside her. "I do hope you can make him understand," she said, smiling. "If not . . . well, I'll have no choice but to pack my bags and move right in." He smiled back at her—there wasn't a trace of humor in his smile—and she said, "Goodbye, Reverend Daybreak," and went to the door and I followed her out like a puppy.

Neither of us said anything until we were clear of the now-deserted church grounds. I said then, "You amaze me sometimes, lady. Where did you get all of that stuff in there?"

"It just came to me."

"Good thing it did. I wasn't doing too well."

"No, you weren't. Another thirty seconds and you'd have been calling him a crook and a charlatan."

"He *is* a crook and a charlatan."

"Maybe. But he doesn't think so."

"I thought you'd gone nuts at first. I couldn't figure out what you were doing."

"Women's wiles, my dear."

"Yeah," I said. "Well, that put an end to it; you hit him right where he lives. We won't have any more trouble with Dunston."

"Lord," she said fervently, "I hope not. I would *hate* to have to follow up on all those threats."

"You don't mean you'd actually move down here?"

She gave me an enigmatic smile, and then sneezed in the middle of it. "What do you think?" she said as we reached the car. "You old fornicator, you."

NINETEEN

It was after two when we got back to San Francisco. I was pretty hungry by then, but there was no time to even grab a sandwich; I would be cutting it close as it was, getting to the Fairmont in time for my three o'clock appointment with Margaret Prine. I dropped Kerry off at her apartment and hurried downtown and up onto Nob Hill and parked more or less legally on Taylor Street, opposite Grace Cathedral and around the corner from Mrs. Prine's fancy apartment house. I was exactly one minute late when I walked into the hotel.

The Fairmont has been a San Francisco landmark for close to eighty years and is still one of its finest luxury hotels. It has posh bars and restaurants and shops, a couple of suites that would cost you a grand a day *if* you had the right pedigree, a twenty-nine-story tower addition built in the early sixties, and a lobby notable for its late-Victorian elegance: dark, brownish marble pillars and staircases, ornate wood-paneled ceiling and walls, antique furnishings. If you're wearing a hat when you walk in there you invariably find yourself taking it off. It has that effect even on lowbrows like me.

The lobby was moderately crowded at the moment; I walked the length of it, feeling out of place and looking for an elderly woman with a gold-headed cane. There were plenty of elderly women and even a couple of canes, but none of the latter had a gold head. I made another circuit and then decided I ought to sit down somewhere, before one of the security people spotted me and took me for an undesirable. There was some plush maroon furniture near the entrance to the Squire Restaurant, opposite the hotel's main entrance off Mason Street. I parked myself on an overstuffed couch and watched people move in and out, back and forth. And waited.

At 3:20 I was still waiting. Maybe Ozimas didn't go to Big Sur after all, I thought. Maybe she got hold of him and he told her he didn't know any dealer in antique miniatures named Charles Eberhardt, and that made her balk at keeping our appointment.

I was fretting with that possibility when I saw her. She came in through the main entrance and stopped and held her cane up in front of her in a discreet away, so that the gold head was visible. I got off the couch and went her way, taking my time so I could size her up. From a distance she looked small and frail in a bulky fur coat, like somebody's nice old white-haired grandmother—one who happened to have a couple of million dollars or so. Up close there was no mistaking the toughness in her seamed and rouged face and her shrewd gray eyes, the imperiousness of her bearing. Or the fact that she was a woman who knew what she wanted and usually got it, one way or another.

"Mrs. Prine? I'm Charles Eberhardt."

She looked me up and down, once, as if she were examining a

161

curious artifact. If the artifact made any impression on her she didn't show it. She said, "How do you do, Mr. Eberhardt. I apologize for being tardy; I was unavoidably detained."

Sure you were, I thought. She'd been late on purpose—I understood that now. A double-edged ploy, no doubt, designed to test Mr. Eberhardt's sincerity and to froth up his eagerness to sell her a Cosway snuff box.

I said, "No apology necessary, Mrs. Prine."

"You've bought the Cosway?"

I smiled at her. "Shall we go into the lounge, where it's more private?"

"No. It's too dark in there. I'll want to examine the piece, of course."

"Of course." I gestured toward where I'd been sitting before; none of the furniture there was occupied. "Over this way?"

She nodded and we went that way and took opposite ends of the same lumpy couch. She said, "Now then, Mr. Eberhardt, the Cosway."

I said pleasantly, "Now then, Mrs. Prine, my name isn't Eberhardt and I don't have any Cosway box." I told her what my name *was* and that I was the private detective she wouldn't talk to last week. I also offered her one of my business cards.

She didn't take the card; she looked at it as if it were something unclean. Looked at me the same way, with a sprinkling of contempt and malice thrown in. "I do not care to be lied to," she said in a chilly voice, and started to get up.

"I think you'd better stay a while," I said. "I know you've got Kenneth Purcell's Hainelin snuff box; I know you paid Eldon Summerhayes seventy-five thousand dollars for it four months ago."

She went rigid. She seemed to pale a little, too; at any rate the rouge on her cheeks appeared redder now. The look she gave me this time was one of hatred. She said in a biting whisper, "Blackmail."

"Not at all, Mrs. Prine. I don't want anything from you except the answers to some questions."

162

That pushed her a little more off balance, which was where I wanted to keep her. The way to handle Margaret Prine, I had decided, was the same way Kerry had handled the Right Reverend Clyde T. Daybreak.

"Questions?" she said. "What questions?"

"About the Hainelin box. About where Summerhayes got it and why everybody pretended it was lost when Kenneth fell."

"I don't have to tell you anything," she said.

"That's right, you don't. But how would it look for you if I took my information to the authorities?"

"I admit to nothing. You can't prove I have the Hainelin."

"Maybe not," I said. "But does it matter? Kenneth Purcell was murdered, Mrs. Prine; I think I *can* prove that. So was his brother. How would you like to be arrested as an accessory to double homicide?"

"Accessory?" The hatred was still in her eyes, but so was uncertainty, now, and the emotion I most wanted to see: fear.

"That's right. The Hainelin box may be important evidence in Kenneth's murder. You bought it and are holding it without having informed the authorities of the transaction; technically that's suppressing it, and suppressing evidence in a homicide case is a felony."

"I had nothing to do with Kenneth's death!"

"Whether you did or not, you could still be tried on a felony charge. A good lawyer could probably get you off—but what about the publicity? What would that do to your reputation?"

She clamped her mouth shut as a group of people passed, on their way into the Squire Restaurant. She didn't speak when they were gone, either; she was thinking over what I'd said. The seamed skin of her face had the look of parchment stretched too tight around the shape of her skull, so that it might tear at any second.

It didn't take her long to make up her mind. Not much more than a minute had passed when she said in a stiff, controlled voice, "Ask your questions."

"Where did Summerhayes get the Hainelin box?"

"From Alicia Purcell. Or so he told me."

"How did she come to have it?"

"He said she found it among Kenneth's effects."

"When?"

"Two days after his death."

"Then why did she keep up the pretense that it was lost?"

"She told Eldon she needed cash. If she had reported finding the box it would have legally become part of Kenneth's estate; she would not have been able to sell it until his will cleared probate."

"That sounds pretty flimsy," I said. "She sold it illegally anyway, didn't she?"

"I'm sure I don't care how it sounds to you. I am only telling you what Eldon Summerhayes told me."

"Meaning you didn't care how flimsy it sounded, or how illegal the deal was, as long as you got the Hainelin."

Her lips pulled in tight at the corners and her eyes snapped at me. But she held her tongue.

I said, "Why did Mrs. Purcell need such a large amount of cash?"

"Some sort of investment, I gathered."

"You gathered. Didn't you ask Summerhayes?"

"No. I did not."

"Did he tell you how much he paid her for the box?"

"Seventy thousand dollars."

"So his commission for arranging the deal was five thousand?"

"That is correct."

"That is incorrect," I said. "He paid her fifty and kept twenty-five for himself."

That surprised her, and it made her even angrier than she already was; I could see the anger like sparks in those sharp gray eyes. But it also served to tighten her control. When she spoke again it sounded as though the words were being squeezed out through a roller press.

"If you are telling the truth," she said, "that is a matter between Eldon and myself. It has no bearing on anything else."

"Maybe it does, maybe it doesn't. Have you had any contact with Mrs. Purcell since you bought the box?"

"Hardly."

"Why 'hardly'? Don't you get along with her?"

"I despise her. She has the morals of an alley cat."

So do you, Maggie, I thought, in your own sweet way.

I said, "How about Kenneth? What did you think of him?"

"As little. He was a boor, a drunkard, and a womanizer."

"Uh-huh. Who do you think pushed him off that cliff?"

"I don't believe anyone pushed him, no matter what you say. His death was an accident."

"His brother's wasn't."

"I know nothing about that."

"Did you have any contact with Leonard after Kenneth's death?"

"Certainly not. I told you, I know nothing about his murder." She drew herself up even straighter and pointed the gold head of her cane at me as if it were a weapon. "Now are you quite finished with your questions?"

I wasn't, but asking any more wouldn't get me anything: the set of her jaw and the look in her eyes made it plain that she'd said all she was going to say. If she knew anything else it would take an official inquiry to get her to admit it.

I said, "That's all for now, Mrs. Prine. You can go."

"How generous of you." She got slowly to her feet, using the cane as a fulcrum; I didn't much feel like being a gentleman, not where she was concerned, so I made no effort to help her. When we were both standing she said, "Do you intend to tell anyone about what we have just discussed?"

"If you mean the police or the newspapers, no. Not unless it has a direct bearing on either Kenneth's death or Leonard's."

"If you do I will deny having spoken to you. I will deny having purchased the Hainelin box and I will see to it that Eldon Summerhayes denies having sold it to me. I will also speak to my attorneys about suing you for harassment and defamation of character."

"You're a nice lady, you know that?" I said. "I wish I had a granny like you."

Her tight little mouth worked; if we had been somewhere other than the lobby of the Fairmont, somewhere alone, she might have spit in my eye. As it was, she settled for a contemptuous sneer and then turned abruptly and thumped off across the lobby.

Back in the car, I looked up the Moss Beach number in my notebook and called it on the mobile phone. Alicia Purcell was in; she answered herself. Her voice was cool, but she didn't sound unhappy to hear from me again—not yet.

"Have you found out anything new?" she asked.

"As a matter of fact, yes. I've just had a long talk with Margaret Prine. I know all about the Hainelin snuff box."

". . . What do you know?"

"I know it didn't go over the cliff with your husband," I said. "I know you sold it to Eldon Summerhayes for fifty thousand dollars four months ago, and that he in turn sold it to Mrs. Prine. What I *want* to know is why you lied about having it."

There was a lengthy pause. When she spoke again the coolness in her voice had frozen into solid ice. "I resent you meddling in my private affairs."

"Meddling is one of the things I get paid for," I said. "Answer my question, Mrs. Purcell."

"And if I refuse?"

"Then you'll answer it for the police."

"I've done nothing illegal. The box was mine to sell as my husband's legal heir."

"Not until his will clears probate."

"All right, yes, I admit that. But I needed cash after his death; he left me cash-poor."

"So you needed the fifty thousand for living expenses."

"Among other things, yes."

"What other things?"

"Nothing that concerns you."

"Suppose you let me be the judge of that."

"Oh, all right. There were things I wanted—clothing, jewelry."

"Wouldn't your husband let you buy them when he was alive?"

"If you must know, no, he wouldn't."

"But you told me the other day you never wanted for anything the entire time you were married."

". . . I wasn't being completely candid with you then."

"And you are being candid with me now."

"Yes."

"How did you get the Hainelin box?"

"Kenneth gave it to me."

"When?"

"Before he left the house. When we talked in his hobby room."

"Why did he give it to you?"

"I asked him to. He'd been drinking so heavily . . . I was afraid he'd lose it."

"He just handed it over?"

"Yes."

"No argument or anything?"

"No."

"Did you argue about anything else at that time?"

"We did not. Why do you ask that?"

"Your housekeeper said he was upset when he left the house. Any idea what he was upset about?"

"None whatsoever."

"What did you do with the box after he gave it to you?"

"Put it with the other pieces in his collection."

"Left it there after his death?"

"Until the next day, yes. Then I removed it."

"Hid it, you mean."

"Hid it. Yes. Are you satisfied now?"

"For the time being."

"I suppose that means I'll be hearing from you again."

"I thought you wanted to hear from me," I said. "I thought you were very concerned about things I've been finding out."

She hung up on me again.

On the way down California Street I called Kerry's number; I was starved—all I'd had to eat today had been some toast for breakfast

—and I thought maybe she wanted to go out for an early dinner. But her line was busy. So I drove on home, and tried her again from there. Still busy. Talking to one of her women friends, maybe. Or her mother, Cybil, who was a former pulp writer and lived in Pasadena with Kerry's father, Ivan the Terrible, also an ex-pulp writer, and who would cheerfully talk your ear off if you gave her half a chance.

I rummaged around in the refrigerator. There wasn't anything in there I wanted to eat except an apple, and it turned out to be mushy and I threw it away after one bite. I opened the cupboard and found a can of ravioli and opened it and ate the little buggers cold, right out of the can. Kerry would have been horrified, but I've been eating cold ravioli for years; it's the only way to eat the canned variety, which isn't really ravioli at all. The kind native Italians make by hand and serve hot, *that's* ravioli. The cold canned stuff is a whole different taste treat.

At five o'clock I tried Kerry again and finally got through to her. She'd been talking to Cybil, as it turned out—filling her in on our visit to the Church of the Holy Mission and the number she'd done on the Right Reverend Daybreak. She said dinner sounded fine, but she'd just had a sandwich and wouldn't be hungry again for a while. We settled on seven-thirty and a fish restaurant we both liked out on Geary Boulevard.

I sat down in the living room with a can of beer. So now where was I, after the session with Margaret Prine and the telephone conversation with Alicia Purcell? I now knew for sure that Mrs. Purcell had hidden her possession of the Hainelin box from the authorities, that she'd sold it to Eldon Summerhayes, and that Margaret Prine now had it. So? Did the box have any direct bearing on Kenneth Purcell's death? It didn't look that way, unless Alicia was lying about her reasons for secreting the box, or holding something back. But why would she lie? What would she hold back? I had no good answer in either case. And that put me right back where I'd been two days ago, smack up against a dead end. The only concrete lead I'd turned up with all my running around and maneuvering, it seemed, was Danny Martinez. He was the key to the whole case. Without him, there was no way to make sense out of it, to put it all together.

Or was there?

The telephone rang. I went into the bedroom and answered it, and Tom Washburn said, "I just came back from the house. I . . . well, I couldn't make myself go over there until today. I'm sorry, I just couldn't."

"Don't apologize, Mr. Washburn. Did you find anything in Leonard's papers?"

"Nothing pertaining to Richard Dessault or that man Ozimas."

"Something else?"

"Well, I don't know. A photograph."

"What sort of photograph?"

"You'd better see it for yourself. I don't know what it means; it probably doesn't mean anything. But I think you should look at it."

"Are you still at the house?"

"No. I'm back at Fred's."

"What's the address there again?"

He told me, and I said, "I could come by around seven or so." On my way to Kerry's, I was thinking. "Is that all right with you?"

"Yes, fine. I'll expect you."

A photograph, I thought as I rang off. Which reminded me of the one I'd taken out of Danny Martinez's farmhouse. I found it in the pocket of my other suit coat and looked at it again. And it bothered me again in the same vague way it had yesterday in my office. Or was it something associated with it that was responsible for the bother? I couldn't seem to get a grasp on whatever it was. Too many things whirling around inside my head, too many confusing elements that kept me from seeing any of them clearly.

I started out into the kitchen to get another beer, and the telephone rang again. I did an about-face back into the bedroom, picked up, and a familiar voice said, "This is Melanie Purcell."

She was one of the last people I expected to hear from. I said,

169

"Yes, Melanie," and managed to keep the surprise out of my voice. "What can I do for you?"

"You still want to see Richie?" The way she said it, I thought she might be angry or uptight about something.

"Yes, I do. Where is he?"

"At the houseboat. He came back a little while ago." There was a pause. "He was gone two days," she said.

"Gone where?"

"He wouldn't tell me. I don't care anyway, not anymore. That's why I called you."

"Where are you?"

"One of the neighbor's boats. I slipped out when he got into the shower. Listen, I think he's going out again pretty soon. He acts all excited about something."

"I can be there in half an hour," I said. "Can you keep him around that long?"

"I guess I can try. But you better hurry."

"What kind of car does he drive?"

"A white Trans-Am."

"All right. Thirty minutes, Melanie."

TWENTY

It was full dark when I got to Mission Creek. There was not much of a moon tonight and patchy clouds mostly obscured its thin, pale hook-shape; but nightlights strung along the floating walkway and aglow in boat windows and portholes, lights both moving and stationary on the freeway terminus high above, made it easy enough to see. I cut my headlamps just after I made the turn off Fourth onto Channel Street, beyond Blanche's Café.

On the way down here I had been of two minds as to what to do about Richie Dessault, assuming he was still around when I arrived. One was to brace him, see what I could wrangle out of him by guile and intimidation; the other was to hang around out of sight, wait for him to leave, and then follow him and see where he led me. I had pretty much decided that following him was the best of the two alternatives. Melanie had said he was excited about something. Maybe his emotional state had nothing to do with Danny Martinez or the Purcell murders—maybe he was just tired of Melanie, if not of Melanie's money, and had found himself another bunny to burrow up with for a while. But if his excitement *was* related to the case, then I stood a better chance of finding out what it was by shagging him. I could brace him later, when we got to where he was going; or tomorrow or the day after that, if tonight didn't pan out.

There was nobody that I could see on the embankment, and all of the dozen or so vehicles slotted in at its edge were dark. I let the car drift off the road to the left, lightless, and coasted to a stop in the shadows cast by an express company warehouse. From there I had a good look at the parked cars. One of them was a white Trans-Am. It was directly across the embankment from the nearest of the access ramps, fifty yards or so from where I was and at an angle to my left.

I shut off the engine, rolled down the window so I could listen to the night sounds. The swishing passage of freeway traffic, a ship's horn somewhere in China Basin or out on the Bay, a woman's skittish laughter from one of the anchored boats—all distant and random. Otherwise the creek area, surrounded as it was by industrial outfits and the Southern Pacific yards, all almost entirely deserted on a Sunday night, seemed even more isolated and self-contained than it did during the daylight hours.

I didn't expect much of a wait and I didn't have one. Less than two minutes had passed when Dessault came hurrying up the near ramp and through its security gate; the nightlight there made a pale nimbus of his blond hair, letting me identify him.

He moved across the flat of the embankment, startling a couple of the geese that appeared to live there—I could hear their annoyed honking, see one of them flapping its wings—and got into his Trans-Am. I waited until I heard the deep-throated roar of the engine before I started mine again. He backed out my way, pointed west toward Sixth; and that was the direction he went, not driving fast but not driving slow either.

I let him get a hundred yards down Channel Street before I put on my headlights and pulled away from the warehouse. Following him dark would have been foolish business. If he was the kind of driver who checked his rearview mirror periodically, there was enough light in the area to let him see what was behind him; and he would be a lot more apt to pay attention to a car without its lights on than he would to just another set of headlights.

He made the turn onto Sixth and I did the same. It was deserted and much darker down along here—drayage and freight-forwarding companies and part of the SP freight yards on the east side, and on the west, fenced-in lots mounded with creosote-soaked lumber and other materials that the railroad used for repair work. Here and there nightlights cast thin yellow wedges above empty loading docks. The only other illumination came from the beams on Dessault's car and the beams on mine.

We went about a quarter of a mile. Dessault was nearing the intersection with Sixteenth when he surprised me by making an abrupt left-hand turn; the Trans-Am disappeared between two of the warehouses. When I got to that point I found an unpaved, unmarked access road that served a drayage firm on one side and some kind of truck storage yard on the other: big diesel cabs and unhooked trailers looming up out of the darkness, both inside and outside a high chain-link fence. The Trans-Am was about seventy-five yards along, its lights picking up a low, metal Stop sign anchored where the road widened out past the warehouse and the storage yard.

I slowed, thinking, Some kind of shortcut. He knows this area, he knows a faster way to get where he's going.

Up ahead, the Trans-Am moved on past the Stop sign and its lights splashed over rough ground that fronted a criss-cross of SP sidings; splashed over a string of oil tankers, another of boxcars, as Dessault veered to the right. I made the turn just before he passed out of sight, and when he was gone I punched the accelerator a little. I didn't want him to get too far away.

Even though the Trans-Am was no longer visible I could see the glow of its lights against the dark sky, bouncing erratically because of the uneven ground. And then, suddenly, they stopped bouncing and the glow wasn't there any more . . . as if he'd braked fast and shut off the beams. And just as suddenly I knew that was what he *had* done—I knew this wasn't a shortcut at all, I knew what it *was,* and the knowledge put the brassy taste of fear in my mouth.

Trap, goddamn trap. And I had blundered into it like a witless amateur.

I spun the wheel hard left, sent the car into a slashing turn that made the tires squeal and spin up gravel and dirt. But it was too late by then—too damn late. The trap car was hidden over that way, in the clotted black alongside the last of the drayage company's loading docks; it came shooting out at me, dark and formless, like some kind of phantom. Before I could complete the U-turn, it banged into my right front fender . . . impact, crunch of metal . . . and the wheel twisted out of my hands and the car slewed around and came to a shuddering stop that stalled the engine. I shoved back off the wheel and reached for the door lock with my left hand, for the flashlight under the dash with my right —the only weapon I had in there.

But it was too late for that, too. They weren't all in the trap car; one of them had been hidden somewhere else nearby, on foot, and he got to my door before I could lock it and yanked it open and lunged in at me. I fought him, but he was big, bull-strong: I had an impression of youth, of mindless exhilaration at what he was doing. He got one hand on the collar of my suit jacket, the other bunched in my hair, and hauled me out of the car.

The other two were there by then, big and young like the first one—faceless shapes in the darkness, without humanity of any kind, a trio of androids programmed for violence while the one who had activated them stood off somewhere, maybe watching, maybe not, depending on his stomach for this kind of thing. I fought all three of them in a kind of frenzy and for a few seconds I held my own, I did some damage: kicked one of them somewhere in the body, heard him grunt, hit another one in the face and felt his spittle spray my cheek. But I had no real chance against them, none at all. One of them kicked my legs out from under me and once they got me down on the ground I was finished.

I kept trying to fight, trying to get my legs under me again—until one of them hit me or kicked me in the head, full-force, behind the right ear. Then everything went a little crazy. I heard somebody yelling . . . and it was me because there was blood in my mouth and throat and my voice got caught in it, mired in it, and I felt as if I were strangling. All three of them were using their feet on me now and out of the pain and the craziness a thought swirled up: Cover your head, cover your groin, don't let them hurt you down there. I managed to roll onto my side, to curl up with one arm over my head, one hand covering my privates. And they kept kicking me, and after awhile I stopped feeling anything and just lay there curled like a fetus with the blood raging in my ears, gagging, fighting desperately not to cry or whimper, I will not cry or whimper, I will not give them the satisfaction of that. Then they weren't kicking me anymore and one of them was shouting something; but I couldn't understand him and when he realized that he got down beside me, rolled me onto my back, yelled his message in my ear. Even then the words were filtered through the blood-roar, so that only some of them got through to me.

"Lay off," he seemed to be saying. "No more investigate. Understand? No more, drop the Purcell, next time kill you, understand?"

I passed out.

I must have passed out because the next thing I was aware of was pain, savage and pulsing in my left side, my head, my left hand. But nobody was hurting me anymore, or looming over me or shouting at me, and I sensed they were gone. I was still lying on my back, choking a little on my own blood. I turned my head, coughed my throat clear.

Quiet now, no more roaring in my ears, just the far-off warning blast from a locomotive. Hear that lonesome whistle blow, ask not

174

for whom it blows it blows for thee, oh God they did a job on me, they beat me good, what if I wet my pants? I was suddenly terrified that I had lost control of my bladder. I felt down there—and I was dry. That calmed me, made me more lucid. I tried to open my eyes; the right one was stuck shut and when I put my hand up to it it felt swollen, sticky. Through the other eye I could see the clouds moving overhead, then a little of the crescent moon, then only the restless clouds again. The locomotive's air horn sounded another time. Couplings clattered distantly; there was the steel-on-steel rattle of a train moving through the night.

I rolled over onto my side. The pain was so bad I almost bit through my lower lip. But I couldn't just lie there, it was cold, I was aware of the cold all at once and I started to shake. *Freeze to death out here.* I tried to get up; the pain drove me back down again. I looked around for my car and it was there, over near the loading dock, driver's door shut; the headlights were dark, they'd shut them off before they left because lights might attract attention. It seemed a long way off, halfway across the world. Phone, the mobile phone . . . what if they'd disabled it? Can't drive in this condition. Can't even walk.

I started crawling toward the car. It was slow work; I blacked out once, or maybe it was twice, and all the way the pain was like something eating at me, something tearing at me with claws and a muzzle that was smeared with my blood.

Pay for this, Dessault. Make you *pay* for this.

And I kept crawling, and finally I reached the door and pulled myself up a little at a time until I could take hold of the handle and depress the latch and pull it open. I crawled up onto the seat in stages, using the door handle and then the steering wheel. Lay there gasping, hurting.

The phone, pick it up.

Picked it up. Listened.

Working, it still worked.

I made a call somehow, didn't even think about who I was calling, just did it. Please be home . . . and he was home. Eberhardt. I tried to talk to him but my mouth was broken, the words came out in little broken pieces that didn't seem to make any sense. But they must have made sense to him, after a while, because I heard him say, "Don't move, for God's sake don't move. I'll call an ambulance. I'll come there myself."

I lay on the seat feeling dizzy, feeling sick. Knew I was going to vomit and tried to push myself back out of the car and couldn't do it and vomited on the floorboards.

Passed out again.

And came to when the ambulance got there, and talked to the medics, and talked a little to Eberhardt when he showed up.

And passed out for the last time on the way to Mission Emergency Hospital.

Two cracked ribs. Concussion. Dislocated middle finger on my left hand. Bruises, cuts, abrasions too numerous to list. I was lucky, the doctor said. There didn't seem to be any serious damage to my eye. Nor any internal damage. That was the main thing: no internal damage.

That's what you think, doc. There's internal damage, all right —plenty of it inside my head. And somebody's going to pay for it. Dessault, Melanie, the three sluggers, anybody else who might have had a hand in this.

Lay off the Purcell case?

No way. No frigging way!

TWENTY-ONE

I spent Monday and Tuesday in bed, my bed. I saw no one except Kerry and, briefly on Tuesday, Eberhardt; I ate nothing other than some soup Kerry insisted on feeding me. Mostly I slept. A beating like I'd taken is a shock to the nervous system, a trauma to the psyche, an embarrassment to the ego; no matter how much rage, how much desire for revenge there might be inside you, you don't just slap on some tape and liniment and walk away from it, the way people do in movies and crappy novels. You need rest, time to heal. For a man my age, anything else would have been like playing Russian roulette with more than one bullet in the gun.

Kerry hung around part of the time, even while I was sleeping and even though I did not really want her there. She put on a nice smiley front, but the fact of the beating, the physical evidence of it, had shaken her—almost as badly as that time I'd got shot in Eberhardt's house. Eberhardt didn't take it too well, either. He'd gone to Mission Creek Sunday night, after taking me home from the hospital, and braced both Dessault and Melanie. I'd told him it wouldn't do any good and it hadn't. The girl admitted to calling me but said she'd done it out of a momentary fit of pique, no ulterior motive and not because Richie had told her to; she also said the two of them had made up after he'd explained his absence the past couple of days—he'd gone on a fishing expedition with a friend who owned a boat. Dessault said he didn't know anything about any thugs, or that I had been following him through the freight yards. That was a shortcut he used all the time, he'd said, was it his fault if the goddamn city was full of creeps and muggers? We had nothing on either of them and they knew it; they thought the law couldn't touch them. And they were right: the law couldn't.

But I could.

Not for a few days, though—not until the busted up Humpty-Dumpty put himself back together again. So I slept, and little by little I mended. And sometimes while I slept I dreamed. Most of the dreams were bad: distorted replays of the assault jumbled together with images of Leonard Purcell crawling through blood that was no longer his, that was now mine. Once I woke up yelling and found myself thrashing around on the floor, fighting off the shades of those faceless attackers. Kerry wasn't there at the time, and it was a good thing she wasn't. Not only because the incident would have frightened her, but because I would not have wanted her to see my face just then, the naked truth of what I was thinking.

If any of them had been in the room—Dessault, the three sluggers, any of them—I would have killed them all.

But I had other dreams too, much less fearful and without any psychotic aftermath. They were like film montages: faces, objects, juxtaposed and often superimposed in no apparent order. Leonard Purcell, the Hainelin snuff box, Melanie, Alicia, the photograph of Danny Martinez and his family, the cliff behind the Purcell home, Dessault, Tom Washburn, Elisabeth Summerhayes sitting alone among the ruins on Sutro Heights, Margaret Prine, Alejandro Ozimas smiling at me across his breakfast table while the freaked-out blonde picked her cinnamon roll apart and his house boy mouthed the words *Fuck you* behind his back, Eldon Summerhayes, the housekeeper Lina, the Martinez farmhouse and the crucifixes on the wall, Dessault running away from the barn . . . other images that I couldn't quite identify. There were voices, too, but I could only hear parts of them, the way I had only been able to hear parts of the one slugger's shouted threats. *"Deadfall so sorry fall how could you I know who pushed him two thousand dollars extortion the big gold rush fuck anything in pants disgusting little shit challenge man of my tastes whosoever toucheth her shall not be innocent lousy goddamn pervert once bitten twice shy lust is what binds them claws like cats like challenges like proof like profit like deadfall . . ."* None of it made any sense, and yet it did, I knew it did, it was all there and all I had to do was take the montages apart piece by piece, find the missing images, separate the voices and add the missing words. Except that I couldn't, not while I slept and dreamed and not while I was awake because I couldn't think clearly yet, my mind and my body were both still healing.

On Wednesday morning I felt well enough to get up for a while. My left side, where I had the two cracked ribs, gave me hell whenever I moved too suddenly. So did my concussed head. I had tape around my middle, adhesive and gauze here and there, a splint on my sore finger; when I looked at myself in the mirror I thought I resembled a mostly unwrapped mummy with a three-day growth of beard. But it wasn't funny. Nothing was funny right now.

Kerry had insisted on unplugging the phone the past two days and I hadn't argued with her. A few people had called Eberhardt at the office, including Tom Washburn; Eb had told me that when he stopped by on Tuesday evening. Nothing new on the case, though. Everything on hold, waiting for me to wade into it again, stir it up again.

I plugged the phone back in and called the office. Eberhardt said, "You sound better today. Feel better too?"

"Enough to get out of bed for a while."

"How's the eye? Swelling down on it yet?"

"Yeah. I can see out of it all right."

"Another few days, you'll be back in harness."

"Another few days, hell. Tomorrow, maybe."

"Hey, come on, hero, they cut you up pretty bad—"

"And now it's my turn to cut somebody up. Don't argue with me, Eb; I'm in no mood for it. Anything new this morning?"

He sighed. "Washburn came by twenty minutes ago. Dropped off that photograph he found."

"What's it of?"

"Alicia Purcell, he says. You want me to bring it over there?"

"When you get a chance. Anything else?"

"Nada. Well, Ben Klein got a lead on the whereabouts of Danny Martinez's in-laws in Mexico—Cuernavaca, he said. But you know how it is with the Mexican cops. Be days before Ben gets word, even if Martinez is there and they pick him up."

"No other calls?"

"That's it."

"If there's anything else let me know right away, will you? I'm not unplugging the phone anymore."

"Will do. Just take it easy, okay? Thing's will keep for the time being."

"Sure," I said. "But I won't—not much longer."

I went back into the kitchen and heated up the rest of Kerry's soup and ate it with a slice of bread. I wasn't hungry, the food had no taste, and chewing the bread made my face hurt; but I ate it all just the same, for strength. Afterward I moved around for the same reason, shuffling from room to room; I was so damned stiff and sore from the beating and from lying in bed two days that I needed the exercise.

I got tired before long and sat in the living room and tried to think it all through. Still no good. Too quiet in there: I could hear the silence and it made me restless, edgy. I turned on the TV and stared at a movie that I didn't really see. That made me drowsy, and I went back to bed and slept some more, and when I woke up it was dark outside and Kerry was there. I found her in the living room, curled up on the couch, reading one of my pulps.

"Hey," she said when she saw me come out in my robe and slippers, "you sure you should be out of bed?"

"I was out for three hours earlier," I said. "Didn't do me any harm."

"How do you feel?"

"Not too bad. I'll live."

"Well, you'd better." She let me have one of her chipper smiles. I didn't smile back; I did not feel like smiling, even for her. "Want something to eat?" she asked.

"Pretty soon. How long have you been here?"

"Couple of hours. Since five."

"Eberhardt didn't come by yet, did he?"

"He did. I wouldn't let him wake you up."

"You should have, if he had something to tell me—"

"He didn't have anything to tell you. He just left you an envelope—a photograph, he said."

"Where is it?"

"Over there on your desk."

I went to the desk—an old secretary that I had bought a long time ago, before sixty-year-old Sears, Roebuck junk became "antiques" and quadrupled in value—and opened up the manila envelope that was sitting on it. The photograph was an eight-by-ten color glossy, professionally done. A full-length portrait of Alicia Purcell wearing a slinky black low-cut gown with glittery stuff on

180

it; she had struck a provocative pose and was smiling moistly at the camera. I turned it over to look at the back. And there was an inscription, in green ink, that said: *For Leonard. Love, Al.*

Things moved around inside my head—but that was all they did; nothing came of the movement. I looked at the photo for a time. Then I said to Kerry, "I want to make a call," and went back into the bedroom and dialed the number where Tom Washburn was staying.

When I got him on the line I let him tell me how sorry he was about what he called my "ordeal," and then I said, "I've just seen the photo of Alicia Purcell. Where'd you find it?"

"In Leonard's study. It was tucked away in one of his business files."

"That's an odd place, isn't it?"

"Yes. If she gave it to him, I can't imagine why."

"They weren't close, as far as you know?"

"Well, he seldom spoke of her."

"When he did, what did he say?"

"He said she was cheap. He couldn't understand why Kenneth married her."

"Did he ever call her 'Al' instead of 'Alicia'?"

"No. Never." Washburn paused. "Perhaps it was Kenneth who gave him the photo, for some reason."

"Can you think of one?"

"No, I can't. If only Leonard hadn't been so *private* . . ."

"I'll find out, Mr. Washburn," I said. "I should be back on the job in a day or two."

"So soon? But your partner said you had cracked ribs and a concussion . . ."

"They're healing."

"Aren't you . . . I mean, you're not afraid they'll try to hurt you again?"

Yes, I thought, I'm afraid. You're always a little afraid in this business—more than a little when something like Sunday night happens. But you learn to live with it. And right now what I was feeling was a great deal more rage and determination than fear.

I didn't say any of that to Washburn; it was not the kind of thing I can articulate. I said only, "Don't worry about that. You hired me to do a job; I intend to finish doing it."

Kerry wasn't in the living room when I went out there again. I heard her in the kitchen, bustling around, and I smelled meat frying. It made me hungry—much hungrier than I'd been earlier in the day. I took that as a positive sign. If I could eat with appetite I was capable of putting my pants on and facing the world again.

We had hamburger—"It's about time you ate some solid food," she said—and a spinach salad, and I drank a little beer with it. Afterward we sat in the living room and talked about neutral topics. At ten o'clock I chased her out. And when she was gone I was sorry about it, yet relieved at the same time. I wanted to be alone; I didn't want to be alone. Ambivalence.

Christ, I thought, I need to get out of here.

Tomorrow, I thought. If I can walk in the morning I'm gone.

I went to bed. I was afraid I might have difficulty getting to sleep, because I had done so much sleeping the past three days, but it didn't happen that way. I put the light out and I went out with it.

Dreams.

Faces, places—the same as before. And some new ones too: Alicia Purcell in the slinky, low-cut black gown, smiling. Danny Martinez's son Roberto, smiling.

Voices, old and new. *"Deadfall so sorry love Al once bitten whosoever toucheth fall how could you . . ."*

All through the night, dreams.

Morning.

A little after seven, by the nightstand clock.

I lay in bed remembering the dreams and the voices, and I knew I was close. Don't try to force it; it'll come. I got up, donned my robe, went into the bathroom and had another look at myself.

Not too bad. The swelling was completely gone from my right eye and the lemon-brown discoloration around it had begun to fade; I could see as well as ever, except for a faint blurriness at the far periphery of my vision. Two other bruises were fading even more rapidly. The face might draw some looks, but nobody was going to be startled or frightened by it.

I flexed my body a little, testing my ribs. Still some of that tearing pain; I would have to be careful how I moved. My head didn't hurt at all, but that might be a false sign. Head wounds, concussions, could be tricky. Still, my mind seemed perfectly clear . . . clear enough, anyhow.

Yeah, I thought, I'm ready.

But not right this minute; it was too early to expect to get anything done. I went into the kitchen, made some coffee and a couple of soft-boiled eggs and a piece of toast; ate at the table in there. Went back to bed with a second cup of coffee, to wait and to do some more thinking. Tried to sit up, but my ribs felt more constricted that way, so I stretched out and pulled the blankets over me.

Went to sleep again.

It was an odd sleep—deep and dreamless for a long while, then shallow and restless and heavy with more dreams, and finally not quite sleep at all, just that kind of drifting doze where you're poised on the edge of wakefulness and dreams and reality intermingle.

Photographs, I thought or dreamed.

Love, Al.

His name is Roberto, he's a nice little boy.

Photographs.

Deadfall.

So sorry.

Fall how could you . . .

Love, Al.

Photographs.

Danny Martinez.

Crucifixes.

Roberto.

Lumber, remember the lumber?

I woke up. Sat up so fast that pain ripped through my side and I had to jam my teeth together to keep from crying out. I was soaked in sweat, panting as if I had run a long distance—and in a way, that was just what I'd done.

I had it now . . . some of it, maybe even most of it. And I knew where to look for the rest. Bad, worse than I'd thought, uglier than I'd thought. Simpler than I'd thought, too. That was why it had taken me this long to figure it out. Too many complications, and most of them false trails, miscalculations, red herrings. The forest for the trees.

What time was it? I looked at the clock, and the hands read 1:03. I stared at them; I had slept another five hours, slept away half of the day. Thursday—another Thursday. Everything of any magnitude on this case seemed to happen on Thursday, including its beginning and now maybe its ending.

I got out of bed, stripped off my pajamas in the bathroom—they smelled medicinal and sweaty, and so did I—and took a careful shower. Then I got dressed, went back to the bedroom. My notebook was on the dresser; Kerry had rescued it from what was left of the suit jacket I'd been wearing Sunday night. My car keys were there too, thanks to her and Eberhardt having retrieved the car. When I checked through the notebook I found that I hadn't copied down Claudia Mitchell's telephone number. I could call the office, get it from Eberhardt if he was in, but I did not want to talk to Eberhardt right now. So I dialed 411 instead. There was only one Claudia Mitchell listed—the right one, as it turned out.

Her sister wasn't there, but she gave me a number where Ruth Mitchell could be reached. The former Mrs. Leonard Purcell did not want to talk to me at first, not about anything so personal as what I was asking; but I convinced her it was important, that it would help bring Leonard's murderer to justice. She answered my questions finally. And they were the right answers, the ones I had expected to hear.

One more thing to check out, one very important thing. I did not have to go do it myself, I did not want to go do it myself; it would require work, the kind I was in no shape for—hard work, bad work. Call Ben Klein, I thought, lay it out for him, let him take it from here. But I couldn't do that. It was *my* case now, mine to finish unraveling, mine to put an end to one way or another. Personally.

You sound like Mike Hammer, for Christ's sake, I thought. What's the matter with you?

I watched a man die, I thought, I *felt* him die. And they beat me up, they hurt me bad. That's what's the matter with me.

I got the car keys off the dresser, put on my old tweed overcoat to guard against a chill, and went out. Wishing I owned a gun to take with me, and damned glad I didn't.

TWENTY-TWO

The car didn't handle right. When the trap car rammed it on Sunday night the impact had done more than just cave in part of the right front fender; it had screwed up the steering gear somehow, so that that side felt loose on turns and shimmied badly at speeds above thirty-five. I didn't like driving it this way, but at the moment I had no choice. I held my speed down and put blind trust in the thing hanging together for another sixty miles or so.

I drove straight down the coast on Highway 1, taking it very slow through the bad snaky stretch at Devil's Slide. The weather had turned poor again—heavily overcast, gusty winds, mist sailing in ragged streamers along the edge of the sea. There was not much traffic. I kept my mind blank as I drove; I did not want to think about what lay ahead. Time enough for thinking when I finished what I was on my way to do.

When I got to Moss Beach it was a little after three. I turned inland through the village, went out Sunshine Valley Road, picked up Elm Street a little while later. And a little while after that I was again looking at the deserted expanse of the Martinez farm.

I parked where I had the first time, in the middle of the dusty yard, and got out in slow, careful movements. Driving hadn't bothered me too much, except for the jouncing of the car as I crawled over the rutted access lane; that had made my side and my head hurt. My joints ached, too, as I stepped away from the car. Old, I thought. Old and badly used.

The wind blew hard and cold here, made pained moaning noises in the surrounding woods, flapped a loose shutter at one of the house windows, spun a rowel on a rusty weathervane atop the barn; I was glad I had thought to put on the overcoat. I stood looking around for a time. Everything seemed as it had been nearly a week ago. But looks can be deceiving; I ought to have remembered that little homily before, saved myself a lot of grief. They might have been here in the interim, one or the other or both of them. It depended on how secure they felt . . . no, on how secure *she* felt.

Without thinking about where I was going I crossed to the house, climbed the porch stairs. Delaying tactic, but so what? The front door was still closed, as I had left it last Friday. I turned the knob and it opened and I went inside.

Nothing different about the front parlor; the dark-wood crucifix was still there on one wall. I moved through the kitchen, the dining area, the child's room, into the bedroom Danny Martinez had shared with his common-law wife. Nothing different there either. The bronze, silver-trimmed crucifix still hung above the bed. And the photo of young, laughing Roberto Martinez was still wedged between the frame and the glass of the oval mirror.

Crucifixes.

Photographs.

Man packs up all his belongings, clothes and things, crap from the bathroom medicine cabinet, loads up his old pickup truck and clears out for Mexico—that's the way it's supposed to look. But he's a religious man; why would he leave the crucifixes behind, particularly the one in here? Even if the break-up of his family had soured him on his faith, this crucifix was an expensive piece of craftsmanship and he had been a poor man all his life. No reason for him to leave it behind, none at all.

No reason for him not to have taken the photo of his son, either. You could understand a man not taking the other photo, the one of the three of them: he might not want to keep anything with the woman's image on it. But two different people had told me Danny Martinez doted on Roberto. And the photograph there on the mirror was a fine one, little boy laughing, nobody in it but him— the kind of photo no loving father could bear to leave behind.

Photographs and crucifixes. And I was a damned poor detective for not having realized these things before.

Back through the house, down the stairs, over to the car. I leaned inside, unclipped the flashlight from under the dash. And then hesitated, feeling tired and sore and a little sick to my stomach. The wind slapped at me, and I shivered—but it was more than just the cold that put the tremor on my body. Get it over with, I thought. But it was another minute or so before I could make myself move toward the barn.

The one door was still open, canted at an angle on its weak hinges. I went through the opening. The sour odor was the same —or maybe it wasn't, maybe it was stronger. I breathed through my mouth so I wouldn't have to smell it. The shadows in the corners, under the hayloft, up around the eaves seemed denser today because of the heavy overcast outside. I switched on the flashlight and played its powerful beam over the stack of lumber, the carpentering tools scattered nearby. Then, slowly, I made my way toward the rear, to where the horse stalls were.

The second stack of lumber still stood in the one on the far left. I moved that way, put the light on the two-by-fours and sheets of plywood piled haphazardly along the back wall. Not much, really. Just enough to cover about a third of the packed-earth floor.

What was it doing here? That was the question I should have asked myself last Friday, just as I should have asked myself why the crucifixes and the photograph of Roberto were still in the house. Nothing back here but the otherwise empty stalls; nothing that needed repair; nothing that would warrant lugging two-by-fours and plywood sheets from the front of the barn all the way back here.

Only one reason for the lumber in this stall, then: to hide something underneath it.

I let the light slither over the bare earth. It was marked, chewed up here and there by shoes or boots, by pieces of lumber, maybe by a tool of some kind. Yeah. But the marks and gouges didn't look fresh. Nor did the lumber seem to have been disturbed since my first visit. They hadn't been back in here; that seemed certain.

I had no stomach for the rest of it, and I was afraid of the exertion. But I had to do it, I had to be sure. I wedged the flash into a crack in the boards separating the stall from its neighbor, positioning it so that it illuminated the lumber. There were three of the plywood sheets on top; I tackled those first, carried them out one at a time and dropped them back a ways. The two-by-fours were next: same thing, one at a time. The first few trips weren't too bad, but then I lifted one of the pieces wrong, even though I was bending and lifting in slow motion. The pain cut through my side, made it difficult for me to breathe for a few seconds. Started my head aching again, too. I rested for a time, but the pain lingered and so did the shortness of breath. Live with it, I told myself, you've lived with worse. Don't think about it. Don't think about anything.

It took me more than twenty minutes to clear the stall, double the time it would have taken if I'd been healthy. Wrapped in the heavy overcoat, I was drenched in oily sweat by the time I finished; but I hadn't dared take the coat off, not as cold as it was in here. My knees felt shaky and I had to sit down for a couple of minutes before I did anything else. But not there in the stall; not anywhere close to it. Not with the smell that came from the spaded-up earth under the last two sections of plywood.

There was an old three-legged kitchen stool near the workbench; I sat on that, breathing through my mouth, not thinking about anything. When my legs felt all right I got up again, found a shovel among the tools near the main stack of lumber, took it back to the stall. And began to dig.

The earth was soft, moist; the work would not have been hard except for the constant bending and straightening that aggravated each stiffened joint, worsened the pain in my side and the dull pounding in my head. During the next ten minutes I had to stop and rest three times. If the body had been down deep I might have had to give up the job altogether. But it wasn't down deep; it was buried a little more than twelve inches below the surface.

The shovel blade bit into something yielding and the poisonous, gaseous stench of decay spurted up at me. I recoiled, gagging. When I turned back finally, reluctantly, I was looking at an arm —a man's bloated arm, blackened fingers acrawl with bugs, bulging out of the remnants of a blue chambray shirt.

I had finally found Danny Martinez.

I could not have faced any more digging, even if it had been necessary; the stench was sickening enough as it was. Ben Klein on the phone last Friday: *We didn't even get a smell of this guy Martinez. Jesus Christ!*

Shaking a little, I threw the shovel down and pulled the flashlight out of the crack in the boards. The beam slithered sideways, made something gleam in the mound of dirt I'd created—something red and shiny. I leaned over that way, trying not to gag again, and held the light on it up close.

Part of a fingernail, torn raggedly on one end: a woman's long fingernail painted a bright crimson.

I left it where it was; no point in removing incriminating evidence. I had to get out of there. The stench was so bad it made me feel as if I were suffocating. I followed the light across the barn, shut it off when I got outside. Stood in the chill wind with my head back, sucking air until my chest cleared and the nausea was gone. Then I went to the car and got inside and started the engine and sat huddled and shivering, waiting for the heater to fill up the space with warm air. Thinking again. Remembering.

Elisabeth Summerhayes: *I hate women who mark men, the ones with claws like cats.* She had been talking about Alicia Purcell. But Mrs. Purcell had short fingernails now, short and painted a bright bloody crimson. Why would a woman who habitually wore her nails long cut them short? A whim, maybe. Or maybe she'd had no other choice; maybe she'd torn one of them off, damaged others, doing manual labor of some kind. Like digging. Like burying the body of a man she'd just murdered.

You don't like to think about women having the physical and mental capacity for digging graves, for lugging heavy plywood sheets and two-by-fours to cover one up; you can get so mired in the weak-sex–fair-sex myth that you lose sight of the fact that a woman, given the proper impetus, can pretty much do any job a man can do. Alicia Purcell was wiry, strong. And determined. And as cold-blooded as any black widow spider making dinner out of one of her mates.

She'd killed and buried Danny Martinez, all right. The broken fingernail in there proved that. She hadn't had any help with that part of it; the help had come later, in making it look as though Martinez had pulled up stakes and disappeared to parts unknown. She'd needed somebody to pack up all his belongings, load them into Martinez's pickup, drive the truck away somewhere and get rid of it. That was where Richie Dessault came in.

It had to be Dessault. From all indications he hadn't known Martinez personally; so how had he known it was Martinez I was talking about—I hadn't even known it myself at the time—when I asked Melanie if she knew anyone who spoke with a Latin accent? My visit last Thursday, my investigation, was what had sent him out here the following afternoon. He'd come skulking through the woods because he hadn't wanted to be seen driving into the farm, hadn't wanted his car out in plain sight if anybody showed up. His purpose: either to make sure he hadn't left any traces of himself when he'd done Alicia's bidding, or to see if he could find out just what had been going on between her and Martinez. She wouldn't have told him about the murder, the body buried in the barn, any of the rest of it; she was cunning and he wasn't and she would not have left herself wide open to any more blackmail. No, she'd have made up some plausible-sounding story, something quasi-legitimate at the worst, to explain the need to get rid of Martinez's belongings and truck. Dessault hadn't questioned her at that point, if he'd ever questioned her. She'd have had him hooked by then, with sex as the bait. She'd have seduced him just as she had Summerhayes and countless others.

Just as she had Leonard.

That was the key to the whole thing, not Danny Martinez. Once you realized that Leonard had to have also been one of her conquests, you understood everything else that had followed. Seduction was not only a weapon with her, not only a means to an end, it was a motivating force in her life. All men were fair game—*all* men. And homosexuals were right up there at the top of the list because they presented the greatest challenge. She'd tried to seduce Alex Ozimas, hadn't she? Ozimas: *Not that I'm irresistible, of course; it was merely that she considered seducing a man of my tastes a stimulating challenge.* Sure. So why not her husband's brother, too?

Confirmed homosexuals couldn't be seduced by a woman, of course. But Leonard hadn't been quite as gay as everyone, including poor Tom Washburn, believed him to be. He had not only been married once, he'd been sleeping with his ex-wife now and then during the year prior to Kenneth's death. Claudia Mitchell on the phone last Saturday, talking about her sister: *If I told her once after the divorce I told her a hundred times—good riddance. I warned her. Once bitten, twice shy, but she never listens to me.* Ruth Mitchell had confirmed it when I'd contacted her earlier this afternoon. She had gone to his office one day to ask his advice on a legal matter, there had still been a spark of attraction between them, one thing led to another—*mostly, I gathered, at her instigation.* The right (or wrong) woman could still get Leonard into bed, if she knew how to play her cards right. And Alicia Purcell was a grand master when it came to playing cards of that sort.

So Leonard, good old secretive, duplicitous Leonard, had been screwing Alicia too, right under his brother's nose, right under Washburn's. And they had succeeded in keeping their affair secret until the night of the party last May. That night, not much past nine-thirty, they had been alone in the library; Mrs. Purcell had admitted as much. They must also have been indiscreet in some way—discussed the affair, maybe even engaged in a little stand-up passion play; she was the type who'd find that kind of dangerous activity exciting. And they'd got caught: Kenneth had overheard them or walked in on them. There hadn't been any big scene at that point, even though Kenneth was drunk; he knew what kind of woman his wife was, they'd had an open marriage, so it wasn't likely he'd have assumed the role of the outraged husband. He had probably been more stunned than anything else. At any rate he'd stalked out of the house, passing Lina in the kitchen, and gone straight to the cliffs to be alone, to come to terms with what he'd just found out.

Pure speculation on the rest of it: Leonard had followed belatedly, using another exit from the house or going through the kitchen himself while Lina was out distributing canapés to the guests—his intention being to talk to Kenneth, apologize, beg forgiveness . . . something like that. Alicia either went with him or had followed soon afterward. There had been a confrontation out there in the darkness high above the sea, and it had turned violent. Kenneth was drunk and he'd had time to nurture his anger; maybe he'd attacked Leonard, maybe they'd struggled, maybe Leonard had given him a shove and over he'd gone.

I was sure of this much: Leonard was either directly responsible for his brother's death, or had blamed himself for causing it.

Guilt and remorse and grief might have cracked him up then and there if it hadn't been for Alicia. She'd calmed him down, convinced him to cover up their part in Kenneth's death and to keep their affair a secret. Not because she cared about Leonard; she was looking out for herself. She didn't want to be implicated in her husband's death, not in any way. An unquestioned fatal accident guaranteed her inheritance, insured a hassle-free future —or so she must have thought at the time. She'd coached Leonard in what to do and what to say to the party guests, to the authorities when they came; and because he was weak, and riddled with guilt, he had gone along with her. He'd played his part well enough; even his tears when the body was discovered had been genuine. But he'd been crying as much for himself, I thought, as for his dead brother.

Before they returned to the house, Alicia had done one other thing: she'd picked up the Hainelin snuff box, which must have fallen to the ground when Kenneth's coat pocket was torn during the struggle. That was the real reason she'd kept it hidden from the police, and later sold it to Summerhayes on the QT: she hadn't wanted anybody asking how it had come into her possession that night.

The two of them alibiing each other had fooled everybody into believing she was in the clear—me included. No one suspected Leonard, the devoted brother, of having had anything to do with Kenneth's death; if he said he was with Alicia, then that cleared her, too. Nobody had seen either of them leave the house or return to it, so there was nobody to dispute her word or his. Nobody, that is, except Danny Martinez.

Martinez had just finished making his delivery when Kenneth was killed. Either he'd been drawn out to the cliffs for some reason and had seen it happen, or more likely, he'd been near the house when Alicia and Leonard came back and had overheard an exchange of dialogue that told him what had happened. But they hadn't seen or heard *him.* And for his own reasons he hadn't come forward to tell what he knew. Alicia, at least, must have felt that she and Leonard had got away clean.

But then, after nearly six months, Martinez's life had come apart and he'd decided to use his knowledge for financial gain. He'd called Leonard, only to mistakenly talk to Washburn instead. Martinez, as quoted by Washburn: *Your brother didn't fall off the cliff that night, Mr. Purcell. He was pushed. And I know who pushed him.* Washburn thought Martinez was trying to sell Leonard the name of his brother's killer, and so had I; but that hadn't been it at all. The purpose of Martinez's call had been blackmail, not extortion. And when he finally had reached Leonard with his demands, Leonard had paid off to the tune of two thousand dollars. That had apparently not been enough for Martinez; he'd made the fatal mistake of trying the same blackmail scam on Alicia. And she'd paid him off with death.

Thursday night, two weeks ago. Not more than a couple of days after she had killed and buried Martinez. Leonard must have talked to her about the blackmail business; he was scared, he was still guilt-ridden, maybe he'd even threatened to make a clean breast of everything to the police. She couldn't have that, not after the drastic steps she'd already taken to protect herself. She arranged to see Leonard at his house, alone, while Washburn was out for the evening. With the intention of murdering Leonard, too, to keep him quiet? Possibly; she'd gone in the back way and she'd brought a gun with her—the same gun she'd used on Martinez, probably. Still, you'd think a woman as shrewd as she was would have picked a safer, more isolated place to commit premeditated homicide. It could be she'd brought the gun as a precaution or a threat or a last resort; it could be they'd had words, and she let slip what she'd done to Martinez, and Leonard threatened again to go to the police. In any case she shot him.

Leonard, dying: *Deadfall . . . so sorry . . . fall, how could you . . .* Only that wasn't quite right. He'd been delirious, mumbling, blood in his throat obscuring the words, and I had misheard one of them. He hadn't said *fall, how could you.* He'd said *Al, how could you.*

Al. Love, Al. Love, Alicia.

Ray Dunston, quoting the Bible far more aptly than he'd ever know: *Can a man take fire in his bosom, and his clothes not be burned? Can one go upon hot coals, and his feet not be burned? So he that goeth in to his neighbor's wife; whosoever toucheth her shall not be innocent.*

Another week had passed, and Tom Washburn had brought me into it. I'd asked Mrs. Purcell some probing questions, so probing that she had lied about having tried to seduce Ozimas because she was afraid I might connect her sexually to Leonard. And then I'd found out from Lina about Danny Martinez. Either Alicia had asked the housekeeper what she'd said to me, or Lina had volun-

194

teered the information; whichever it was, she learned that I was on to Martinez. To find out just how much I knew or had guessed, she'd tried to use her favorite weapon—seduction—on me too. Then, later, I'd discovered that the Hainelin box had been in her possession and that she'd sold it to Summerhayes, and had confronted her with the knowledge on Sunday afternoon. I was definitely getting too close for comfort. Sex wasn't going to work on me, so she'd used Dessault again (he might even have been with her when I called; she could easily be the reason for his two-day absence from Mission Creek)—this time to arrange a beating to force me off the case.

Love, Al.

That was the bulk of it. Some of the smaller pieces were still missing, others figured to be somewhat different than I had postulated them, but I was sure all the essentials were right. The full story would have to come from her. Not that the details were vital. Even if she didn't confess, even if she tried to bluff it through, there should be enough hard evidence to convict her. The fingernail in the barn, for one thing. Dessault, for another; he was the type to sell out his own mother if he thought it would save his ass. She might still have the gun, too. In the end there'd be enough.

It was warm in the car now, too warm: I was sweating again. I turned the heat down halfway. Outside, dusk was settling. It was already dark among the trees; their shadows, and those thrown by the barn and the house, crept out toward me across the yard. Time to go, I thought, and I put the car in gear and swung it into a U-turn that made the weak right side tremble. Time to get the rest of it done.

Time to face the black widow in her nest.

TWENTY-THREE

N ight had fallen when I turned off South Lake Street, onto the private drive that led up to the Purcell home. The road surface wasn't as bad here as on the one coming into the Martinez farm, but the car's front end was substantially looser now; I thought it might go at any time. I drove up the hillside at a crawl.

The parking area at the end of the drive was dark: the half-dozen night lanterns atop the garden wall hadn't been put on. There were three cars sitting there—the dusty BMW I'd seen on my first visit, Richie Dessault's white Trans-Am, and a sixties-vintage MG roadster that I didn't recognize. Through the filigreed gate I could see that the garden was also dark but that light showed at the front of the house, made blurry by the mist that swirled in raggedly from the sea.

I put my car next to the BMW and sat there for a few seconds, listening to a voice inside my head that said, Dessault's here, that's all right, but she's got other company. What's the sense in bracing her now? What's the sense in bracing her at all? Let it go, for Christ's sake. You don't *need* any more of this. Then I stopped listening to the voice and got out of the car, into a blustery wind thick with the smells of salt and the offshore kelp beds.

The gate wasn't shut all the way, so I didn't have to bother with the bell or the intercom system. I shouldered through the open half, followed the crushed-shell path between the rows of rose-bushes. The light at the front of the house was coming through a window and also through a wedge between the door and the jamb. I stopped, looking at the open door. From inside, distantly, there was the sound of music—something classical, something with a lot of stringed instruments. No other sounds filtered out to where I stood.

Frowning, I put the tips of my fingers against the door panel and pushed it inward. Went past its far edge by a couple of steps, into the empty front hall. Nobody in the formal living room that opened off of it, nobody on the carpeted staircase to my right or up on the second-floor landing. I thought about calling out, announcing myself, but I didn't do it. I didn't do anything except stand still, listening to the music: it was coming from upstairs, over on the south side.

Something wrong here, I thought.

Something bad here.

After a time I crossed to the staircase and climbed it, slowly, reluctantly. A central hallway went both ways upstairs; I turned left, to the south. Four doors gave on it in that direction, two open, two closed. The open ones showed me a bathroom and what looked to be a spare bedroom; I didn't pause at either one. At the far end, on the right, a strip of light showed under the bottom of the second closed door; the music seemed to be coming from in there. Bedroom? Her bedroom? I kept moving, and I was only a few feet away when the familiar smell registered on my olfactory nerve.

Cordite. Burnt gunpowder.

My chest got tight and my head began to ache again. I quit walking and leaned against the wall; the palms of my hands were suddenly as wet as if I'd dunked them in water. No more, I thought, I can't look at any more death today. But I was not the kind of man who could walk away from something like this without *knowing*. The curse of my existence: the constant, compulsive need to *know*.

I tried to take a deep breath, to steady myself; the pain in my side turned it into a shallow grunt. I shoved off the wall, a little rubber-legged now, and went ahead to the door. It was shut all the way. Inside, the classical orchestra was playing something sweet and gentle. Violins. Mood music. Music for lovers.

I opened the door and went in.

Bedroom, all right. Death, all right. I felt the impact of it in my stomach, the same sickening pain as when one of the sluggers had kicked me on Sunday night. White room: white walls, white furry carpet, white canopied bed trimmed in white lace. Red room now: red on the sheets, red on the headboard and the canopy and the lace trim, red on the furry carpet. Spent shells on the carpet, too, four of them, ejected from an automatic weapon. Stereo record-changer in one corner playing the violin music. And the acrid smell of cordite strong in here, overpowering the faint musky scent of perfume.

They were both naked, both spattered with blood—both dead, I thought at first. Dessault was lying half on and half off the bed, head down and arms outflung to the carpet, one bare foot hooked around a canopy post; he had been shot twice, once in the small of the back and once under the right shoulder blade. The two bullets that had entered Alicia Purcell's body, one in the area of the sternum, the other through the upper curve of her right breast, had driven her back against the headboard. She was leaning side-ways against it with her legs spread wide—a position made all the more obscene by the torn flesh and the ribbons of blood.

Broken glass on the hardwood floor, broken china plates and cups and saucers, blue-and-white patterned stuff with some of the shards speckled with crimson. And Leonard Purcell crawling away, one hand clawing at the wood, the other crooked under him in a vain effort to stem the flow of bright arterial blood. Dragging sounds, crunching sounds: trying to crawl away from death.

Ending as it began for me, in a welter of blood, in a strange house with me looking at the end products of human corruption: wrong place at the wrong time. The same helplessness, the same futility. The same pity. The same pain.

Why? I thought. Why this way?

And I was pretty sure I knew.

There wasn't anyone else in the room, and the door to the adjoining bath was open, letting me see that it was empty. White drapes were only half drawn across a picture window in the back wall; beyond the glass were trees half-obscured by darkness and fog. I looked out at them until my stomach settled and I felt I could move again without being sick.

Dessault was the closest to me, but I didn't go to him. There was no way he could still be alive; the one bullet had shattered his spine. Whosoever toucheth her, I thought. I went around on the near side of the bed, still with that rubbery sensation in my legs, and took hold of Alicia Purcell's wrist, felt for a pulse. Just a formality, an automatic gesture . . . but it wasn't. She was alive. Faint pulse, weak and fluttery. Up close this way, I could see that blood was still leaking out of her wounds. She'd lost a lot of it in the few minutes since the shooting; if she lost much more she *would* be dead.

There was nothing I could do for her, nothing I dared do for her; I was no damn good with first aid and if I tried to move her, to staunch the flow of blood, I was liable to do more harm than good. A door on that side of the room opened on a walk-in closet; I found a blanket inside, shook it out. The position she was in made it difficult to cover her. I did the best I could and then backed off, looking for a telephone.

No phone in there. I went out and down the hall, down the stairs, hurrying in spite of the hurt in my side. No phone in the living room, either, where did they keep the goddamn telephones? Out of the living room, down the hall toward the rear . . . the kitchen. I turned in there, looking left and right, and on one wall was one of those antique wooden things, the kind with the two exposed bells and the fake crank. I went to it, caught up the bell-shaped receiver, heard the dial tone.

Heard a voice say behind me, "Put it down. Don't call anybody, I don't want you to call anybody."

It was as if a door had been opened and the cold wind let in from outside: the words put a tremor on my neck, freckled my skin with goosebumps under its layer of sweat. I took the receiver away from my ear, slowly, and replaced it on the wall unit. Put my arms out away from my body and turned, slowly, to face her.

She was standing just inside the kitchen doorway; she must have been somewhere at the back of the house, hiding, waiting. The gun in her hand was an automatic, what looked to be a .38 Smith & Wesson wadcutter—not a big gun but big in her tiny hands. She was holding it in both of them, to keep it steady; the muzzle was about on a level with my chest. But it wasn't the gun itself that frightened me. It was those vulpine eyes of hers. They were bright, glassy, on the wild side so that the cocked one seemed even more erratic. It was not just emotion that had made them that way. She was on something—coke, probably. And cocaine made a person's behavior unpredictable, volatile if that person was worked up to begin with.

"You saw them, didn't you," she said. It wasn't a question. "They're dead, both of them. I shot them."

"Your stepmother's still alive, Melanie."

"Is she? I thought she was dead. Richie's dead, isn't he?"

"Yes."

"Oh God," she said, and I thought she was going to cry. She'd been crying before: her acne-blotched cheeks were stained with drying tears. But then she shook her head and her mouth firmed and she said, "No, I'm glad he's dead. He deserved to die."

"She'll die too if I don't call a doctor pretty soon."

"I don't care. I want her to die." Her nose was running; she took her left hand away from the .38 and swiped at it. "You know what they were doing when I walked in on them? You want me to tell you what they were doing?"

"No," I said.

"They weren't just fucking, oh no, they were . . . they . . ." She broke off, as if she couldn't articulate the thing she'd witnessed. "I loved him," she said. "I *loved* him and he was doing that with her. *With her!*"

I didn't say anything this time. She was still holding the gun with just the one hand, still pawing at her runny nose with the other.

"I knew he was seeing somebody," she said. "Staying out all night, five nights in three weeks, lying to me, I knew he was getting it on with somebody else. I asked him and he said no, he wasn't . . . lies, lies. I had to know who it was. You understand? I had to know. That's why I followed him this afternoon. I couldn't believe it when he came here. I thought, it's not her, it can't be *her,* he's here for some other reason. I waited out in the car. I waited and waited, but he didn't come out so I went in and I heard them, they were laughing, God they were laughing and she said, 'Come on, Richie,' she said, 'Do it just like I tell you, Richie,' she said . . . I couldn't listen anymore. I wanted to hurt them, I hated them both, I wanted to *kill* them . . . this is my father's gun, did you know that? He taught me how to shoot, did you know that?"

I stood unmoving, silent, watching the gun, watching her finger slide back and forth over the surface of the trigger.

"He always kept it in his study," she said, "in a box in the bookcase. It was still there, she hadn't moved it. I got it and I went up there to her bedroom and they were naked . . . they were . . . it made me sick and I shot him and she screamed and I shot her I shot them both I killed them . . ."

Her face was screwed up and there was wetness leaking out of those bright, glassy eyes again; she looked old and gnomish, as if she had fallen prey to some rapid aging disease—a pathetic, tragic figure, an ugly duckling torn apart by love and hate. But I couldn't feel anything for her, not yet, not while she had that gun in her hand.

"Melanie," I said gently, "you're not going to shoot me, too?"

"What?"

"Do you want to shoot me, too?"

"No," she said. "Not if you leave me alone."

"If I promise to leave you alone, will you put the gun down?"

"No. Promises are lies. I don't want to hear any more lies."

"I won't lie to you, Melanie."

"Yes you will. Everybody lies to me. All my life, lies, lies and bullshit. Don't you think I know what I am? Don't you think I look in mirrors and see what I am?"

"Melanie, please put the gun down."

"No. I've got to get out of here, I don't want to stay here any more. I *hate* this house. You won't let me go if I put the gun down."

"Where do you want to go?"

"I don't know. Just away from here."

"You'll have to talk to the police sooner or later. Wouldn't it be better to do it now?"

"Fuck the police. You think I'm afraid of them?"

"You don't have to be afraid of them."

"Well I'm not. I don't care what they do to me. I don't care about anything anymore."

"Not even who killed your father and your uncle?"

"No."

"I'll tell you anyway. Leonard was responsible for your father's death. Alicia helped him cover it up. She's the one who shot Leonard. She killed Danny Martinez, too."

It was too much for her to comprehend all at once. She shook her head, said, "What?" and shook her head another time. The gun wavered a little in her hand—a little but not enough.

"It's true, Melanie," I said. "She murdered two people in cold blood. And she got Richie to help her cover up what she did to Martinez. Don't you want to know the full story? *Why* she did all those things?"

"Kenneth? She killed him?"

"No. It was Leonard."

"Why would Leonard do that?"

"Put the gun down and we'll talk about it."

"No. You said Richie helped her."

"Helped her cover up the Martinez murder. But he didn't know it was a murder."

Another headshake. Another swipe at her runny nose. The longer she stayed confused, the better my chances were of talking that gun out of her hand. "Your face," she said, "Richie did that. He beat you up."

"He arranged for it, yes."

"He made me call you," she said. "He said they were only going to scare you, make you leave us alone. More lies. I didn't know they were going to beat you."

"It's all right, Melanie."

"It's not all right. He did it for her, didn't he."

"Yes."

"Did everything for her, killed my father . . ."

"No, it was Leonard who did that. Richie didn't kill anyone; he didn't know Alicia had killed anyone. He just made it look like Danny Martinez had run away—"

"I don't *know* anybody named Danny Martinez. What are you talking about?"

"Martinez delivered groceries here, the night your father was killed. I told you about that at Blanche's, remember?"

"No." Her headshake was violent this time. "You're confusing me," she said. "I don't understand what you're talking about."

"Why don't we sit down at the table over there? I'll explain it all to you from the beginning—"

"No! Shut up, why don't you just shut *up?*"

I shut up. The automatic wasn't steady in her hand, but her finger was tight now on the trigger.

"I've got to get out of here," she said. The bright stare shifted away from me for an instant, over to the side door that led outside; but the cockeye seemed still to be fixed on my face. "I can't breathe, you're not letting me breathe!"

I wasn't breathing either. I might have confused her too much; the look on her face now was one of burgeoning paranoia, the kind that can explode into violence at any time. I stood rigid, poised, ready to throw myself at her. She could get a shot off before I reached her but the sudden movement might cause her to shy, to miss. It was the only chance I had if she decided to shoot and telegraphed her intent. If she didn't telegraph it . . .

She didn't decide to shoot. She said, "Get out, get *out,*" talking to herself, not to me, and took a couple of herky-jerky steps sideways into the kitchen: parallel to me, toward the side door. Then she stopped, and bit her lower lip, and rubbed at her nose; and then she moved again, crossed to the door in that same herky-jerky way. Fumbled for the knob, got the door open. "Don't come after me, I'll kill you if you do." And she was gone.

Some of the tension went out of me, just enough to loosen the rigidity of my body and let me move, too—without hesitation. I couldn't let her go, the shape she was in, no matter what the risk to me; if she tried to drive she was liable to kill somebody else, an innocent party, with that MG of hers. And if my calculations were right, she only had one bullet left in the automatic's clip. A Smith & Wesson .38 wadcutter held five rounds; she'd fired four into Dessault and her stepmother, and in her condition she probably wouldn't have thought to reload.

I got to the door, yanked it all the way open, stumbled through. She was thirty feet away, out from under the portico, half-running toward the front of the house. I yelled her name and the sound of my voice brought her up short, brought her around to face me. I saw her arm go up and I ducked instinctively, dodging sideways; the gun cracked, glass shattered somewhere to my right, and I banged into one of the metal garbage cans, upset it, almost fell over it with pain tearing in my side.

"Melanie!"

It came out like the ghost-echo of a shout, low and strangulated; I couldn't seem to get enough air into my lungs as I righted myself. She was still standing a few feet away, the gun extended at arm's length—pulling the trigger frantically now, the hammer making audible clicks as it fell on the empty chamber. I staggered toward her, and she threw the gun at me, just the way you see them do it on television, and turned and ran. But not toward the front garden this time; to the north, away from the house, into the black tangle of the woods.

I ran after her, with one thought boiling in my head: The cliffs, Christ, the cliffs! The trees swallowed her, but I saw through a blur of sweat where she went into them—the path, she was on the path. My side and my head were on fire when I got there and I was sucking air with my mouth wide open, still not getting enough; it felt as if something hot and dry was being forced down my throat, into my lungs. I plunged ahead, let the woods swallow me. Couldn't see anything except grayness far ahead, the vague shape of her like something impaled against it, the tree trunks like prison bars in a nightmare. I tripped over something, fell, got up. I couldn't run anymore because I couldn't see, couldn't breathe; I had to feel my way along, blundering off the trail, back onto it, one hand up in front of my face to fend off low-hanging branches. The dark pressed in on me, added to the feeling of suffocation, so that I had to fend off the cutting edge of panic as well.

I heard her somewhere ahead, or thought I did; then all I could hear was the blood pounding in my ears . . . no, it was the boom of wind-roiled surf, colliding with the rocks at the base of the cliff. Jog in the path—I almost ran into a tree before I realized it. And there she was, twenty yards away, out beyond where the trees thinned. Standing at the edge of the cliff, stiff and still against the fog like a condemned prisoner against a crumbling gray wall.

Melanie!

I yelled the word but only inside my head: I had no voice. I lurched to my left, threw an arm around one of the slender tree trunks just before my legs gave out. Clung there gasping, trying to clear the dizziness out of my head.

Melanie might have been some kind of alfresco statue, both arms down at her sides, unmoving. I couldn't see her face clearly, couldn't tell what was written on it. But she didn't move, didn't move, didn't move—and my throat opened up, my lungs worked, the feeling of suffocation faded and strength came back into my arms, my legs. My mind was clear again. I let go of the tree and took a slow step toward her, still deep in the tree shadows so that she couldn't see me. She couldn't hear me, either, because of the wind and the surf's hissing cannonade.

Another step. Another—

And she moved, turned to her right abruptly and took a couple of small shuffling sidewise paces toward the edge. Leaned out a ways, with the wind whipping her frizzed hair, swaying her thin gangly body. Looked down, I saw her look down. Then she straightened again, and either saw or heard me somehow because she swiveled her head in my direction.

"I'm going to jump," she said.

The wind caught the words, tore them apart almost instantly. But I heard them, the awful dull resignation in them. There was no doubt she meant it.

I yelled at her, "No, Melanie!" Hoarse croak: the words couldn't have carried to her. I yelled them again, took another step.

"I have to," she said, "I have to jump. Richie . . . Richie . . . I killed him. Oh God, I killed him!"

Coming down off the coke high, that was it. The full implications of what she'd done settling in on her, the weight of it building a suicidal depression. I took another step. She didn't move. Another step, and I was at the edge of the clearing. No more than ten feet separating us. The twisted shape of the cypress growing up from the cliff face gyrated nearby . . . too far away from both of us for it to be of any use. Nothing anywhere near her except me. And the restless fog. And the black emptiness, waiting out there like something sentient, whispering to her, beckoning to her.

"Melanie, listen to me . . ."

"You can't stop me," she said. "I'm going to do it. I don't have anything to live for now. I don't want to live. He's dead, I killed him. I loved him and I *killed* him."

"Please, Melanie, please . . ."

She put her back to me, put her arms out at her sides like a bird about to take flight, and looked down, looked down . . . and I ran at her, full of terror that was as much for me as for her because this was a high place, because of my vertigo, and I reached her, clawed a hold on her sweater with my good hand

and she jumped

oh Jesus God she jumped with my hand on her

and the sweater tore, I couldn't hold on, and she

she was gone, tumbling over and over, screaming, gone, and I

I staggered, teetered at the edge windmilling my arms

Deadfall!

and somehow I managed to pitch my body backward and to one side . . . breath jarred out of me when I hit the ground . . . and

I was sliding, I felt my legs go over the edge, I clutched frenziedly at the rough surface

and caught onto something, a rock, something, and I wasn't sliding anymore, I was pulling myself up and away from the edge . . .

Safe.

I lay with my head buried in my arms, my cheek against the rough sandstone, listening to the hungry feeding of the surf far below, crying a little. But not for Melanie. Not for Melanie, not for anyone in her God-damned family, not for Danny Martinez, not for any of them.

For me. The one I was crying for was me.

TWENTY-FOUR

Sunday afternoon, three days later.

Kerry's apartment.

We had spent a quiet day there, reading, watching tapes of old comedy films on her VCR. It was almost five o'clock and getting dark outside. I leaned over and turned on the end-table lamp. I didn't like the darkness much right now; it made me uneasy. Beside me on the couch, Kerry was silent. She understood.

The past three days had been bad, worse than the three days after my beating: psychic damage was much harder to deal with than the physical kind. Thursday night had been the worst. Police, ambulances, sirens, questions, more questions; floodlights and winches on the cliff, men milling about, working at the retrieval of Melanie's broken body from the rocks; exhaustion, half-sleep, nightmares—always the nightmares, like a preview of hell seen over and over but only vaguely perceived. Friday had been bad, too, but Kerry had been there at my flat, and Eberhardt for a while, and they had made it tolerable. Saturday had been a little better. And today better still. Time would fade it all, blend it with all the other similar episodes, all the other views of pain and death, and make it indistinguishable from them. Scar tissue added to scar tissue, hidden away inside.

Alicia Purcell had survived the shooting, at least so far. She was in critical condition; the doctors gave her no better than an even chance. Ben Klein had talked to her briefly, as had the San Mateo County authorities, but she hadn't told them much—almost nothing, in fact. Maybe she would never tell them anything. That might bother them, but it didn't bother me. What did it matter if I had doped out some of the details incorrectly or not at all? What mattered was that a lot of people were dead—nasty people but people just the same.

Dead people. That was the crux of everything. My life, my job, was full of dead people; my memory and my dreams were full of dead people. How many more could I bury in my own private graveyard? Not many. Maybe none. I was too old, too tired; I no longer had the resistence or the resiliency to deal with so much ugliness. All I wanted, now, was peace, quiet, freedom from the sordid side of mankind.

I kept thinking about retirement.

The idea scared me a little. I couldn't imagine myself not working; I remembered the way I'd felt, the emptiness and purposelessness, when I'd lost my license for a few months a couple of years ago. And yet I kept thinking about retirement. It didn't have to be a full retirement—just from the field. Turn that part of it over to Eberhardt, maybe hire somebody to help him out when we had extra work. Go to the office one or two days a week, do the paperwork, help plan procedure, offer advice if it was needed. Draw half-salary; I could just about live on that, with Kerry helping to share expenses—something we did already. She made a very good salary. I hadn't talked it over with her, but I knew she wouldn't mind; she'd welcome the idea, in fact; it would erase the worry, the vestiges of fear, that had been in her face the past week. We could live like normal people. I could learn to enjoy life again.

It might work. It might.

I kept thinking about it.

The movie we'd been watching—an old Cary Grant farce, *Bringing Up Baby*—ended and Kerry got up to stop the machine, push the rewind button. "That's the last tape," she said. "We can watch some TV, if you want. Or are you hungry?"

"Not yet."

"How about a beer?"

"Okay. It's about that time."

She went off into the kitchen. Came back in a while with a bottle of Bud Light for me and a glass of something clear and sparkly for herself. I pointed at the glass and asked, "What's that?"

"Mineral water."

"Since when do you drink mineral water?"

"Since last week. You know, for a detective you're not very observant sometimes. I must have gone through two cartons of this stuff the past three days."

"How come no more wine?"

She shrugged and gave me a solemn look. "I decided you were right, I'd been drinking too much."

"What made you decide?"

"I don't know, I guess I just got tired of waking up in the morning with a headache and a fuzzy mouth."

I smiled at her, touched her cheek with the back of my hand. "You did it for me," I said, "for my sake."

"Who says?"

"I say."

"Don't be so damn sure of yourself—"

"I love you, Kerry," I said.

Her expression softened and she leaned over and kissed me, gently, not putting her hands on me. "I love you, too. If you were in better shape I'd prove it to you."

"I'm not so sore today. Hardly any pain from the ribs. We could do something mildly exotic."

"Like what?"

I told her like what.

"That might hurt you," she said dubiously. "Let me think about it."

The videotape had finished rewinding. She got up and shut it off, but the TV kept running; I picked up the remote control unit. "While you're thinking," I said, "I'll see what's on the tube. Might be something on I like better than sex."

She wrinkled her nose at me. I punched the channel selector button on the remote; Kerry had cable, so I had a lot of channels to go through. After five or six I didn't pay much attention to the flickering images, because I really wasn't interested in watching anything else.

Kerry said suddenly, with surprise in her voice, "Hey, wait. Back up one."

I backed up one and she said, "Wow, look."

I looked. It was one of those religious cable stations, the kind where evangelists of one stripe or another try to spread the gospel according to their interpretation and every few minutes handsome young guys and wholesomely pretty girls sing rousing gospel songs that are supposed to stir your sense of Christian duty to the point where you'll call in and pledge a generous donation. Right now a guy in a three-piece, dark-blue suit was talking about Sodom and Gomorrah and all the terrible things that went on there, drawing an analogy to all the terrible things that were going on today, right under our very noses, not only in massage parlors and porno movie houses, but in wicked old Hollywood and in New York publishing houses whose editors persisted in "inundating our society with a floodtide of trash"—which struck me as a mixed metaphor—"that uses the printed word to spread a pagan message of filth and perversion."

The guy was the Right Reverend Clyde T. Daybreak, and he was wearing a big blue-and-white button on his lapel that said THE MORAL CRUSADE.

"Looks like he finally got himself a TV show," Kerry said. "I wonder how much it cost him?"

"You sound as cynical as me."

"He's pretty good, though, isn't he?"

"If you're into pagan messages of filth and perversion."

"I wonder—" she said, and the telephone rang.

"If that's for me," I said, "I'm not here."

"It's probably Cybil. Sunday's her day to call."

She got up and went to answer the phone. I watched Clyde T. Daybreak fulminate in his quiet, forceful way, and I didn't find him amusing. What he was advocating was censorship, something I consider even more vile than crusading fundamentalists who use God's name to foment intolerance and to coerce money out of gullible citizens. Pretty soon, mercifully, he quit babbling and the camera pulled back and panned around, letting me see part of his entourage, all of whom were smiling and nodding like marionettes whose strings had just been pulled. I was leaning forward, peering at the faces, when Kerry came back.

"There's Reverend Holloway," I said, pointing. "Most of the Holy Mission mavens are there, looks like, except for—"

"—the Reverend Dunston," she said grimly. "I know. That was him on the phone."

"What? What did he want?"

"Me. He acted as if nothing had happened, as if Daybreak never even talked to him."

"But Daybreak must have." I didn't want to look at the Right Reverend or his congregation any longer; I shut off the television. "You put the fear of lawsuit into him last week."

"Well, if he did, then Ray's defying him. What if he comes here again? What if he starts bothering you again? What if—"

"Hey," I said, "easy. Don't worry, we'll deal with it."

"But after all we've been through—"

"After all we've been through," I said, "Dunston isn't important. He just doesn't matter." I pulled her down beside me. "What's important is us."

She let me hold her for a time. Then she drew back a little and said, "I've made up my mind."

"About what?"

"About your suggestion. The mildly exotic one. I still think it'll hurt you, but if you're game so am I."

"I'm game," I said.

She was right, as it turned out: it hurt me. But not much, and I didn't care. All I cared about was her. Being with her, loving her. Living a sane and normal life with her.

I kept thinking about retiring . . .